BLOOD BOUND BOOKS

Presents

NIGHT TERRORS III

Editors:

Marc Ciccarone
Theresa Dillon
G. Winston Hyatt

BLOOD BOUND BOOKS

"White Moon Rising" copyright© 1977 by Stuart David Schiff. First published in the anthology *Whispers*, edited by Stuart David Schiff. Copyright © 1984 Dennis Etchison for *Red Dreams*.

All other stories are original to this volume and are copyright © 2014 to their respective authors.

Artwork by Andrej Bartulovic.

Interior Formatting by Lori Michelle

ISBN: 978-1-940250-14-4

First Edition

Visit us on the web at:
www.bloodboundbooks.net

NOVELS AVAILABLE NOW FROM BLOOD BOUND BOOKS:

400 Days of Oppression by Wrath James White

Habeas Corpse by Nikki Hopeman

Loveless by Dev Jarrett

The Sinner by K. Trap Jones

Mother's Boys by Daniel I. Russell

Knuckle Supper by Drew Stepek

Sons of the Pope by Daniel O'Connor

Dolls by KJ Moore

At the End of All Things by Stony Graves

The Return by David A Riley

THE BLOOD BOUND STAFF:

Marc Ciccarone
Joe Spagnola
Theresa Dillon
Karen Fierro
G. Winston Hyatt

TABLE OF CONTENTS

INTRODUCTION

THE **ADVANCEMENT OF** civilization has been measured largely by its reduction of the world's horrors, yet horrors persist. Just as bacteria mutate into more resilient, drug-resistant forms, life's most terrifying aspects seem to evolve into new and startling manifestations the more we try to suppress them. Each new horror—however seemingly modern—is tied to core anxieties that have lurked in the human mind for ages: fears of death, suffering, otherness, intrusion, and the unknown. Fear of a loss of agency, freedom, or identity. Fears that the laws, rituals, and standards we rely on could fail at any moment, sending us plummeting into dangerous and uncontrollable scenarios. A horror story is always an old story. Nevertheless, the innovation and imagination of storytellers affords new shapes, new voices, and new life to dark tales.

The *Night Terrors* series of anthologies by Blood Bound Books offers a doorway into the striking originality and multiform personalities of contemporary horror fiction. I am thrilled to have been part of selecting and editing the stories in this third volume. My first encounter with *Night Terrors* was as a contributor some years ago. A story I'd written in a fantasy writing workshop—which, I might add, I expected to be pilloried due to its grotesque subject matter and "twist" ending—received overall positive feedback from my classmates. This culminated in the instructor suggesting I try to have it published. Two small horror magazines rejected it on the basis that the content itself was a violation of editorial standards. (I was puzzled, as I had encountered far worse violence and child endangerment in the fairy tales read to me as a boy.) Because of these rejections, Blood Bound Books' claim to be "without limits" and looking for "your darkest side" in the original *Night Terrors* was exactly the sort of reassurance I needed to submit my work there. Thus, "Little Piggies" became one of my first published works of horror. I then became a regular on the BBB web forums. (These are no more, supplanted by Facebook—always a new horror, as I said.) There I discovered a community rooted in the pure love of the genre. A few published stories and many passionate Internet discussions later, when Blood Bound Books announced it was looking to expand its editorial staff, I jumped at the chance—and I've been aboard ever since.

Night Terrors III is unabashedly a horror anthology. Horror fandom is passionate, personal, and varied. Every person has his or her own story of discovering the chill of a good dark story. Magical mythology, bloody folktales, gothic novels, horror pulps, dime-store comics, weekend matinees, paperback shockers, late-night spook shows, eerie TV series, surreal art, campfire ghost stories, and modern literary experiments all touched our hearts as individuals and shaped our culture as a whole. This array of forbearers has led horror fiction to exist as a fusion of ancient and modern worldviews, and a collision of high and low culture, as vibrant and strange as any other.

A tour of the many stories contained in *Night Terrors III* demonstrates the multifariousness of today's horror fiction. Earthly threats of human perversion, nightmarish explorations of other worlds, surreal voyages of the mind, fanciful childhood fears, technological innovations run amok, visitations from the darkest past, criminal exploits gone beyond the pale, and the ruinous events surrounding the loss of love, life, or limb—all of this and more comes to life in these pages. Titans of the genre such as Jack Ketchum,

Dennis Etchison, and Steve Rasnic Tem stand among the talents of emerging masters, each offering a stirring example of the literature of fear.

Welcome, dear reader, to *Night Terrors III*. Thank you for joining us. This is horror.

—G. Winston Hyatt

THE RUN

ARIC SUNDQUIST

SAMANTHA WATCHED HER father set the wire trap down on a tree stump. He reached inside the cage and pushed down the pressure plate until it locked in place, then pulled out a plump rabbit, its legs thumping against the wire mesh. He unsheathed his hunting knife and whacked the bone handle against its skull, then slit its neck. Blood drained.

"Hit 'em in the head first," he said. "It stuns 'em so they don't move. You try." He motioned with the knife to the trap next to her.

Samantha glanced at the other rabbit suspended in a homemade snare. Her body went numb. She had no problem helping her father set up traps along the run, and she had no problem cooking and eating the meat afterwards, but she didn't want to kill anything. Her father had always made it a point to do that back home, out in the barn. Not in front of her.

Samantha stared up at the clear blue sky, at the shapes shifting into forest animals. Her fingers poked around in her pocket and she clutched her lucky rock, a Petoskey stone. She loved how the fossilized coral patterns looked like seashells, except they were smooth to the touch.

"Sam?" he asked. "You hear me?"

She shrugged. "Do I have to?"

Her father reset the trap and set it back down on the trail, placing lettuce leaves near the spring mechanism. He grabbed the remaining rabbit from the snare and forced the animal into her hands. "You have to learn. Here, take my knife. Come back when you're done."

He handed over the knife and sheath. Then he reset the snare by folding the sapling over and making sure the string was good and tight on the release. He stood and regarded her for a brief moment. She glimpsed sadness in his blue eyes, or maybe compassion, but she couldn't tell for sure. Then he hefted his backpack up on his shoulders and began his walk back home.

Samantha followed the run for close to a half hour, cradling the rabbit in one hand, the knife in the other. She arrived at her tree fort and rummaged through the bushes. Finding an old Coca-Cola crate, she banged the dirt off and placed the rabbit inside, then set her father's knife next to the base of the oak tree. She climbed up the steps and flung the trapdoor open, sending a cloud of dust into orbit. Her brother Aiden had built the tree fort many years ago, before going to Iraq. It was her favorite place to go when she needed a place to get away.

She quickly found her deck of cards sealed in a plastic bag, then shuffled herself a game of solitaire. She played slowly, dispassionately, her mind wandering, and only made it halfway through the game when a rustling came from the forest. Probably a deer heading down the run to get some apples from the orchards. Sneaking over to the window, she pried open the shutter and peeked outside, searching for movement, hoping to see a deer gliding through the woods like a ghost.

Beneath the forest canopy, a figure darted from tree to tree—a boy, thin but muscular, wearing a blue baseball hat and a white T-shirt stained with sweat. Even from so far away, she could see flies swarming around his head like satellites.

"Hello?" she said.

He froze in his tracks and smiled sheepishly. "You heard me? Oh shit. I wanted to surprise you. How's it going?"

"Fine, I guess."

"What's your name?"

"Sam."

"Sam? Like Samantha?"

"Yup, but people just call me Sam."

"That's cool." He looked inside the crate. "This your rabbit? He's nice."

"I guess. What're you doing out here? This is my dad's property."

"Sorry about that. I didn't know. Was just fishing down at the lake and I saw you walking by. You like to fish?"

"No, not so much."

"I suppose you're one of those girls who likes dolls and stuff."

She smiled, sensing his sarcasm. "Nope. I just like being out in the woods. Never cared much for fishing."

"I see. You alone up there?"

"Yup."

He stepped closer and spoke quieter. "I stole a pack of smokes from my uncle." He pulled out a pack of cigarettes, bright red, and opened them up, smelling the tobacco. "You want one? You can have two if you want."

"I don't know. I never smoked before."

"Really? How old are you?"

"Fourteen."

"You're old enough. I got some whiskey, too." He pulled out a bottle from his back pocket and swished the dark liquid around. The label was peeled off. Then he lit a cigarette with a lighter. "We can have ourselves a little party. What do you say?"

"No, that's okay." She watched the smoke curl around in gray threads. "I gotta be getting home soon."

"You should stay. We can be friends."

"I don't know . . . "

He gave her a hurt look and stared down at his feet. "I see. I bet you got a lot of friends at school and stuff."

"Not really. I'm home schooled."

"Is that right? So you're probably a little weird, huh?" He laughed at his joke, then bent down and grabbed up the rabbit, sticking his face in its fur. "I bet you're nice and soft like Mr. Bunny here."

She was about to say something but stopped.

"Okay, I'm going to come up there now," he said, pitching his cigarette and stomping on the embers. He placed the rabbit back in the crate.

"I don't think that's a good idea. I just wanna be alone."

"You don't have a choice, Sam. That's how life is sometimes, am I right? Things happen and you don't have a choice. Now, I'm going to come up there. You won't like what I'm gonna do, but there's nothing you can do to stop it. And if you tell anyone, I'll kill you."

Her hands began shaking uncontrollably. She tried to calm herself but couldn't. "Go to hell," she said under her breath.

He shook his head slowly, as if scolding a young child, then he walked closer and vanished underneath the tree fort.

Samantha heard scraping against the tree and the sound of creaking wood. She grabbed the rope handle to the door, ready to slam it, and peered down in the hole. The boy climbing toward her looked much older than she had originally thought. Small wrinkles creased around his eyes, and when he glanced up and grinned at her, she noticed his teeth were turning black at the roots.

The man suddenly reached out for her leg. Samantha threw the trap door down with a loud clatter. He ducked just in time. Then she moved the table overtop the door, barricading herself inside.

"Son-of-a-bitch!" he said, striking the door with his fist.

The table rocketed up and nearly tipped over, sending the playing cards fluttering like wounded doves. Then the pounding stopped.

She leaned closer and heard him uncapping the liquor bottle, which seemed odd, followed by the sound of the bottle being dropped to the grass below.

She crept even closer, her whole body tense, listening. Then she screamed.

She tripped and fell on her back. By her feet, a knife blade jutted between the floorboards. Dark liquid covered the blade.

Her foot throbbed. Blood pooled inside her shoe. A strange euphoria seized her, followed by a dull droning sound that made her feel light-headed. She fought the urge to faint and lifted herself up on the window ledge, eyeing a branch a few feet away. It would be risky, but she had no other choice. She needed to get away.

She took a deep breath and jumped.

Samantha's hands connected with the branch. She hung limply, feet pumping the air. The second branch was directly below. She heard the man hit the door and this time it cracked and boards clattered to the ground.

Samantha let go and fell onto the branch below. But instead of stabilizing herself and wrapping her arms around the branch, her foot slipped and she twisted upside down.

Then she was falling.

You have to get up, a voice said.

Samantha opened her eyes to a clear blue sky. She had trouble breathing and coughed in spasms. She tried to stand but fell back down. A figure shifted into view next to her, billowing in a haze of incandescence. The shape coalesced into the form of her brother, dressed in his military uniform. He knelt down beside her.

You have to hide until the sickness passes.

"What?" she said, coughing. "What sickness?"

That's how he kills. He covered Dad's knife in poison.

She tried to stand again but couldn't find the strength. "Are you home now?" she asked. The blood in her mouth tasted vile—metallic and sharp. "Does Dad know you're home?"

Yes, he knows. He wants you to learn about death, not hide from it.

"I don't want to learn. I want you to be safe, with us."

Light spread across her vision, imprinting images, sending her mind spiraling inward. She smelled cleaning chemicals and flowers and saw a mass of people staring at her brother's casket. She stumbled through the crowd and touched his hand and tried to help him out. And then she heard crying from all around and hid under a table and pulled at a loose thread on her dress until the seam unraveled. She saw her father hugging her aunt and then he crawled under the table and held her tight. He held her for a long time and didn't say anything.

Samantha fought against the memories, retaliated against the visions. They finally receded and she was in the woods again, breathing the humid air, inhaling the scent of pine trees. Aiden was dead, she told herself for the first time in months. She repeated it like a mantra and broke down into tears. He was already home, buried in the local cemetery.

She heard swearing from high above and saw the man stick his head out of the window. Her vision swirled and danced and became distorted. And then she saw the man change before her eyes. His face smeared like a painting melting in a tropical sun. His eyes drooped and became dark ovals, similar to a rotting a jack o' lantern left out on a November porch. His teeth grew long and jagged and smoke jettisoned from his ears in smokestack spurts. He wasn't human anymore; he was some sort of monster. Then he put a finger to his lips, motioning silence, and slipped down the ladder. His unclasped belt buckle slapped each step while he descended.

Her brother gripped her arm, helped her sit up.

Run, he said.

Somehow, Samantha found the strength to stand. And then she was running.

~

The woods became one long blur of melted branches and leaves. Her head swam through the trees and she drank up the bees and the dragonflies. She could hear footsteps behind her. And labored breathing. Then she couldn't run anymore. She knew something was wrong with her foot, but couldn't figure out what.

"I can see you!" the man shouted.

She glanced back.

He followed slowly, mechanically, yanking a drawstring attached to his back, similar to a child's toy. The sound of a motor revved and his head flipped open. His band-saw teeth began tearing through the underbrush like a chainsaw, spewing out bark and sawdust. Everything was caught in his path—the leaves, the branches, even the deer and the mice.

Entrails spewed into the heavens.

"There's nowhere to run, my little rabbit!" he said.

Samantha knew her only chance was to lose him in the woods. She darted off the trail and swiped at the ferns blocking her way. The pulpy stalks tore at her skin and cut her palms to shreds. Then the ferns smacked her back with open palms, swearing in some strange swooshing language that sounded like hushed rattles. She told them she was sorry and kept running.

She didn't know how long she ran. Time didn't add up right in her head. She pushed through a thicket of tangled poplars and lost her footing. The world tumbled and she was falling against a large pine tree, out of breath. Her head hit the ground, but it was only a glancing blow. Fireflies dotted her vision and then vanished in flashes of light.

At first she thought about climbing a tree, but she could barely stand up straight. When she closed her eyes, the darkness exploded with pinholes of light and expanded and contracted like an accordion. She held her eyes open with her fingers, afraid to close them again, and listened to the wind become one with the forest sounds—all the rustling trees and ferns and the sounds of the squirrels scampering high above. Everything mixed together to form a symphony.

She tried to stand but pain rocketed through her leg. She unlaced her shoe and wrenched it off, peeling away the sock. The wound was in the arch of her foot. When she touched it, red spilled out in a torrent.

She turned to the closest tree. "I need some of your blood."

The ancient tree creaked and groaned and finally awakened, spreading its branches wide and revealing a beating heart formed out of huge knots. She crept closer and punctured its dark skin with her fingernail. Clear blood squirted over her fingertips in an arterial spray.

She fell back down and applied the pine blood to her foot and the pain shocked her to her core, traveled all the way up her thighs and into the pit of her stomach, clenching down tight. She vomited but not much came up. Then the pain subsided and she applied more of the blood and could feel it harden, sticking her wound together like glue.

She waited until her breathing calmed, then checked her foot again. It still hurt a little, but she could deal with that. As long as she didn't lose any more blood. Finally she slipped on her shoe and forced herself up. She felt strange, like an autumn leaf ready to be swept up by the wind.

Samantha continued onward through the woods for close to an hour, although she wasn't exactly sure. She walked as quietly as possible, checking her foot occasionally to make sure the wound had been sealed properly.

Soon the forest thinned and she saw musical notes hovering over the trees. She knew how to read music and often played the piano at home. But the notes in the sky didn't make any sense to her. They were haphazard and had no sense of rhythm. Then the notes hopped up and down the clefts and she realized she was staring at power lines. The notes were birds perched on the wires.

A memory surfaced, of her walking with Aiden down the

lines and through the looping countryside to the Escanaba River. She remembered picking dandelions and putting some in her hair. And then he told her to feel one of the telephone poles with her hands, and she did, and the electrical current buzzed from deep within, as if it were alive and breathing.

And then something pulled her out of her reverie. The sound of a motor, growing nearer.

The telephone poles acted like beacons, guiding Samantha through the open countryside. She counted each pole as she passed, one at a time, and once she reached number twelve, stopped for a quick breather. Although the world still shifted and tumbled around her, her vision was beginning to clear, and she could finally think more logically. The drug was finally wearing off.

She ran past two more poles and realized her foot was getting worse. At first the pain was distant, but now it began throbbing and sending paralyzing jolts through her body with each step. The drug must have been keeping the pain at bay.

"There you are!" a voice shouted.

The man crashed out of the woods a hundred feet behind her. He was no longer full of revolving saw blades and smokestacks and rumbling motors. Now he looked like some sort of sickly demon, hunched over, eyes bright as coals and a mouth full of splinters and dried blood. An orange leaf stuck to his hat and looked like a feather. It reminded her of the kind of hat Robin Hood wore.

She pointed and laughed. His smile, so full of evil and malice, fell to barely a sneer. He reached up and plucked off the leaf, crushing it into pulp in his hand, letting the remains flutter away in the wind. Then he was running toward her.

She kept her distance—at least one pole between the two of them at all times. Occasionally he stopped to catch his breath, wheezing and coughing and shouting obscenities. She used that time to massage her foot and catch her breath and form a plan.

After the seventeenth pole she decided to take a chance and slip away. She had no idea where the power lines eventually led, but from what she remembered, her house was a straight shot through the woods from her current position. She had to act now.

She waited until he stopped to catch his breath, then crouched down low in the grass and headed straight into the woods.

She moved through the underbrush cautiously, and within minutes arrived at her father's deer run. Her legs were dead tired, and her lungs clenched tight, forcing her to stop. Although the drug was wearing off, she could still feel the effects clouding her mind. A dull ache tapped at her temples with each heartbeat.

She ran until she couldn't run anymore, halting near a sharp bend in the trail. The woods swayed as if she were traveling through an aquarium. The wind kicked up and sounded like a mechanical bubbler purring softly from the heavens.

She recognized her position and a glint of hope grew inside her. This was one of her favorite spots to set snares while her dad hunted for deer. Usually rabbits hugged the corners and skirted beside fallen logs and thick bushes. Those were the best spots to put down traps, creating a natural bottleneck.

"Come on out!" the man said from the woods. "I was just kidding before!"

Her heart dropped. She felt like crying, like beating her fists in rage. Instead she calmed herself and thought about her options. She could barely move, could barely even remain standing. And she was on the verge of passing out. Her only option was to hide.

She hobbled off the trail and stumbled through tangled trees and bushes. She pushed a thick branch out of the way and it sprung back and slapped her in the lip, almost knocking her out. All around, the trees and the ferns laughed in their strange language. They were all mocking her.

"Shut up," she said to the forest, dabbing at the blood on her lip with her sleeve. And then she couldn't stand anymore. She collapsed to the ground.

Samantha broke down and cried. She felt like she had disappointed her brother, who was always so strong, always so confident. She pulled out the tumbled stone from her pocket and held it in her palm. The rock was the last thing Aiden had ever given her—a present from a fossil shop in Traverse City. She wanted to be like him more than anything. Even in his casket, wearing his uniform, he looked so regal, like he could rise up and command troops from beyond the grave.

She closed her eyes and clenched the rock in her fist and fought to gain control.

You can't run anymore, a voice said. *You have to fight back.*

It was her voice this time.

Something happened to her at that moment. It felt as if some unseen force took control of her body, possessing her in steady waves, fueling her, channeling her with inner strength to fight against her own annihilation. She felt like a marionette controlled by invisible strings. She felt strong.

Samantha stood and wrenched off her sweatshirt and unbuttoned her flannel, throwing them both off to the side. Taking a deep breath to calm her nerves, she took aim at the nearest tree and pitched the rock as hard as she could. It struck with a loud *crack*.

On the trail, the man stopped dead in his tracks. Then he darted off into the woods, following the sound, swiping at the bushes with the knife and trampling the ferns like an enraged boar.

He saw her and stopped. His eyes still glowed, like burning embers, and he looked her up and down, noticing her exposed skin. Then he tore off his belt and rushed her.

Samantha wrenched back the branch that had almost knocked her out minutes before. The tension caused her arms to tremble and shudder. She released her hold.

At first she thought her trap had failed, but a muffled cry erupted and the man twitched on the ground, clutching his face, blood funneling between his fingers and staining his shirt dark crimson. Her father's knife fell to the ground beside him.

She didn't hesitate for a second. She jumped forward and struck with her knee. His nose crunched from the impact, and her momentum sent her tumbling forward on top of him. He reached up and tried to throw her off, but she batted his hands away, then planted her knees to his chest, pinning him to the ground.

He continued struggling, but was too weak to do much of anything. Finally he gave up and stared up at her with those strange eyes, face smeared with blood. A smile spread over his lips, a toying smile, as if saying he still won the fight.

All around, the ferns laughed. Some even clapped.

"You have to hit 'em in the head first," she said, mimicking her father from earlier that morning.

His face slipped from amusement to confusion.

Then she picked up her father's knife.

HOMELESS BAGS

DEAN H. WILD

THE WEATHER WAS turning mean again as Larry Parman stepped out, tentatively, from behind the counter marked BAGGAGE CLAIM to watch the storms sailing over Medberg Field. They had managed to reduce the flow of passengers to a trickle around midnight. After that people stopped showing up all together. But it was not the absence of warm bodies in the airport halls that put his hackles up (and they were indeed up, now standing at full attention as a matter of fact). It was, he realized, the lightning—more precisely the way it seemed to glide overhead with a sweeping searchlight type of motion—that tripped the silent alarm in his personal command center.

Across from him, plate glass windows offered a view of the main parking lot and a small clutch of cars huddled in an outer row like abandoned pets. He stood and watched sheets of rain drift past the sodium lights. Crackles of hot white threw swooping shadows across the airport grounds and he squinted against them, wondering why he heard no thunder. Strange lightning. *Strangeling*, his hackle-raising unease dubbed it. And then, like an afterthought: *Something that doesn't belong here.*

Don Ciphers touched his arm and he jumped back what felt like a mile.

"Goddamn it," he barked and then gave the man in the

Medberg Field polo shirt a thin smile. "Who let you out of your cage? The tower's not going to run itself on a night like this."

"Took a minute to stretch my legs." Ciphers shrugged. His usual overwrought nature held a hint of weariness, or perhaps edginess, running on low current because his own alarm system was gearing up. "Everything for us is either grounded or redirected: Skyway, Vagabond Air, you name it. Besides, Feeney's on with me tonight. I've got him watching the boards."

"Feeney's back?"

"Probationary status for the next ninety days."

Larry grunted over his amazement at how ninety days of scrupulously observed performance was sufficient to scrub a near mid-air collision off the face of an already threadbare record.

"I'm surprised they don't send me home when it's this quiet," he finally said. "Flight V22 was the last one to deplane. That was three hours ago. No flights means no bags."

"Corporate bullshit," Ciphers offered. It was a standard response that was always sure to bring nods all around. Then he pointed across the empty expanse of the baggage area. "So, are you saving that one for later?"

"Saving?" Larry asked, already following the directive of the other man's finger.

Medberg Field accommodated all passengers with a single baggage carousel which sat demurely in the corner opposite Larry's desk. The lights in that area were switched down to half capacity in honor of the lack of travelers, and yet the medium-sized travel bag (the type always reminded him of something designed to house bowling balls) seemed stark and obvious sitting there alone on the belt. He wondered how he could have missed it. The answer was simple, that uneasy part of him volunteered: there was no bag to notice . . . until now.

"Did you put Feeney up to this?" he asked. "Or Wayland?"

Ciphers held up his hands in a show of blamelessness. "Told you, Feeney's in the tower. Wayland, he left when they shut down ticketing. If you're as surprised to see that thing as you seem to be, we should probably follow protocol."

The rules were pretty straightforward; they'd all heard them while crammed into training room desks, lined up under harsh fluorescents like somebody's science fair project, hoping to sprout some semblance of compliance. Prevent all interaction by passengers and personnel until security officials can evaluate the situation. Larry weighed this, feeling his unease change to a type of fascination, then he took a few steps toward the carousel. This was Medberg, Wisconsin, after all, not LAX, not Chicago, not fricking BWI. "Let me take a closer look before we hit any panic buttons."

"You know I can't condone that," Ciphers said. "It's failure to act in accordance with—"

"Go back to your tower, then," Larry said. "Show Feeney how to make the little dots on the radar miss each other."

"C'mon, Larry. This storm's got me jumpy enough. Can't we do this by the book?"

"It's got a claim tag," he offered as he stepped closer. "Somebody checked it through somewhere."

Strangeling, like a wave of camera flashes, made him stop. It gave the bag an almost undulating quality.

"Something's not right," Ciphers said. "I say we get Gardner from security down here."

"Old tub-of-guts himself." Larry stooped close to the bag. "By all means bring him down. It'll be great. I can run numbers on this claim tag, you can pick the knots out of your shorts, and we can both listen to him shoot off his mouth the whole time."

"Should have stayed up-top," Ciphers said as he escaped into the half-light of the main passage which led to the concourse hub and security check-in. "I don't have to handle shit like this up in the tower."

Larry decided to forgo any type of parting comment, suddenly fixated on the zipper closure across the top of the bag. It was mottled with mossy flecks of green. For some reason it brought to life memories of a poster he'd seen in a long-ago grade school hallway. It demonstrated the consequences of neglectful tooth brushing with a photograph of an open mouth filled with rotted teeth and infected gums. Each time he'd glimpsed it—on his way to the lunch room or coming back from recess—he was certain the depicted grin was wider, more substantial than the time before, approaching a point where it would be able to munch its way right through the cinderblock wall, or snatch a bit of meat off of a hapless, passing student. Finally, before it could establish a hazardous presence in the real world, it was replaced by a new poster, a wise old owl in a graduate cap reminding one and all to never be tardy. But he often wondered if the grin wasn't still there, part of the building now, lurking just under Mister Owl's paper façade, scheming to one day burst through and finish its hungry work.

He shuddered and leaned closer to the bag. The claim tag was not a modern barcode strip, but a ragged stub attached to one of the hand grips with a loop of pink string. He grasped it and twirled it toward him.

It squirmed, fleshy and living between his fingers. He pulled his hand back with a gasp. The sides of the bag, some sort of scaly black leather, heaved in and out and a sound, deep and throaty, leaked from the zipper closure.

"What the hell?" he heard himself say.

The tag writhed at the end of its string, prodding the air, seeking, tasting. Another growl issued from within the leather belly and its sentiment was undoubtable. It was a warning, not much different than that of a rabid dog hunched back in the dark safety of its coop. The boards of his alarm system lit up. He was unable to take his eyes off the bag, even when he heard footsteps in the corridor.

"Gardner says he'll be down after his break," Ciphers

announced. "Of course he said it around a mouthful of bologna sandwich, and it was the first one in a stack of about four. God, he eats like a pig . . . Why are you standing there like that?"

"Shut up a minute." Larry motioned to Ciphers with a cautionary slow-down gesture. "Get the flashlight out of my desk. We need to see this thing a little better. And bring a luggage cart."

"What's going on?"

"Just do it. And make sure the door to the lock-up vault is swung all the way open. I mean it."

"Lock-up?

"Behind the counter. The little room where I keep the homeless bags when we get them. Do it."

Ciphers rummaged around behind the counter for a moment, then switched on a long-neck flashlight. It bobbed in his hand as he wheeled a flat pushcart away from the back wall. "I'll say it again, Larry. I don't think we should be touching that thing."

Larry stepped lightly to a small utility closet near the counter and snatched a broom from inside. "I don't think we have a choice. Stay close."

He moved up to the bag slowly. Ill will as palpable as displaced air around a thrumming machine seemed to radiate from it. His stomach clenched. He felt wound up and running on too much torque. Unease and fascination had changed again to a type of conviction.

"This is the plan. I'm going to knock that bag onto the cart," he said, "and then you're going to run like your ass is on fire and shove the whole works into lock-up, no matter what you see. Got it?"

"Are you kidding me?" Ciphers looked seriously ill.

"Not even a little." He brought the broom up to show he meant it. "We can talk about it once this thing is put away. Ready? One . . . two . . . "

The lights went out.

Larry froze, his eyes automatically switching to the window overlooking the landing strips. High intensity lamps studding either side of Runway Four, the only open approach for the night, squeezed down to pinpoints and then vanished into the torrential night. No lights burned anywhere, which meant this was everything, the whole show—parking lot lamps, access road overheads and all—and he didn't like the feel of it one bit. Not combined with everything else: the strangeling, the bag . . .

"Goddamn it," Ciphers lamented. His light beam darted around the room in senseless circles. "Why now?"

Because that's how it is when you've just sunk into some unwelcome shit. Larry wanted to say. *And that's exactly what we've got here.* He kept it to himself because it seemed unbidden to speak into the smothering blanket of dark.

A growl, low and full of dark promise, rose into the air.

"Was that—?" Ciphers asked, training the beam on the bag.

"Yes." He raised his broom defensively.

The bag made another of those loose inhale-exhale motions. Its tag darted into the air, two short jabs, and then its zipper mouth unlaced, spreading open like a snarl to show not standard issue zipper teeth but a series of tiny hooks.

Ciphers backed away a step. "Oh Christ, look at that. Where's Gardner? He needs to—"

"No," he managed to snag Ciphers's wrist in the near blackness. "I don't think we have that kind of time. Can't you feel it? In the air?"

Ciphers seemed to consider this, then planted a shaky hand on the push rail of the luggage trolley once again. Beads of moisture shone on his forehead. "Let's contain it then, whatever it is."

Larry clutched up on the broom and rested the bristles against the side of the bag. "If I'm wrong, if this isn't as bad as I think it is, I'll buy you a beer, or whatever you tower guys like to dr—"

An earsplitting yowl erupted from the bag's insides. Its

open maw snatched at the broom and clamped onto the bristles. Larry jumped, instinctively lifted the broom, and swung it toward the luggage cart like a fisherman attempting to land a huge and improbable catch. As if aware of the forward motion at its disposal, the bag released its hold at the apex of the swing and flew through the air, directly at Don Ciphers. It plowed into him. Its zipper mouth battened on his chest and immediately began to gnaw.

"Oh God." Ciphers squealed and fell flat out in the dark. The flashlight tumbled to the floor and rolled away. "Oh God, oh my God. It's biting me. Biting!"

Without thought, Larry cast the broom aside and scrambled forward. The emergency hallway lights came to life. A wash of strangeling accompanied it, making everything seem over-bright. Ciphers was on his back holding the bag away from himself but the opening chomped and snapped, stretching toward him like anxious lips. Shredded patches on the front of his shirt glinted with blood. Before he could think better of it, Larry clutched the exposed underside of the bag. It was hot and writhing in his hands.

"Let go, Don. C'mon," he demanded.

Ciphers did not so much let go as he did shove the bag away. Larry drew it against his chest, clenched down and bolted for the lock up room. Putrid air, organic, revolting, whorled out at him from the depths of the bag's maw as he ran. He caught a glimpse of Ciphers's blood in its teeth. A second later he flung the bag into the lockup room and shoved the door closed with both hands.

A hazy after-image seemed to shimmer over the lock-up door as he backed away. The image was a door as well, heavier and slower-moving, studded with rivets and streaked with rust. He glared and let it register for only a second, then the shimmer-image caught up to the tangible Medberg Field door and was gone. From behind it came a muffled snarl and a metallic scraping sound; tiny teeth on the interior of the homeless bags chamber.

"Oh God," Ciphers labored at climbing to his feet, looking like the world's oldest track runner at the starting block.

"What's all the fuss?" came a voice from the semi-dark hallway. A hulking form plodded toward them, a set of keys in one hand and a high-powered flashlight in the other. A security badge floated in a sea of uniformed chest flab. It caught the light like a bright and intense eye.

Larry felt winded, so it surprised him when his own voice came out like a commanding bark. "It's about time, Gardner. We've got a situation here."

"An orphan, the way I heard it," Gardner said with dry importance. He smacked his lips, clearing away the last vestiges of bologna and mayo. "I was also told it's on the carousel. Why ain't it on the carousel? Don't tell me one of you numbnuts moved it."

"It's in lock-up." Larry rested a hand against the homeless bags door.

Gardner wobbled his jowly face as if he hadn't heard correctly. "What the hell for?"

"It's not a regular leave-behind," Ciphers slogged into a pool of emergency light to inspect his wounds. His hands trembled. "It chewed me, for Christ's sake. Look. It *chewed* me."

The flashlight in Gardner's meaty hand made an evaluating sweep. The corner of his mouth twitched and his eyes grew narrow. "Look, I know it's quiet tonight, and you guys are bored but, passengers or no passengers, I got power outage protocols to follow. I don't have time to play."

"We're not playing," Larry said with the last of his authoritative tone.

He rapped on the door to the lock-up and what was inside responded with an infuriated yowl. The door shuddered as a small leathery body dashed itself against the backside.

Gardner's eyes widened. "What have you got in there?"

"We don't know," Larry said.

Ciphers held out crimson hands. He looked like a man

lost in a dream. "It looks like a small suitcase. I swear to God. That's what I thought it was until it—"

"Chewed you, yeah. I got that." Gardner nodded and fixed his gaze on the door to the homeless bags room. "Open it up."

Some of the color drained from Ciphers's face. "What? You can't."

"You heard me."

Larry made an imploring motion at the door. "Damn it, Gardner, I told you we're not messing around."

"Neither am I." Gardner reached around and pulled a small handgun from a holster at the small of his back. It looked like a toy in his thick, dimpled hand.

"That's a firearm," Ciphers said, as if needing to broadcast the presence of such unwelcome things in the hallowed halls of Medberg Field.

Gardner's mouth was touched by a smirk that seemed to say *damned straight*. He trained the gun barrel and his flashlight on the door, two-fisted aiming. "Open it up, Parman."

Larry took out his key ring. The space inside the homeless bags room grew quiet as he undid the lock and opened the door just a crack. *It's getting ready*, he thought, his heart racing.

"Now stand over there," the security man said, motioning back toward Ciphers.

"There are no emergency lights in there," Larry offered. "I should hold your flashlight—"

"Over." Gardner said impatiently and flicked his light toward Ciphers. "There."

Larry stepped away. Strangeling lit the entire baggage area making it seem suddenly unfamiliar, strangely cavernous.

"He shouldn't have that gun," Ciphers said in a hoarse whisper. "Not concealed like that. Who does he think he is?"

Larry barely heard him. The interior of the Medberg Field baggage area wasn't exactly modern, but the walls were plain and clean, and he knew them well. At the moment, however, they had changed to crude steel beams and cinder block. The ceiling above him was a reinforcement grid of bare girders. These images shimmered like a transparent overlay and it made him think of the homeless bags door. He blinked hard as if to clear his vision. The strangeling ended. The overlays went with it.

"Did you see that?" he asked the other two men. He wondered if what had opened up was opening up wider and wider with every stroke of strangeling.

Ciphers's voice, nearly a shriek, shook him out of his thoughts. "Gardner, don't!"

The homeless bags door banged open. Gardner hunched in the doorway like a man peering into a dense fog from his back porch, flashlight in one hand, gun in the other.

"Godamnit," Larry lamented as he rushed up. "Are you crazy?"

He heard Gardner speak a single word, high and almost childlike. "Jeepers."

The bag lunged out of the dark, skating along the floor as if on a coiled spring. Larry was directly behind Gardner and he got a straight-on view of the bag's gaping mouth as it skidded into the security guard's flashlight beam. More than that, he got a look *into* the mouth, pillowy and slick, funneling down behind the teeth to form a fleshy gullet, mottled, greenish, pulsing.

He expected Gardner to jump back, perhaps even beat a retreat back down the dark hallway toward a more sensible world of protocols and bologna. Instead the man took a step forward and dealt a forceful kick. The bag seemed to meet the blow and fold around Gardner's ankle. It did not flinch. Instead, it bit down, hard.

Gardner hopped backward, keeping his foot with the bag aloft, drawing a bead down the barrel of the handgun. At the same time Ciphers ducked in, the baggage counter flashlight reclaimed and wielded with war club intensity. Strangeling surged. Larry's instincts pulled him back a little more just as Ciphers brought his flashlight around.

The rigid head of the flashlight missed its mark by only an inch and cracked sharply against Gardner's elevated shin. Gardner let out a high yelp and his grounded foot skated out from under him. He toppled backward with violent force, his feet momentarily trading places with his head. Ciphers dodged to the side, but not before Gardner's shoe clipped his cheek and sent him reeling into the gloom. The next second Gardner landed with a meaty thud. The bag sunk its teeth deeper in defiance of the jarring drop and Gardner screamed. Every part of him tensed, including his trigger finger. The sharp and deafening gunshot that followed found its mark: Gardner's own free and still-elevated left foot. Next to it, the other leg remained aloft and rigid, the bag humping and tearing away, uninterrupted. Gardner screamed again.

Larry leapt forward. The broom was there at his feet and he snatched it up, unaware he was standing on the handle until the resistance nearly tripped him. At the last moment the handle snapped leaving him with a much shorter, albeit sharper weapon. He rushed up and spoke directly to Gardner, although it seemed the man was already lost in a fog of pain and panic. "I'm going to knock it off of you. Just don't shoot me."

The bag dug in deeper and this time blood welled between its fish hook teeth like crimson spring water. Gardner screamed and tensed again. Ciphers, his right eye swelling shut where he'd been caught by a flailing shoe, scrambled over and crouched near Gardner's hands, reaching for the gun. "Give that over before you blow—"

The gun discharged. The bullet entered Ciphers's throat just below the jawline and bust out of his right eye socket, turning it into a red and roaring hole. He toppled over, mouth still working as if to finish his sentence.

Larry cried out, a rush of mournful horror as he watched Ciphers fall. Across the room something moved, detached itself from a shadowy corner and lurched stealthily along the wall, too deeply shaded by the gloom to be identified, other than it was small, no more than three feet tall. No time, he thought and turned back to Gardner.

"Jesus," Gardner squealed, kicking at his attacker with his gun-shot foot. Judging from the ragged rift in his shoe, he may have lost some toes. "Do something, Parman!"

"Try to hold still," Larry said.

He brought the broom handle around, adding an upward scooping motion at the end. The ragged wooden point struck black scaly hide and gained some purchase. The bag tore free and flipped through the gloom, its mouth working like a trout's, gulping air, and it landed on its side a few feet away. Larry descended on it before it could right itself. He brought the broom handle down in a two-handed jabbing motion. The point punched through the leather and sunk in neatly, making a wet yet resistant crunch. The bag let out a gargling sound, twitched once, and then fell still. Thick liquid, cloudy and greenish, began to leak over its hook-teeth and pool on the floor. Larry pulled the handle out and then speared it again for good measure, his mouth hard and fixed in a scowl.

Behind him, Gardner reached for his chewed right leg, his gun forgotten on the floor at his side. He seemed to be a neophyte attempting his first-ever sit-up and not quite making the cut. What Larry could see of the shin and calf between the shreds of uniform leg was the consistency of raw hamburger. It bled profusely. The other gun-wounded foot painted the floor with its own crimson squiggles.

"What do I do now?" Gardner slurred between gasps and sputters. He caught a glimpse of Ciphers's motionless form and wailed. "Ah God, what do I do?"

Larry glanced at their surroundings. "Get up."

"Can't," Gardner lamented. "Ah God, I can't."

"In case you hadn't noticed, things are changing around here and not necessarily for the good."

As if to punctuate his point, a volley of strangeling lit the place. Larry twisted his head upward. The overlay image was there, much clearer now. He could see pits of rust in the metal ceiling girders, and strands of shaggy black material dangling down like moss in a Deep South cemetery. It blew slightly in a passing breeze up there.

Almost here now, Larry thought and backed up, his shoe sliding through a puddle of blood near Ciphers's head. *Almost all are here.*

Distantly, beneath the rush of wind and rain, he heard a droning sound from outside, steady and familiar. A grave chill settled over him. *Propellers.* He looked around at the windows as they came alight with strangeling—they were small windows now, reinforced with wire mesh. In front of them were contoured plastic chairs, every third one sidled by a standing ashtray-type apparatus and a metal post fitted with a length of thick chain. Small signs on the walls demanded PLEASE RESTRAIN YOUR BAGS. WANDERING LUGGAGE WILL BE CONFISCATED. Further along were what appeared to be banks of pay telephones, low to the ground, gleaming like chrome memories. No dials or number pads fronted these phones. Only a single pushbutton. House phones, perhaps. His mind touched upon these things but dismissed them easily.

No need to figure out any of it. It's not for us. It's something they use over there. Over There, which is becoming Over Here.

"Parman?"

He looked around at Gardner who was propped up on his elbows gazing into the belly of the baggage area. Things were back to the Medberg Field he recognized, for the moment anyway. However, four more suitcases, larger rectangular ones, were scattered around the room, one of them busily shuffling left-right, left-right, along the edge of the carousel. Another ran its zippered mouth open, closed, and open again, as if stretching long unused muscles. When its mouth was open its teeth bloomed outward, coppery crescents that rippled and glinted.

Gardner eyed them, a filament of panic beginning to glow behind each pupil. "Where in the hell did they come from?"

"Someplace we're not supposed to know about." He reached down to take Gardner's meaty arm. As he did this he checked the ceiling again. As he feared, there were places up there that appeared as gray smudges now, permanent fissures as if this Medberg Field were a layer of flaking paint showing other strata underneath. "Someplace that's landing right on top of us, brought down by the storm, maybe. Come on."

Gardner tried to stand but sat right back down with a barely stifled scream. "I'm not going anywhere," he panted. "Hurts too much."

One of the new arrivals shuffled over to the defunct, speared bag, leaned as if to consider it, then let out a long, low moan. It shuddered as it vocalized, its sides jiggling like an amorphous sac.

Gardner stared at it with his hot filament eyes. Most of the color had run out of his jowly face. "What are they doing here, Parman?"

"They're waiting," he said, marking each suitcase with an evaluating glance. "That's mostly what you do in an airport, isn't it? Wait?"

Then he looked toward the parking lot windows. Strangeling lit the night. A dozen or so man-shaped forms stood in the rain watching the building with rapt contemplation, unmindful of the downpour pelting their coarse, fabric-like skin. Grommeted nostrils and black bead eyes gleamed. Mouths, which were slanted lines of zipper, seemed fixed in expressions of mute distaste. They began to plod through pavement puddles, scarecrow gloves for hands, faces seamed and greenish like worn army duffels. He could see more of them farther back, hooking around from the landing field where he knew an unfamiliar version of a four-prop plane sat with a portable gangway rolled up to the side. He wondered if Feeney had given them clearance to land.

Larry took up the gun and handed it go Gardner. "Here. Worst case, the door to the homeless bags storage area will lock behind you."

Gardner goggled. "What are you going to do?"

"I'm going to try to work something out," Larry said, and indicated the words PLEASE RESTRAIN YOUR BAGS which showed permanently above the windows now.

Gardner began to crawl toward the lock-up, his flabby arms working overtime. The floor beneath him was no longer smooth Medberg Field tile but plates of craggy fitted stone. "Your funeral."

The largest of the bags pivoted in small increments, gauging the large man's struggles with a greedy type of patience, its string and tag switching in the air with calculation.

"Yeah," Larry said. "Maybe."

There was a side exit leading to the parking lot about twenty paces up the hall, just out of reach of the emergency lights. He strode toward it, mindful of the shapes outside as they filtered close to the plate glass, searching for entry. He could see thirty or more, a couple of them female, one cradling a dripping infant-sized bundle to its chest.

In the room behind him the carousel came to life, filling the space with the thump and rattle of cargo riding down the conveyor, bag after bag. Larry felt a sick knot drop into his gut as he estimated the amount of cargo in an average plane load. A moment later Gardner let out a high and pain-filled scream. It ended wetly and abruptly. There were no gunshots.

He pushed the door open and was met by the shuffle of canvas feet. Strangeling flourished and revealed the tarpaulin faces within arms reach, milling together.

"Welcome to Medberg Field," he said with a sick grimace, all the while thinking *please, oh please God, restrain your bags.*

No response on those faces. Vacant. He noticed how the

throats and chests of greenish fabric were covered with snags and rendered holes, scrapes. Rips. Roughly handled. Careworn. Telling.

All the strength left his body as they ambled past him and took seats in the rows of plastic chairs, hands folded and waiting almost primly.

He sat down hard on the craggy floor. Behind him the familiar hum of the baggage carousel changed to something piercing, a chitter of inconceivable working parts. *All here now*, he thought, *it's all here.* Leathery cargo hopped off the moving track, tags aloft and writhing as they mingled and nudged. Some made low sounds over the hunched bodies scattered on the floor but most pressed inward expectantly; owners on alert as the last of their sodden luggage shuffled in on canvas legs.

He rested his head in his hands and waited, his unease back and twisting up into a brand of pure revulsion. Perhaps if he didn't move they would disregard him, dismiss him as a lone, strangely upholstered bag. Ownerless.

Homeless.

Outside, another plane touched down.

LISTEN

JACK KETCHUM

LISTEN. JUST LISTEN. That's all I want from you right now.
All right.

Maybe we'll fuck later, I don't know.

Sure. Okay.

I've got you for the whole night.

Eight hours. Yeah. One question. Why me? This place is gorgeous. I presume you looked through our book online. And why the cuffs? That's two questions. Sorry.

You looked . . . open, intelligent, attentive. Like somebody I could talk to. And honest. You looked honest. What? What's funny?

Honey, there are folks who'd say there isn't a whore in all of Boston you'd call exactly honest.

Whore? Not escort?

Escort on paper. Escort on your arm, sure. In the bedroom . . .

Listen, if I'm wrong I'm wrong. To me, you look honest. You're also very pretty. But you already know that. I wanted somebody pretty.

Why not beautiful? Rachel, Lee Ann? I don't exactly fit your décor.

I wanted pretty.

Okay. So how come the cuffs? They're new aren't they. I can tell from the leather.

I bought them day before yesterday. I was afraid of what you'd think.

What I'd think?

That I might . . . that you might feel threatened. Scared. This way you won't feel threatened.

That bad, huh?

Yes. That bad.

You sure you can't get out of them?

Want me to try again?

No, I don't think you need to do that. But do you mind if I admit to being scared a little?

No. Not at all. Light a smoke for me, will you? They're over there on the table.

(Pause.)

Thanks. You should be.

What? Scared?

Yes.

That's reassuring.

That's why the cuffs. If you want, you can tie me to the bedposts.

No. Behind your back is fine.

There's a good single-malt there. Have some.

Don't mind if I do. You?

Not right now. Give me another hit, will you?

Sure. Okay if I have one?

A smoke? Sure. Go ahead.

(Long pause.)

Tell me about yourself.

I thought you wanted to talk about you.

I do. In a minute. I don't need to hear everything. Just give me the CliffsNotes version. You know CliffsNotes. You're a student, aren't you.

How'd you guess?

You're young. You're lovely. You're . . .

Putting myself through school, yes. Good observation.

That's part of what I do. Observe.

What else?

Hmmm?

What else do you do?

We'll get to that. You don't much want to talk about yourself, do you.

Not really. Not particularly. I'm not that interesting.

Everybody's interesting. If you see them clearly enough.

To see me clearly enough would take you more than eight hours. And then you wouldn't get to do any of the talking, would you.

Now see? That's interesting.

No it's not. It's just me being glib, that's all. It's a problem I have. Being a smartass. Especially in nervous situations.

One last hit, please.

Sure. Here you go.

I make you nervous?

Of course you do. A little. You're my first client who's ever felt the need to put on handcuffs just to talk. Good scotch, by the way.

Thank you. Glad you like it.

Okay, the CliffsNotes version. Grew up in L.A., three older brothers, no sisters. My father was a dentist.

Was?

Cancer, two years ago. Mom, your basic housewife. Reads a lot. My brother Matt still lives with her. My major's political science. Minor in English. I like to write.

You're going into politics?

I'm interested in Ethical Politics. And yes, I know, it sounds like an oxymoron. You can't know how many times I've heard that. But it's more about working out problems of social justice and ethics than it is about Democrats or Republicans or anything. It's about changing public discourse to reflect the tension between the rights and interests of the majority and the rights and interests of the minority. About empathy and morality. And I don't mean any of that bible-based crap.

I told you you were interesting.

That's about as interesting as I get. Do you want me to take my clothes off?

I think I'd like that.
(Very long pause.)
Very nice.
Thank you. How about yours?
We'll leave them on for now.
You have a hard-on, Charlie. Okay to call you Charlie?
Sure.
You have a hard-on, Charlie.
It happens sometimes.
So what did you want to talk to me about? Should I sit on the bed?

Yes, sit on the bed. One question. I'm a pretty smart guy. I've read a bit about Ethical Politics myself. As I see it, it's about *collaboration*. And collaboration is as much about conflict as it is about cooperation, am I right?

Absolutely. Conflict and resolution of conflict.

So. Are we in conflict? You and I?

No. Why would you think that? We're in a transaction. You're paying me for a service. No harm, no foul.

But you're wrong. I'm here to hurt you. To do you harm.

Your hands are cuffed behind your back, Charlie. And as you can see, I'm a big girl.

Yes, you are. Even so. I think I'm going to lie down now. Will you lie down with me?

I'd like another scotch, please. If you don't mind. You go ahead, though.

You're nervous again. I've made you nervous.

You just told me you want to hurt me, so I'm a little nervous, yes.

Have the scotch.

Thank you. I think I will.

(Pause)

Where did you say you lived? Where you grew up, I mean.

Los Angeles. Pacific Palisades, to be exact.

I know Pacific Palisades. You come from money, then. So what are you doing hooking?

I prefer to make my own way. My mother and I aren't on the best of terms. When do we get to talking about you?

Soon. You say your mother reads a lot.

I . . . yes . . . so?

Reads by the pool, does she?

As a matter of fact . . .

How old would you say I am?

How old? I'm not great at guessing. Mid-fifties?

Forty-nine. I suppose I haven't aged all that well. My life's been . . . complicated. And you're what? Twenty-five?

Yes. Just this month. How did you know we have a pool?

Let's just say I *am* good at guessing. Finish your drink and lie down here. I want to tell you a story.

Yeah. About time we talked about you. But if I'm gonna lie down I think I'd like to take you up on your offer. About the bedposts.

Okay. No problem.

(Long pause.)

There.

Feel better now? More secure?

Yes.

You didn't ask me what I do for a living.

So what do you do for a living, Charlie?

I'm a contractor. I own my own construction company. Been in construction since I was a kid. Three years of college was all I could take. I guess you could say I had a case of wanderlust. I was good with my hands. And my body wasn't soft like it is now. So I traveled a lot. Crewed on, crewed out. Pay was always good and I wasn't stupid. I worked myself up to foreman and I saved my money. Made some very good investments. Bought Apple in '96, would you believe it? I learned how to bid and how to balance the books. And then who to *hire* to bid and balance the books.

So now you're a rich guy.

Yes I am.

Got a wife? Family? If you don't mind my asking.

No. Never.

Never wanted that?

Never. Not in my game-plan. You?

Someday maybe. Great big maybe on that.

You don't like children?

I didn't much like them growing up, that's for sure. When I was a kid. Now I don't know any.

Why didn't you like them growing up?

I don't know. Well, yes I do. Of course I do. When I was around ten, eleven, I hit I guess what you'd call an awkward stage. I got fat. You get fat at that age, you get teased. You get treated this certain way. You can't be part of anything. It's not that you're overlooked—you're not—you're looked at too much, like you're not exactly part of the human race. You take a lot of shit. Kids can be fucking mean, you know?

(Pause.)

You weren't fat when I knew you.

(Pause.)

What?

You were a slim little thing. Your hair was very fine, thinner than it is now. You wore it in a ponytail.

(Long pause.)

You'd have been eight years old. I was thirty-two. You were my second.

Your what?

I built your pool. The one your mother reads by. I was crew. 444 Ocampo Drive. Shallow end about thirty feet from the house as I recall. I was on backhoe that day. You remember?

You were . . . ?

Don't get up. Picture me with long hair and a lot fewer years on my face. I had all my hair back then.

You . . .

You liked to watch the backhoe tearing up the lawn. You were curious. You brought me a glass of lemonade. Your mother was in the kitchen talking to the foreman. I drank the lemonade very fast and took you by the arm into the tall shrubs you had there separating your house from the one behind it and held you down and forced your mouth open. You remember now?

You motherfucker. You motherfucking son of a bitch.

Don't get up. I told you I was going to hurt you, didn't I? It was very fast. You cried. Not too much. I told you to limp a little and tell your mother you'd stubbed your toe on a rock from the lawn and you did. Because I told you that if you didn't say that, if you said anything else, I'd have to kill her. Kill the both of you, actually. I'd done one other little girl before you. I held out for a long time. You were my second.

How did you . . . why are you telling me this? Who the fuck are you?

I'm Charlie, Sarah. Yes. I know your real name. Are you surprised?

What the fuck? What the fuck do you want from me?

Sit down. Reach into my pocket here.

(Pause.)

What am I supposed to do with these?

You were the second. Since then there have been fifteen others, Sarah. Fifteen more. The last one, only a week ago. And I don't just use their mouths anymore. You got fat, Sarah. You had your awkward stage. I have to wonder what some of them will go through. Some of those fifteen. I don't really care, but I do wonder. I only know about the first one. And you.

What . . . ?

Her name was Michelle Burton. You may have read about her. She had an argument with her live-in boyfriend. Piled her two children by two separate marriages into her car and drove them into a concrete divider at seventy miles an hour on FDR Drive in New York. It made the news. The children were two little girls, four and three years old. Michelle was twenty-seven, two years older than you.

(Pause.)

That bottle you're holding. Open it. Go ahead.
(Pause.)
Potassium cyanide. Are things becoming clearer now?
Wait a minute. Wait one fucking minute. You tell me about this Michelle person. She killed herself. Okay. I mean, it's not okay, but okay. But if you think I'm inclined that way, if you think I'm going to take what's in this bottle you're nuts, you're out of your fucking mind. My life is just fine, thank you very much. Despite what you did. Despite what you did. And yeah, you fucked me up for a long time. But that was then and this is now. So you can go screw yourself. Turn yourself in to the cops. Jump out your pretty picture window here. Blow your fucking brains out!
You're emotional. You misunderstand. But you're close. The capsule is for me, not for you.
Excuse me?
Sarah, I'm tired. I'm exhausted. I have no friends. Not even sure what that word means. I have no real enemies. I've probably gone as far in life as my work will take me. Success, making money, manipulating the system, it's nothing, it's not *fun* anymore. I'll do what I do again, you know. To another little girl and then another. It's the only thing in my life that really gets me, the only thing I really care to do. But it doesn't *last*, Sarah. I'm high for a day, high for a week, and then . . . I'm running on empty. I don't have the courage to do this myself. I tried. I had one of these on my tongue. I couldn't bite down and I couldn't swallow. I just couldn't do it.
So you want me to . . . you're asking me to do you a favor, Charlie? Me?
With a good single-malt chaser, yes. I figured you'd hate me enough.
(Pause.)
Right. Sure. And I go down for murder, Charlie. You fucking asshole. I'd love to help you out here. If you knew what I went through. It would give me great pleasure to see you dead. But no way am I . . .

Nobody knows you're here, Sarah. This is a private home in a brownstone apartment building. No doorman. And as you see, I have the entire floor. You passed nobody on the stairs, did you.

No, but . . .

Of course not. The neighbors go to bed early here. That's why I asked for you at one in the morning.

Bullshit. I mean, Rebecca knows . . . the service . . .

Rebecca, yes. Nobody knows you're here *except* Rebecca. And she won't tell. Rebecca was number four.

What?

She took it much harder than you did. Maybe because she was twelve at the time, almost a teenager. Difficult age. Still a virgin, though. Before, I mean.

You're lying. That's not possible.

I did thorough due diligence on both of you. I know where *all* my girls are, Sarah. I always do. All seventeen. Well, sixteen, now. Quite a coincidence, isn't it? Small world. Six degrees of separation, that kind of thing. Listen to me. You've never been arrested. Your fingerprints are not on record. You've *never been* here.

(Pause.)

I could do it. Couldn't I.

Of course you could.

(Very long pause.)

Interesting. Mind if I use your phone?

That depends on who you're calling.

I was really just being polite, Charlie. You're cuffed to the bedposts. I sort of doubt you can stop me.

(Pause.)

Hi, Wade. I'm fine, thanks. But I need a favor. I'm at a client's apartment. 33 West Cedar Street. Do you think you can come over?

Sarah . . .

How long, do you think?

Sarah, I don't . . .

Okay, that'll be fine. Third floor. I'll buzz you up. Thanks, Wade. See you soon. Bye.

What are you doing, Sarah? What the hell is this? Who's this Wade person?

He's a friend. A good friend. He and I dated for a while a couple of years ago. He was getting over a very bad marriage and I was his rebound girl. We were fun together. Met at the City Bar over on Exeter, got to talking over scotches. Not as good as your scotch, Charlie. But we hit it off. He's a good man, a compassionate man. And he knows how to listen. By now he pretty much knows my life story, all of it, and he doesn't judge. But here's where it gets funny, Charlie. Those six degrees of separation you talked about? One of the things that we talked about was what you did to me back then. He was especially interested in that. He's BPD, Charlie. Sexual Assault Unit. How's that for small world?

(Long pause.)

I'm going to get dressed. I'm going to have a smoke and a scotch. You can join me if you like. I'll give you a hand. But what you can't *do is take one of your little death pills. You're going to live, Charlie. And when Wade gets here you're going to tell him all about number seventeen. Who she is and where she lives and exactly what you did to her. Everything. Wade told me his stories too. Stories about his wife, but also about his job, you know? I gather he can be very persuasive.*

(Pause.)

Oh, quit it. Come on. Cut it out, Charlie. Struggling won't help. Consider this Ethical Politics in action, okay? We'll collaborate. Resolve our conflict. The tension between the rights and interests of the majority versus the rights and interest of the minority, know what I mean? In this case, you're the minority, Charles. And the majority? The majority will have your ass three ways to Sunday at Cedar Junction. You know that. Cons don't like baby-rapers much, and for me, thinking about that's going to be a lot nicer than killing you. All we need to do is see you get convicted. Shouldn't be hard. Get you in the papers, on the net. Maybe on TV.

(Pause.)

Then all they have to do inside is pay attention . . . just listen.

MAN HOLDING RAZOR BLADE

JOHN MCNEE

HEY SLUT. JUST a remnder 2 sleep with 1 eye open tonite in case you think Id forgot how u FUCKED MY LIFE WHORE. Only a matter of time til I find you so sweet dreams bitch.

Nasreen was up to her elbows in dishes and soapy water, so Hannah had to hold the phone up to her face. She squinted and then gasped. "Wow."

"Yep," said Hannah, slumping back down onto the sofa. Nasreen's hallway segued into a kitchen-slash-living room without widening so much as an inch, demanding a set-up where the sofa, pushed up against the wall, was only two feet from the kitchen counter and close enough to catch spray from the tap.

Nasreen shook her head in astonishment. "That's . . . intense. Are they all like that?"

"The next one will probably be nicer. He alternates."

"Does it frighten you?"

Hannah gave her a look like she'd asked a stupid question. "I'm here, aren't I?"

Nasreen exhaled loudly, then went back to scouring a baking tray. "If it were me I'd just delete them. Unread."

"Can't. I have to save them all for the police."

"What are they going to do with them?"

"Going on past form? Not a lot."

Hannah's relationship with Darren ended the third time police were called out to settle one of their arguments. She declined the offer of medical treatment for various fresh cuts and bruises but was finally persuaded to make a statement.

A few days later, Darren Howe, 32, appeared in court to plead not guilty to charges of domestic assault and behaving in a threatening or abusive manner. He was released on bail subject to the condition he not communicate directly or indirectly with the complainant, Hannah Gillespie.

She started on the night shift that evening, returning home in the early hours of the morning to find her front door ajar, carpets soaked with pig's blood and the word CUNT scrawled in excrement on the inside of her bedroom window. Turning on her phone to call the police, she discovered a text from Darren reading: This is just the start. Welcome to Hell.

The officers who went to arrest him learned he had never returned to his bail address.

"You might want to think about finding somewhere else to stay," a sympathetic constable advised her. "Somewhere he doesn't know about. Just until we track him down."

Nasreen's sofa was the latest to which she'd fled. The flat, situated in a half-empty council block, wasn't much, but it beat sleeping in the Women's Refuge. Hannah stood up when her phone sounded again, returning to Nasreen's side to display Darren's latest: I no we could sort this out if u just called. No1 gets me like u do. U know that. U just make me so fuckin mad sumtimes xxxx

"He's no poet," Nasreen said. "I don't know how you managed two years of that. Honestly. You always attract the nasty ones." The way she said it had a trace of judgment that Hannah did her best to ignore.

Nasreen didn't date, didn't believe in sex before marriage and would probably end up wed to whichever young doctor her mother picked out for her. Hannah didn't stand a chance of making her understand, so she just shook her head. "I don't know. It all feels like such a bad dream. All I want is for it to be over. I just wish . . . What's that?"

"Hmm?"

"That." Hannah pointed out the window, across the courtyard to the high wall separating the complex from the street.

"Oh. *That*."

The wall had been painted with a graffiti mural—Banksy by way of Hieronymus Bosch, just about visible in the orange glow of the streetlights. It depicted the slope of a hill on which a large bonfire blazed. Numerous naked, deformed creatures danced around it, engaged in various acts of debauchery and self-mutilation. In the foreground, with his back to the flames, stood a dark-skinned man in a brown, pinstriped suit, a shining blade clutched in his fist.

"It was painted by an artist who lives in the block around the corner," Nasreen said. "Asylum seeker. He's quite well-regarded, apparently."

"It's horrible," said Hannah.

"Yes." Nasreen sighed. "It is. Nobody asked him to paint it. I woke up one morning and there it was. Put me right off my cornflakes."

"But isn't it council property?"

"It is. And they were told. And were all set to scrub it off when the press got a hold of it. You can imagine the story— renowned artist fleeing persecution in his homeland creates first new work in three years only for jobs-worth council cleaners to wash it away. Then some arts collective got involved, it became this whole big thing . . . The council backed off and now we're stuck with it."

"That's . . . ridiculous." Hannah couldn't help smiling. She squinted through the window, trying to make out more of the mural's details in the half-light. One of the dancing figures was a three-legged man doing a jig on feet made of knives.

Another was a fat, bald man with a neck like a python coiling round and around his pink body. "Did anyone try talking to the guy who painted it?"

"He's nuts. I'm not kidding. Mrs. Stewart—she lives across the way—objected to having to pass it every morning and complained to him directly. He responded by painting her into it. She's the one on the far right eating her own intestines."

"Ewww."

"Yeah. I haven't seen her since. I think she takes the long way round these days." The rubber gloves snapped as Nasreen peeled them off. "And on that delightful note . . . I'm going to bed."

"Ah. When are you on?"

"Eight till ten. The winter shifts are a killer. You?"

"Not till two."

Nasreen smiled. "I won't even see you. Keys are by the door. Don't forget them. I'll try not to wake you on my way out."

"Don't worry about it," Hannah said, dropping back onto the sofa. "I haven't really been sleeping for a while now."

"Maybe turn your phone off," Nasreen suggested, on her way to the bathroom. "Just a thought."

Hey SLUT. The dripping of the tap roused Hannah from a troubled sleep, busy with fears and threats. The words of his text message hovered before her as she opened her eyes, lingering in electric white, unwilling to fade back into her subconscious just yet.

She'd always been a vivid dreamer, prone to waking hallucinations. Talked in her sleep, too. She remembered a time waking up next to Darren, rolling over to see a giant gray moth eating his face. She'd screamed, slapped the moth away and chased it into a corner of the room, then collapsed, weeping against the bed.

Darren had grabbed her and she'd turned to see his face ragged and bloody, eyes bulging out of lidless holes, teeth grinning in a lipless red mouth. He'd shaken her, shouted, and she'd watched, stunned, as the wounds faded, his flesh healing itself in a few seconds. The moth, still fluttering madly in the corner, faded a moment later.

The neon words floating above Nasreen's sofa would fade too, if she wanted, but the drip took precedence. Letting the words hang where they were, Hannah rolled out from under her duvet, reached out for the counter top and pulled herself onto her feet.

Fire danced through the window. Hannah peered out and saw a bonfire in the courtyard. A man stood a few feet in front of it, silhouetted against the scarlet flames. The high wall behind him was bare brick.

As Hannah watched him, the man raised his head and stared back at her.

She blinked. He stared back.

She blinked again, hard, and shook her head. He stared back.

Feeling the weight of exhaustion pressing down, she sighed, tightened the handle on the tap and went back to the sofa. She slid beneath the covers and floating words, and watched the hallucinatory light from the bonfire flickering on the wall as she drifted back to sleep.

She left for work at 1pm, too tired to function properly, having forced herself to get up an hour earlier. She hadn't heard Nasreen leave to start her 14-hour shift, but woke more than once to the sound of her phone vibrating. She didn't read the texts till she was crossing the courtyard, choosing them over study of the bonfire graffiti, now safely back on the high wall where it belonged.

Ready to talk? the first message read, sent at 8:05 am, after what Darren must have assumed was a restless night.

Dont u dare fucking ignore me cunt! I'm sick to the fucking back teeth of being treated like shit by a cheatin cow lik u! That one sent at 11:38 a.m., after he'd had plenty of time to get a few beers down his throat and build up a good head of hate.

Hannah was almost out of the courtyard when she finally gave in to temptation, raised her head from her phone, and looked at the painting. The man in the pinstriped suit stared right back at her. The artist had deliberately painted him in such a way that his glowering black eyes were trained upon her right up to the moment she passed through the gate onto the street.

Work was a welcome distraction from her fears and fatigue. She wasn't worried about Darren tracking her down there. It was a big hospital, with plenty of security staff. For twelve hours she could switch off her phone and busy herself with the much more serious problems of the patients filling up the psychiatric ward.

It was only after her shift ended at 2 am that she remembered how exhausted she was. On the bus back to Nasreen's she fell asleep and had to be woken by the driver, who was considerate enough to yell when they reached her stop.

Hannah waved her thanks and staggered out into the empty street. Her eyes were half-closed as she navigated the chilling darkness, and she was ready to let out a half-hearted little cheer, keys already in hand, as she passed back through the gate.

Heat hit her like a wall. She lurched left, throwing her hands up against the flames.

The courtyard was ablaze—burning debris piled high in the center quad. The same bonfire from the painting, the one from her dream. Orange embers floated all around her, spinning through air that shimmered in the scorching temperatures. Smoke stung her eyes and nostrils. She felt the burning air dry her throat when she gasped.

Somewhere, beyond the inferno, a woman screamed.

Her eyes watering from the smoke, almost blinded by the

light, Hannah started to run in what she hoped was the direction of the flat. Though she was moving away from the fire, the heat seemed to intensify with every step. She could feel the hairs being singed on the back of her neck.

Wiping tears from her eyes, she saw the door to Nasreen's block and, just a few feet ahead, a figure crouched on the ground, turned away from her.

"Hello?" She coughed, drawing closer. "Hello, are you okay?"

It was an old woman. Hannah could make out her white bouffant and flower pattern scarf poking out from the collar of her anorak. She was hunched, head moving busily up and down. Hannah could hear the sound of her lips smacking and feared she might be choking.

She rushed forward and was reaching out her hand when the woman turned and faced her.

Hannah recoiled at the sight, breath catching in her throat.

The woman had a length of red flesh between her teeth. She fed it into her mouth with blood-slick hands, tugging at great loops that spilled out of a hole in her gut and hung wet and heavy between her legs. When she saw Hannah, the woman's eyes widened behind her thick spectacles. Her mouth popped open, spraying scraps of quivering entrails and saliva. "Wrong one!" She shrieked through pink froth. "Wrong one! Wrong one! Wrong one!"

"What's that?" The voice came from over Hannah's shoulder. She spun around to face something lumbering towards her, its features hidden by the bonfire's radiance. All she could see was that it had too many limbs to be human, yet it spoke with a man's voice. "What is it?"

Another figure appeared beside him, this one with a grand, bulbous head atop a stick-thin body, like a pumpkin on a pencil. "She says we got the wrong one," he said, raising a slender hand to point at Hannah. "That's the one he wants."

Hannah turned and ran. Dodging the grasping hands of

the old woman, she sprinted for the door. It was unlocked. She had the handle in her fist and was pulling it toward her when she heard another voice close behind.

"Hannah, wait . . . "

She froze and looked round to see a man stepping out of the shadows. He wore a brown pinstripe suit and clutched a straight razor in his hand. His dark-skinned face looked heavily scarred, but she realized after a moment what the crisscrossing lines were—brush-strokes. Oil-painted flesh come to life. "You know me," he said.

"No."

"You do." He took a step closer. She could sense others moving in around her. "You just . . . don't remember right now."

"*No!*" She threw the door wide and dashed up the stairs.

"Hannah!" His voice echoed in the stairwell.

She charged down the hall, Nasreen's keys already jangling in her hand. She unlocked the door, slammed it behind her, and threw her body up against it.

"Naz!" She yelled. "Naz!"

No answer.

Keeping her back pressed to the door, she slid down to the floor and sat there, panting and shivering.

Dark hands and faces were pressed against the kitchen windows. Deformed, fire-ravaged horrors. She saw them peering in at her, but they made no attempt to break through.

"They can't get in." Clutching her knees to her chest, Hannah squeezed her eyes shut and whispered the words like a mantra. "They can't get in, can't get in, can't get in . . . "

She woke with the dawn's light, starting awake on the floor, unsure at first of where she was or how long she'd been asleep. When she'd gathered her senses as best she could, she ran to the windows and looked down into the courtyard. It looked normal, of course. No bonfire. No monsters. Painting back on the wall.

"Naz!" She called, marching through to the bedroom. "Naz!"

She opened the door and turned on the light. The bed was empty.

Hannah went into the bathroom and washed her face while she tried to make sense of the evening's events, however impossible the task appeared. To have left the flat, Nasreen would have to have physically dragged her away from the door without waking her. She was certain that had never happened, which meant she never returned to the flat at all.

Hannah took out her phone to call her and found six messages.

U sucking his dick rite now? Hope u fuckin enjoy it while it lasts.

Dont prtend u dont read these. I know u.

U forget how well I fuckin know you.

And so on. Hannah felt tears welling up in her eyes and clenched her fist tight, feeling her nails bite into the flesh of her palm.

"Get a grip," she told the bathroom mirror. "Get a fucking grip already."

She was out the door a few minutes later, planning to go to Nasreen, wherever she was. She didn't know yet but would find out on the way. Anything was better than sitting alone in the flat, feeling her mind slipping away from her.

The painted man's eyes were on her as she neared the wall. Defiant, she glared back at him, then halted.

There was something different about the mural. A new splash of color on the hillside, the details becoming clearer as she approached. In between Mrs. Stewart the organ-muncher and a nine-legged flesh crab stood a new member of the merry band. A slim woman, her black hair tied back in a pony-tail, had been stripped of her clothing and was now being fitted with a dress of molten metal. Lengths of searing hot chains had been wrapped around her body and were being wound tightly about her arms, scorching her skin with their touch.

Hannah stared at the woman's features for a long time, amazed that a face so contorted in agony could still be so easily recognizable.

"I call it 'Man Holding Razor Blade,'" Gleb said, through teeth the color of mustard.

It had taken Hannah most of the day to find him. Almost all of the flats in Nasreen's block were empty and the few that weren't were occupied almost exclusively by the most unsociable, unhelpful people. However, she eventually received clear instructions on where to find "the lunatic Russian painter" Gleb Kulesh.

He wasn't Russian. He was keen to make that clear when they met. He hailed from Belarus, where he had enjoyed a celebrity lifestyle, the toast of the international art scene. But when his affiliations with certain political factions got him into trouble with the government, he fled, and landed in the UK as an asylum seeker. He had been in the country for years, living in squalor, unable to work, unable to sell his paintings, cut off from his friends and family, resentful of his own government and that of the UK, where he was effectively a political prisoner.

All this he told her in a barely comprehensible rant while she stood in his doorway.

He settled down some once she managed to make it clear her interest was only in his artwork, and invited her onto the balcony outside his flat, where they shared a drink from a bottle of something that looked like vodka, but was labeled "spirit drink."

"But what is it?" she said, referring to the painting. "What's it about?"

"Aaah . . . " He tried to fix her with a meaningful stare, but his bloodshot eyes had trouble finding hers. "Is like fairy tale."

She frowned. "I doubt that."

"Comes to me in dream," he said. "A golden firefly, while I sleep, creeps in my ear and sings song of this man."

Hannah's frown deepened. She tilted her empty glass towards the bottle. "We don't have fireflies in Scotland."

Gleb's grin widened, showing yet more yellow teeth and the gaping spaces in between. "And yet . . . Sing to me she does, telling story of cursed man, doomed to wander the land of nightmares. All he knows is fear and horror, till one night meets beautiful maiden. She dreams of him in her sleep. They fall in love, yet she must wake up. And when does, she forget."

"Forget?"

He nodded. "Forget him. Forget she loves him. He weeps, searches the land of nightmares till he find her again, and does, when she is sleep again. And again they fall in love. But she must wake up. Forgets. And again and again. So he has plan, yes?"

"What plan?"

Gleb poured them both another shot. "He invades dream of great artist. Tells to paint picture of him on wall, looking out, yes? So he may see his beloved in the waking world. So he may woo her and . . . win her hand. You understand?"

Hannah nodded, though she wasn't sure if she did or even wanted to. "Then what?"

Gleb shrugged. "And then . . . nothing. I get out of bed and I paint fucking picture. And fucking people want to take down, others not, bullshit, bullshit, bullshit." He knocked the shot back.

Hannah dropped her head into her hands, battling to grasp a coherent thought. "But . . . then . . . why? Why Mrs. Stewart?"

"What?"

"Mrs. Stewart. Why paint her in? And why paint Naz?"

Gleb screwed his face up in confusion. "I don't know what you mean . . . "

~

She dragged him to see the painting for himself, pointing out the malformed caricatures of Nasreen and Mrs. Stewart from a good six feet away. Though Hannah was keen to maintain an appropriate distance, Gleb was happy to get up close and personal with his work.

He leaned in, till his nose was almost pressed against the bricks. He brushed his hand across the paint, tracing figures with his fingers. The examination lasted several minutes and was conducted in silence, while Hannah did her best to ignore the man with the razor blade's glare. It seemed to her there was a touch more venom in those eyes than when they'd last met her own.

"Hmph." Gleb clapped his hands together and straightened up.

"Well?"

He looked at her, smiled, and pointed his finger at the image of Nasreen, swathed in glowing metal. "I did not paint this."

She swallowed. "No?"

He shook his head. "No." His finger moved to Mrs. Stewart. "Or this." The flesh crab. "Or this." He pointed at the figure of a woman walking on her hands, two cinder-black babies clutched in feet like eagle talons. "Or this."

Hannah was slow to respond. "You're . . . certain?"

He nodded. "Most certainly, yes. Not my work. Is good, though. Is very like. Could be. Almost very could." He grinned. "You . . . know artist, yes?"

Hannah's head reeled. She could feel the burn of his cheap vodka where it had stuck in her throat, threatening to bubble back up out of her mouth. "No. There is no artist."

Gleb's grin faded. It was clear he didn't understand what she meant, though he was doing his very best. He pointed again at Nasreen's screaming face. "Her. You say she disappeared?"

Hannah nodded. "Vanished. I think they all did. I think he took them."

Gleb frowned again. He looked at the man with the razor blade, then turned back to Hannah. The look he gave her was pitiable. "Is . . . only paint."

Hannah closed her eyes and swore a few times under her breath. She pressed a hand to her throbbing head while clawing through a tangle of disjointed thoughts, trying to find the words that would make him comprehend. It was almost a relief when her phone sounded, giving her an excuse to turn away.

The text, from Darren, read: This is your last chance.

Hannah read it over twice, then laughed, sighed and replied: "Probably."

"That's the thing about love though, isn't it? It's dangerous." Darren stared at her from under a thick fringe of dark, glossy hair. He didn't look the violent kind. Hannah had to wonder how many of them did. "That's what we've got. Makes you do things you'd never dream of doing."

They sat at a corner table in the nearest pub. The landlady had just called last orders.

Hannah was silent for a moment, giving him a chance to think about what he'd just said, then leaned forward and replied, "You poured pig's blood on my fucking carpets."

He grinned sheepishly, like a boy caught with his hand in the biscuit tin. "Yeah, I guess I did, didn't I?"

Hannah could feel her temper rising. "That's the least of it!"

"Hey. You did some pretty terrible things yourself."

"Like what? Telling the truth?"

His expression hardened. "You know *exactly* what I'm talking about."

She pulled back and bit her tongue. He could still put the fear in her, even in the middle of a crowded bar.

"I'm sorry," he said, after they'd passed a few moments in silence. "I've been trying to tell you that all night. I want us to put what's done behind us. I want to spend the rest of my life making you happy, but before I can do that I need you to go to the cops, ask to make a fresh statement, delete the texts . . . "

"There's still the bail breach."

"That's okay," he said. "I'll take whatever they dish out it if it means I can have you back again. I love you, Hannah." He took her hand in his own. "And whatever happens between us . . . that's nobody's business but ours, right?"

In a frantic few seconds her mind's eye played a slideshow of painful memories: her own face, bloodied and bruised, eyes ringed red with tears, scratched skin, red smears on the walls, broken glass shards twinkling on the rug . . . The final image was of a dark man on a burning hillside.

"They're closing," she said. "You should . . . come back to the flat. For a drink."

Darren's arm was linked with hers as they crossed the street. His touch made her queasy, but she hoped this would be the last time.

"It's late," he said. "You're sure your friend won't mind?" The frosted cloud of his breath swirled towards her through the darkness. She tried not to inhale.

"No," Hannah replied. "She's long gone."

She halted when they passed through the gate. The courtyard was empty—a silent, gray void, chilled in the shadow of the tower block. She looked to the high wall and saw it was clean.

"You okay?" Darren asked.

She forced herself to look him in the eye and for a moment came perilously close to apologizing.

"Hannah . . . " The voice came from their left. They both looked and saw a shadow in the shape of a man.

"The fuck are you?" Darren spat, turning from the shadow to Hannah, searching her face for answers.

"Hannah . . . " the shadow repeated. There was hunger in his voice.

"It's him, isn't it?" Darren sneered. "The one you talk about in your sleep."

Hannah was shaking as she faced the shadow. "You want me?" She startled herself with the volume of her voice.

The shadow nodded.

"Want to win me?"

"You know I do," the shadow replied.

"Now's your chance," she said, pointing at Darren.

"Fuck that," Darren yelled, and slapped her hand away.

The bonfire exploded into brilliant life behind them. A shock eruption of heat and light that threw Hannah off balance and knocked Darren onto the cement.

She leaped over his sprawled body and started to run, heading for the block and the protection of Nasreen's flat. Glancing back, she saw Darren raising himself up onto his knees, hands shielding his face from the blaze.

Gleb's Painted Man stood over him, razor blade open in his fist. His arm snapped diagonally up, then down, and Darren's neck became a gushing fountain of red. He threw his hands against the wound and in a moment they too were painted in blood.

The man glared at Hannah. She put her head down and ran, dodging other monstrous shadows as they grasped for her. She made it into the building and slammed the main door behind her, then tore up the stairs to Nasreen's flat . . . and froze.

The front door stood ajar—a set of crimson-coated keys in the lock.

Hannah was panting, an icy sweat on her skin. They couldn't get into the flat. She *knew* that. She'd seen it for herself. "Naz?" Had to be. "Nasreen?" She pressed forward, into the darkened hallway. "Naz?"

Her reply was preceded by the sound of chains dragging on linoleum. "Yes . . . and no . . . " The lithe nightmare that stepped into view was only barely recognizable as female. The dark flesh clinging to her skeletal frame had melted with the hot steel and wound into tight ropes of skin and metal, twisted around her limbs. Her fingers, peeled back to the bones, drummed on the kitchen counter. "I remember . . . when this was mine."

Hannah's knees buckled. "No . . . "

Nasreen touched her fingers to her eyeless face, now a map of overlapping scar tissue. "Look what he did to me," she said. "So bored . . . of waiting for you."

Hannah was on the floor. She could feel vomit rising in her throat. She turned and saw his silhouette in the doorway.

"Oh Hannah . . . " Nasreen sighed. "You always attract the nasty ones . . . "

Council cleaners came the following Monday, at Gleb's own request. He made repeated assurances that he would not interfere with their work and even agreed to contribute to a press statement voicing his support of the mural's removal.

His decision was made following the latest batch of unauthorized 'alterations,' which he felt went too far in changing the meaning of the piece. The addition of the young man, face down in a pool of blood, he could have perhaps lived with, but not the fresh blood on the main figure's blade or the very prominent blonde woman who had been painted into his arms.

Her face was turned towards the bonfire, so Gleb could not tell who—if anyone—she was supposed to be.

He stood and watched as the cleaners got to work with their pressure hoses and sand blasters. They worked efficiently and, within a matter of minutes, she was gone.

SAILOR'S REST

JAY CASELBERG

THE BEACH AT night is a calm place, a place of warm, damp air and a vaguely whispering breeze stirring your hair. It is all dark purples and blacks, smudged shapes and indistinct. When the wind picks up, the slow sand hiss slides just beneath the blanket of water sounds, harmonizing with the waves. It is a place of simultaneous stillness and movement.

The best of the beaches are replete with dunes, small rises that form a barrier to the rest of the world, a rampart of privacy against the rest of humanity. Tufts of wispy grass stand waving slightly, silent sentinels against the chance interloper. My place of solace, retreat, and to be honest, private coupling, was my refuge—or had been until that night.

I'd never really thought about it before, but after the events of that one late evening, I thought about it more, over and over. Think of those billions of tiny particles, the grains of sand and what might lay hidden amongst the multitude. Buried beneath and within that flat expanse lie many things—bits and pieces of otherness, not originally from there, but having ended up as an essential part of all that which has become the beach itself. Lumps of driftwood, small pieces of wave-smoothed glass, strands of weed, desiccated sponges like hands reaching up in a silent plea, you can find all of them. You can find other things too if you look hard enough or if you are there at the right place and time to see them.

It had been a convivial evening, excellent food, several bottles of good wine, and one or two spirited but affable arguments, as was our wont. There were six of us, and we met regularly in rotation, the next couple in line playing host. It wasn't so much a social ritual as it was a group of friends, enjoying each other's company when we could. We all knew the shapes of our ragged edges and the knots and bumps, all the things that make us interesting. Sometimes the jagged lines became a bit too sharp, but we'd all been friends long enough that none of them really cut deep. There was never any real rancor between us, and the fleeting enmities that transpired soon passed.

"Let's build a beach fire and stay a while longer. Yes, why not?" That was Susan. She was always the one to pounce on a whim and drive the collective group to comply. And so it started.

"Yeah," said Thomas. "I'm in. What about the rest of you?"

He was Jennifer's partner, a bit of a dreamer, one who'd never really grown past his student days, and probably the most easily swayed of all of us. His longish hair and scraggly beard harkened back to days of protests and causes. He had a gentle nature despite all that. Not really the sort to throw bottles or stones. More at home online or fiddling about with web design.

Jennifer's pixie-like features were always touched with a hint of mischievous amusement. She pushed back a strand of her blonde hair and peered at us.

"It's such a fine night, and you two have been so blessed. It would be a shame to waste it. Why not share it? Unless you don't want the unwashed masses partaking of your precious domain . . . " She leaned forward, looking knowingly at each of the others.

We were all warm with the glow of the evening, so

Amanda and I didn't take much convincing. Max simply nodded. He was a man of few words at the best of times. Short and taciturn, he belonged to Jennifer, and "belonged" was really the right term; she carted him around like a possession, not that he seemed to mind. I smiled and nodded, then started clearing the table.

"Oh, leave that, Paul," Amanda said. "We can do it later."

"Yeah, come on," Jennifer chimed in. She was already on her feet.

I spread my hands in acquiescence with a forced sigh. There really was nothing else for it.

Still laughing and giggling, we headed out. Amanda and I had been lucky with our purchase. The house was a low wooden affair, many rooms and a gorgeous glassed-in veranda area where we hosted all of our social events. It had taken a lot of work to make it livable, but it had paid off. You know the expression "location, location, location?" Well, we had that and then some. Across a small rise of dunes lay the secluded beach that we claimed as our own. We were out at the end of town, so the beach didn't get too many visitors, the occasional dog-walker, a lone surfer, and, of course, us, but that was about it. For Amanda and me, it was ideal, but the beach . . . the beach was just there, and it was always just there. It was that which had sold us on the house in the first place, despite its dilapidated condition when we bought it.

Because the long strip of empty shore and dunes was seldom frequented, there was a good supply of old wood scattered across the edges of the grassy hummocks and along the beach itself. It wouldn't take too long to find enough for a decent fire. Max and I set about dragging enough together, while Thomas sat staring at the low rolling, inky waves, nursing one of the remaining wine bottles, wavering slightly as if pushed by an invisible breeze, clearly a little the worse for wear. Jennifer and Amanda sat nearby, their shoes off beside them, their heads together talking about something in low tones. Susan strolled along the shallow water's edge, kicking through the thin slick of saltwater and silver bubbles that marked each wave's retreat. She held her shoes in one hand, swinging them as she walked.

After about ten minutes, Max and I had enough to start a decent blaze and feed it for maybe an hour or so. Amanda looked across at me as the wood began to catch. She nodded across at Thomas and gave me a little frown. I followed her look and then turned back and gave my head a little shake. He was fine. Susan was still strolling along the water's edge, but she soon noticed the light of the fire and headed back up the beach toward us. She squatted down in front of the flames, staring into the heat and moving patterns as Max poked at the logs with a stick, repositioning them slightly.

"Oh," said Amanda. "We forgot the wine."

"Thomas didn't, clearly," said Susan, with a low chuckle and a toss of her chin in his direction.

"What?" he said, dragging his attention away from his vigil. Susan just waved him back to what he was doing.

"There's still some left?" said Amanda.

"Yeah, I think so. There's still a couple of bottles. Yeah, yeah, don't worry. I'll go get them. I hope you're not going to ask me for glasses too."

"Well, you could at least bring a few mugs."

I sighed and pushed myself to my feet, muttering in mock annoyance, and headed back up over the dunes.

By the time I returned with an armload of bottles and mugs, corkscrew shoved into my pocket, the fire was well and truly blazing, and the others were arrayed around it in a loose circle. Fire's funny that way, how it sucks at your attention, drawing you in just to stare, the heat stroking at your face with gentle fingers. Max reached again for his stick, poking once, twice, sending a spray of sparks up into the dark night air. Now with the light of the flames, the rest of the beach was darker in comparison, folding itself around us in deep purple and black. I uncorked one of the two remaining bottles and handed out the mugs, planting the bottle itself firmly in the sand after pouring. I'd poured one for Thomas, but he waved it away, so I kept it for myself. I took a healthy swallow and looked up at the stars, following the smoke, ever upwards into blackness. It was a clear night, moonless, and stars spattered across the vault above. I nearly lost my balance backward as I followed their pattern, but I caught myself and returned my attention to the flames and the mug of wine cradled in my hands. All conversation seemed to have gone out of the evening by then. We were simply content to sit, listening to the low sound of the water and the crackling flames, lost in our own private thoughts.

"Cold," someone said quietly, the word drawn out and long.

I looked around, but everyone seemed fixed on the flames. Maybe I'd imagined it. I scanned the darkness around us, but everything was still. I took another sip of wine and returned my attention to the fire.

"Cold." There was the voice again, barely audible. If I didn't know any better, it seemed to have come from the direction of the fire itself. I frowned.

"Did somebody say something?" A couple of them shook their heads. Amanda looked across at me with a little questioning frown, her features dancing in the firelight.

"You had enough, my man?" asked Max, grinning at me. He took a healthy swallow from his own mug, then lifted it in salute. He looked across at Thomas who still sat, his arms clutching his knees, staring at the water.

Just at that moment, as if prompted by Max's glance in his direction, Thomas pushed himself upright, almost stumbling in the process. He stood swaying slightly where he stood, and then spoke.

"Just going for a bit of a walk," he said. "Be back in a little while."

A couple of us looked up and watched him wander unsteadily away from the fire and into the darkness. His shape became an indistinct blur.

"Should someone go with him?" asked Susan.

"Nah," said Max. "He'll be okay. Let him be."

Max was probably right, I thought. Let him get it out of his system if he needed to. We've all been there, and Thomas didn't need anyone following him to enhance his discomfiture.

He'd be okay.

I watched his shadow in the darkness becoming slowly more ill-defined, barely visible in the gloom. I turned back to the edges of the fire. As I turned back, I shifted, putting my hand down as I adjusted to a more comfortable position.

"Cold . . . "

The sand was damp. A scattering of ash had fallen from the edges of the fire, but it was moist. That didn't make sense. I lifted my hand and looked at my palm. It was grey with damp ash and sand, sticking to the skin, wet. I narrowed my eyes, put down my mug and tried to brush it off with the other hand. I looked down at the place where I had rested my palm, and there was a shine of water in the firelight, marking the depression of my handprint. There was movement there, a slight stirring of sand in water, a pulse, the wetness growing and fading like the beating of a heart.

"Cold . . . "

"Hey, guys!" Thomas called from down the beach. "Take a look at this!"

I turned, having difficulty locating him, my eyes still blinded by the firelight. I stood, the wet sand forgotten at the moment, peering into the darkness.

"Guys, really! Come look at this."

I took three steps away from the fire in the direction of his voice. Slowly, the darkened landscape started to solidify, the grey silver expanse of sand, the darker clumps of vegetation closer to the road and there, I could just make out Thomas's shadow, but there was something else, something that didn't belong.

Around Thomas's feet some sort of flickering light was

crawling across the surface of the beach: purple, orange, flashes of green. It slipped around the edges of where he stood a flat serpentine shadow, paused near him, and then slid around his legs again. I walked toward him, picking up my pace. The others were on their feet now beginning to move as well.

"What is it?" I called. He was some way down the beach.

"I don't know. Man, I'm not imagining this?"

"No, I can see it too," I yelled.

"Careful, baby," Jennifer called.

We were all increasing our pace now.

As we grew nearer, the light seemed to intensify, become more solid. It bunched together, grew. Thomas took a step back. It grew taller before him. He took another step to the rear, his head leaning back to look at the top of the growing rope of light. We were still not close enough to see clearly.

Purple, green, orange, it coiled like a thick tree trunk, sending out branches now, branches and twigs, becoming a dimly pulsing tree, looking solid.

As we closed the gap, the details became clearer. Not a tree, no, but hands, bits of hands and arms, all twining one around the other. Pale flesh, some with no flesh at all, questing, fingers plucking at the empty darkness of the sky.

"My God," said Susan as she pounded along beside me. "What the hell is that?"

We could see Thomas clearly now, though framed in flickering purple and orange light, a beach fire, but a fire of some other form. The light looked cold, fluorescent. He stood with his mouth open staring upward.

Our pace slowed as it became even clearer. I stopped where I was, my hands on the top of my thighs, trying to catch my breath.

I straightened slowly, barely able to believe what I was seeing.

"Thomas," I said in a loud voice. "You all right?"

"Thomas?" said Jennifer. Her voice was full of worry.

A flicker of something flashed across Thomas's face.

"I . . . " he said.

He tore his gaze from the tree of writhing hands, looked toward us, his mouth open as if he was about to say something more. He reached out to us, imploring.

In that moment, two of the tree's branches swooped out, sweeping Thomas into their grasp, bearing him aloft above the central trunk. He was bathed in crawling light, held firmly in the grip of many hands.

"Thomas!" Jennifer screamed.

"What the . . . ?" That was Max.

"Oh God," Thomas cried out. "It's cold. So cold."

With a rush, the hand-tree retracted, collapsing back into the sand, taking Thomas's suspended form with it. It was just gone, and with it went the ethereal light that had pulsed throughout it. We were plunged into darkness, gazes fixed on its afterimage.

Still struggling to comprehend what I had just witnessed, I rushed forward to the spot we had last seen the thing. Jennifer was screaming. There was nothing, nothing but blank beach and a pool of moisture slowly disappearing into the sand. I fell to my hands and knees, scrabbling at the place where the tree-like thing had withdrawn, like an eel retreating to its darkened undersea hole. There was nothing but wet sand within my fingers, the smell of old seaweed all around me. I started to dig. Max leapt over to join me, shoving aside lumps of dripping sand too. Both of us were digging, but there was nothing but sand and more sand, all wet and oozing with seawater. Amanda had her arms around Jennifer's shoulders, trying to still her screaming.

Slowly, Max and I got to our feet, scanning the beach, looking for any other sign, turning around and around. Susan stood transfixed, staring at the spot where Thomas had disappeared.

We searched the beach in the darkness. We looked out at the water. All of it was to no avail. Even the damp circle in the sand soon faded away to nothing. The only thing to mark the spot was a shallow depression and some heaped sand piles where Max and I had dug.

Amanda was the one who reported it, in the end. She turned out to be the strongest of us. As always, she was the sensible one. Thomas had gone into the water for a nighttime swim and simply disappeared. It was dark.

"Why did you not report it immediately?"

She spun some tale about going swimming, drinking too much. Told them that we had simply believed that Thomas had been playing some sick game with us, that was all. We could hardly tell them the truth of what we had seen.

Thomas's body washed ashore a couple of days later, and they came back to us.

"He was fully dressed. How do you explain that?"

"He was drunk. We were all a little drunk. We'd had a good night."

They clearly weren't satisfied, but they left us alone after that. We did not go to the funeral. We couldn't face Jennifer or Max or Susan. To join together would be an acknowledgement of what had happened.

I do not know if our fire had drawn them, seeking the heat that they had lost for so long, hungry for the memory of what it felt like to be alive. And why they took Thomas, why that happened, we will never know.

The police told us about their findings, asked us the routine questions. I will always remember one of the last things they said though, before they finally left us alone.

"All very strange. It was clear that he drowned, but it was peculiar. For some reason, his lungs and his stomach—both—contained an unusual amount of sand. Is there any way you can account for that?"

Jennifer hasn't spoken to us since that night, and Max and Susan keep their distance. In a way, that makes it easier.

Over time, things wash up on the beach, bits and pieces, flotsam and jetsam from the hungry depths of the ocean. All those dead ships that have fallen to a watery grave over time, all the dead sailors. There are parts of them too: tiny, tiny specks of their mortal remains, bits that are left after the ocean and the fish and the other creatures have done their work. They say that ghosts may haunt the resting place of their mortal remains. We, the remainder of our little group, we are sure that's true. We've seen the proof.

The beach . . . the beach was just there. It was always just there.

It will always be *just there* as long as we stay.

Amanda and I stare through the back window, out in the direction of the dunes and what lies beyond, my hand slowly stroking the small of her back, and I'm not sure how long that will be anymore. Neither of us is.

THE DEAD BOY

PAUL TREMBLAY

DAVE

THE BEDROOM DOOR spasms in its frame. In the pitch-dark I'm blindly stumbling away from my bed. Thick with the molasses of sleep yet hyper-aware because of the apocalyptic assault on my bedroom door, I am of multiple minds. One mind warns of bitey bed frame corners and the pair of sneakers stubbornly abandoned in front of my bureau. Another mind remembers the bedroom door is locked, when it normally isn't.

We locked it because we had appointment sex. Jeanne let me take her from behind. We don't use that position very often. It was all wonderfully awkward. We were loud, and after, we giggled sheepishly, like we were clumsy teenagers who couldn't believe we got away with it.

Adrift in the dark somewhere between the bed and my bureau, a part of my bifurcated mind thinks about our loudness, her curly black hair forming rings around my thick fingers, her twitching shoulder blades, the orgasm that started in my toes.

Jeanne says from the depths of her pillow, "Is Ryan out there?"

Ryan is our four-year-old son. I have difficulty processing what she means by *out there*.

Ryan frantically hammers on the bedroom door with fists that must have grown to the size of moons. He cries and yells words that aren't words. There are too many vowels to be real words.

I say, "I'm coming, hold on. The door is locked!" My voice sounds angrier than I intend. Though maybe I am that angry. I am still a being of multiple minds.

I open the door and Ryan stands there, shivering in the secret chill of a night terror, something that has become an almost nightly occurrence. His eyes are as wide as a confession. He sees through me, through the room, into some hallucinatory dreamscape, one in which I am the most terrifying being imaginable. That look, it hurts. He's not consciously giving it to me, of course. Maybe that's worse. Maybe his unconscious is being more truthful. Those artificial layers of niceties and social custom at which a four year old is already so frighteningly adept are stripped away, here in the dead of night, and I'm left with his natural, primal, instinctual fear of his father. I'm not his pal, his hero, his daddy, but a man he fears for now, a man he'll tolerate later, and eventually a man he'll strive to overcome, to conquer, or worse, a man he'll simply dismiss.

I reach out and say, "Shh. It's me. It's Daddy," but stop before weakly amending with: *I'm not so bad, buddy, really.*

Ryan ducks and dodges in silhouette. He avoids my touch, recoiling, curling into a ball, then uncurling and flailing with more arms and legs than he should have. He calls for Mommy, his raspy voice breaks, like he's called for her, without answer, for his entire life.

Suddenly and irrationally angry—as if there is any other kind of angry—I hiss at him. "Come on, Ryan. Everything's fine. Just go back to bed." It's all I can do to keep from saying *just go back to fucking bed.*

A handful of hours ago, I was hurrying through a prayer, hoping to complete it before Jeanne finished brushing her teeth. I asked a God I don't really believe in to protect Ryan and help me be a better father. I would never admit to Jeanne that this atheist-by-day silently offers these lukewarm, leftover talismans from my childhood at night. After the prayer, I imagine myself playing catch with an older Ryan, teaching him to ride his bike, sharing my favorite books and movies, training him how to deal with bullies. I generally drift off to sleep while helping some version of future-Ryan gracefully tiptoe through the minefield of adolescence.

Now, I stand here like some ancient sentinel with *none shall pass* on his lips as well as on his blackened heart, and I hate Ryan and his skinny arms, the non-existent biceps I could engulf with my hands; I hate the way he cries for Mommy, his please-sir-may-I-have-some-more whiney voice; I hate how easy his tears come, how *lousy* he always is with tears; I hate his terror, his scardey-catness, his overall and obvious physical and emotional vulnerability; I hate his dark curly hair which is so unlike my fair and thinning hair; I hate that he's a little me but more a little her; and I hate how right now we both know I am the monster.

Ryan leaks past me and through the doorway, winter air through a drafty window. He runs to the bed and climbs into Jeanne's arms. I look at the clock. It's 2:35 a.m. I have to be up in less than three hours.

I sigh and it's louder than a shout. It's too dark for me to see the look Jeanne shoots me, but I feel it.

She says, "Dave, you *can't* be mad at him," despite all of the evidence to the contrary that I am in fact able to be mad at our sleep-walking, jive-talking, cuter-than-any-button, four-year-old son.

Then she says to Ryan, "I'm here, baby. It's okay. It's me. Mommy's got you. You're safe."

I sigh again, despite myself, despite knowing better, despite knowing neither one of them deserve it. But Jeanne should not keep calling Ryan a baby, particularly in times of crisis. He's not a baby. She's not helping him; she's hurting him each and every time she utters that word. That word will fray his character. His yet undeveloped resolve will be as threadbare and fragile as a generations-old teddy bear missing its button eyes. Doesn't she realize Ryan needs to be forged, made stronger, tougher, and that we can't always protect him, and that we shouldn't always protect him?

Ryan continues to scream against his unseen demons and his shivers become full body convulsions. It's the unexpected violence of these convulsions that flip a switch in my bifurcated head, and now my stomach plummets and pools inside my feet. Maybe there's something seriously wrong with Ryan and he is beyond my help. Is he having a seizure? A mental break? Hospital scenarios with diagnoses of rare mental disorders dance in my head like evil sugar plum fairies.

I watch them from the doorway. My self-removal from the scene is a fitting punishment for what I previously thought about Ryan. He cries harder and louder, rubs his arms like a junkie scraping off the impossible insects of delusion. He screams, "No!" and, "Get away!" and then, "Mommeeee!" repeatedly until the word loses coherence, the grouping of sounds unrecognizable and menacing in their transformation to meaninglessness.

Jeanne tries to lie down beside Ryan, but he thrashes around too violently, and threatens to fall off the bed. She moves Ryan to the middle of the mattress, placing him on his back and on top of an inside-out, black t-shirt of mine. Earlier, I placed the t-shirt over the wet spot. That's generally my job post-coitus. To cover the offending spot, I always choose one of my t-shirts from the dirty laundry and never one of her garments as if to prove how considerate I am.

Jeanne coos softly to Ryan, telling him that he's okay, that Mommy's here, that he's safe. She goes on all fours above Ryan, pulls him closer to her, or more accurately, she lowers herself onto him. I assume she's nose to nose with him now, kissing his forehead, and wiping tears from his cheeks. I can't know for sure because from this bedroom doorway vantage,

I'm removed, I'm a fly on the wall, I'm someone else's outer-body experience, and all I can see is the backside of Jeanne's crouch. She lowers herself further and lies on Ryan. His spindly legs snake out from between Jeanne's thighs. His cries and screams become far away, muffled, suffocated. Jeanne says, "I've got you, Ryan. You're right here with me. I'm holding you."

When I eventually come back to bed, Ryan's convulsions have stopped, so has his crying and screaming. Jeanne rolls off Ryan, scoots him into the middle of our bed, then she lies on her side and rests an arm on Ryan's jewelry-box-sized chest. His eyes are closed and so are hers. Jeanne's breaths are heavy at first but become deeper, finding their sleep rhythm almost instantly.

I watch her arm on Ryan's chest. I watch for the rise and fall. There isn't any. Ryan isn't breathing.

I breathe out a long, loud exhale, and it's not one of my previous anger-sighs; I swear it's not. Almost on the verge of tears myself, I say, "I love you both so much. Good night." I turn over and resist the urge to mentally recite another feckless prayer.

JEANNE

Dave shuts off the alarm and bumbles toward the bathroom, bear that he is, comically holding his hand over the crotch of his tight underwear briefs. Dave has never been modest, so I'm oddly touched that he's cognizant enough to feel the need to protect us from the sight of his obvious and silly morning erection. I also feel a wave of physical revulsion, and I'm ashamed and alarmed to admit it's a feeling I've had more often lately. More times than not I blame myself, believing there's some nameless *lack* within me that explains these fits of shallowness toward his evolving, or devolving, appearance. In the checkered history of his mane of hair (he was once the proud owner of an un-ironic mullet), it has never been described as lush, and now it's reduced to a sad collection of wisps and tufts, scattered on his scalp like cotton balls stretched too thin. His weight gain has leavened his once solid, muscular mass, and dulled the masculine angles of his face. With the addition of coarse hair and volcanic acne on his back, the very notion of physical intimacy has become a considerable mental challenge for myself. So much so, we rarely have sex without me having a few drinks first. Last night was no exception.

Before leaving for work Dave leans over the bed, purposefully yet gently imposing his body weight on mine, and kisses Ryan on the forehead. He has already stopped kissing Ryan on the lips, and I wonder how long it'll be before the manly man stops kissing our son altogether. He says, "Love you, buddy. Proud of you," in a quivering voice, one full of apology for how poorly he behaved last night, for his silent recriminations, his accusatory sighs directed toward me and my perceived coddling/babying of our only child. Dave kisses my cheek on the recoil, and he smells nice; chemically clean, yes, but enhanced by that earthy, animal *him* smell. And just like that, I'm in love with him all over again. Which is to say that I'm madly in love with this moment. After thirteen years together, I admit that I am not in love with this man, my husband, my partner, my competitor. I'm in love with a collection of moments that I desperately hoard and scrapbook. There simply needs to be enough of those moments to keep the gears from grinding.

With Dave gone, I put my arm back around Ryan and say, "Your father loves you very much, baby." My voice echoes in the cavernous bedroom, the words frantically searching for escape rather than purchase. Ryan's skin is a cold shower and there's no hope of my falling back to sleep. I shift my hips and sit up in one motion, and feel a cold dampness on my thigh. "Oh, Ryan," I say, failing to hide a hint of admonishment he certainly doesn't deserve. I throw back our thick comforter and the rest of the covers, exposing us both as well as unleashing a choking stench. The t-shirt beneath Ryan is soaked through with urine and his bowels loosened as well. I forgot about the wet-spot T-shirt, and I'm appalled that Ryan spent the evening on top of it.

"Oh, my poor, baby."

I'm momentarily overwhelmed by the amount of tasks that must be done. After inwardly stammering, I start on myself, peeling off my nightshirt, shorts, and underwear, depositing them inside one of the soiled sheets. Next, I tend to Ryan who is as still as a pillow, and take off his underwear and roll him onto his side. His body is stiff but not inflexible, however, the purplish-red color of the skin on his back and buttocks is shocking. Having volunteered as a nursing home aid in my teens, I slowly recall that the discoloration is the likely result of gravity and pooling blood. I press my thumb, wet with tears, into his livid back, hoping to, I don't know, change the skin coloration, if only momentarily, but there's no effect. There's no change. Tears drip off my face and onto various parts of my body, and I've never felt so naked. I pull the t-shirt from under him, and lay him back down on the bed. I wipe him off as best as I can with a towel, then I tug the rest of the sheets and blankets off the bed and from underneath him until he is alone on a bare mattress. I consider depositing the pile of everything that was soiled into a garbage bag instead of washing it, but throwing it all away would be too easy.

I bring Ryan into the shower with me. In the harsh light of the overhead compact fluorescent bulb, his skin is as gray as wet newspaper. The water is hot enough to turn my skin an angry red and fill our dying world with steam. I try to prop Ryan standing up in the corner of our boxy shower stall; instead he slumps toward the drain and curls around my feet. Stereotypical rigor mortis has not set in; perhaps not enough time has passed; perhaps he's too young and his muscle mass is too insubstantial. I stand above him, straddling his prone form, and dump an entire bottle of shampoo on us both. I take my time washing our heads of dark curly hair. I sing him one of his favorite songs as I do so, using the fake British accent I always use. The accent pleases me more than him, always.

After the shower, I dress in a long sleeve t-shirt and sweatpants. My hair is still damp and un-brushed. The bed is remade with clean sheets, blankets, and hastily fluffed pillows. Ryan again lies in the middle, though closer to my side of the bed, and he wears a set of astronaut pajamas. Do kids dream of being astronauts anymore? I carefully cut his toenails and fingernails. While worrying that I'm cutting too close to the skin, I lose track of a few clippings. I run my hands along the bed sheet searching for them.

I put the clippers on my nightstand and then brush his curly hair, which is my curly hair. I say, "I know, my fingers make a poor comb." (Something my mother said to me when I stubbornly refused to brush my own stubborn hair.) "I don't know if this will help or not. I don't want to make your night terrors worse, Ryan, but it's perfectly normal to have them." (With the loss of his healthy pink color, his lips have all but disappeared into his mouth, which is stuck half-open, not half-closed.) "What I mean by 'normal,' is that there's nothing wrong with you. I hope you weren't afraid that something was wrong with you." (I lift his right arm and bend it at the elbow, then flex his wrist and fingers, and massage his tiny muscles, in an effort to keep any encroaching rigor mortis at bay.) "I'm not saying this right at all, am I?" (I work on his other arm, slowly.) "My parents—your Grammy and Grampy—never said I had night terrors, per se, but when I was a child, about your age, I had a recurring nightmare." (I make it a point to never talk dumb, or talk down to Ryan, and instead treat him as an equal, or a better, my husband's issue with my sometimes referring to him as "baby" notwithstanding.) "It was and is a truly awful, terrifying nightmare, one that I've never spoken about with anyone

else. My mother begged me to tell her about it, but I refused."
(Some nights my mother would read *The Velveteen Rabbit*
to me after I woke up screaming.) "She would claim that I
would more easily overcome the nightmare by putting it into
words, by coolly and clinically analyzing what so disturbed
me." (I'm not sure why I'm telling you this now, Ryan, other
than I have to open my mouth and say something.) "She
wanted to empower me, which, now that I'm a parent, I
understand is the proper approach." (I've moved on to his
left leg, bending it at the knee, massaging and molding his
nascent quadriceps and calf muscles.) "The truth is, I was
afraid that I couldn't accurately describe what had me so
frightened and that it would all sound silly and totally
ridiculous, which meant I was silly for being frightened at
all." (I will not and cannot tell him that the real reason I
didn't want to talk about the dream with my mother was
because I was afraid that if I talked about it and then still had
the nightmare, I would never be rid of it.) "In the nightmare,
I was at my grandparents', which was an old, dusty, creaky,
but wonderful three-family house." (How is it possible that
my own beloved Grammy and Grampy, the people with
whom I spent my childhood Sundays and holidays, are dead
and have never met Ryan?) "My grandparents lived on the
first floor and various other family lived on the other two
floors." (A motley rotation of the family ghosts: unmarried,
seemingly asexual uncles; divorcee aunts; cousins struggling
with their disastrously young, out-of-wedlock family.) "The
front door and staircase of the house was rarely if ever used.
It was as good as blocked off with boxes of old *National
Geographic*s piled in the front hallway." (I have his right leg
in my hands now, and I pretend the skin beneath the flannel
is warm.) "My brother and I would play post office on the
front stairs, sliding old postcards and letters down the
perfectly letter-sized space between the banister and the wall.
The postcards were from Canadian relatives who may or may
not have been deceased for a long time. Neither of us would

dare go beyond the second floor landing, down a small hallway, on its brown and curled linoleum, and around the corner to the unseen and unused third floor stairway." (My hands need something to do so I begin again with the bending and massaging of his left arm and I'm gentle because Ryan will not be my velveteen rabbit; worn, tattered, and shabby as proof of my love, as proof of my desperate attempt to make him real.) "I've already given too much preamble, I think. The nightmare is simple enough to understand, particularly if you've ever been less than four feet tall and standing in a dark place that was so much bigger than you were." (Maybe I shouldn't be telling him this; it won't help anyone or anything.) "It starts with me at the top of the stairs, sliding a yellowed postcard down to my brother, who suddenly isn't there anymore." (If only this were a nightmare, with Ryan suddenly not there anymore.) "I'd find myself walking slowly down the second floor hallway, my hand running along the dusty railing, toward the faint light of the curtained window at the end of the hallway; in life and in the dream, those thin, see-through curtains were always closed." (The blinds in our bedroom are closed now; there are no curtains in this room.) "I turn the corner and there is the unseen white door, with its chipped, flaking paint that opens to the unseen stairway to the third floor. I say *unseen* because I don't ever recall seeing them in real life, though I must have. I know it's possibly arrogant to say, yet it seems impossible that I would dream of a part of that house, a house whose nooks and crannies I infested with my presence, without seeing it first." (I think I've always been afraid and that molds me.) "It's when I open that door—and I always opened it, even when I know what's coming—where time speeds up, and I all but float up the dark stairs toward the third floor apartment that wasn't the real third floor apartment." (I again comb Ryan's hair with the poor substitute of my fingers, and they get stuck in a knot) "Inside the apartment I could hear an aunt, cowering somewhere, and I wanted to cower too, the dream wouldn't let me." (Let me cower now.) "On the small landing near the apartment's front door there's a gap in the wood shaped like a rough frame, and in the gap's blackness, in its *lack*, is a face, a human face." (I can't forget the face; I'll never remember the face's features.) "When I saw the face, it was . . . horrible." (My childhood fear is coming true: I am unable to fully explain the terror; my words failing, like everything does eventually.) "If I'd had a snapshot of the face to share with people, I don't think anyone would decry it as unnatural—as in beyond nature—or evil, so that's not it at all. There was some secret context, hidden within myself, speaking to me, telling me this was wrong, that this was the worst kind of mistake imaginable. My brain and body turned into a cold electricity that amped, and I couldn't breathe, and then everything shut down, and I felt myself receding, going inconsequential. It felt like I was dying, and when I woke up gasping for breath and drowning in the continuously crashing waves of nightmare imagery, that face was there in the room with me, even though I was never sure that I was still there with it." (I'm afraid, now, Ryan, that the face I saw was the face I'm looking at right now).

I sit and cry for a bit, then finish by mumbling some anticlimactic, falsely reassuring parental pabulum to my son. I don't think he minds as much as I do. I tuck the blankets beneath his chin, framing his smallness in our bed, which is as large as the sea. I lumber through the house and down into the basement and the laundry room, carrying the lump of soiled sheets. There's only one light bulb that hangs from the unfinished ceiling. I put my hand in a web as I turn on the light bulb, and then frantically wipe my hand on the bag of laundry. After jamming all that I can into the washing machine, I pour in a cup of bleach with a cup of detergent. I twist the knob to *hot*, then I cover my face with my hands, which smell of chemicals only, and certainly of nothing alive.

Now I'm thinking that I shouldn't have changed my

clothes, or the sheets, or even have moved the T-shirt, and left everything the way it was.

RYAN AND THE REALTOR

The realtor opens the bedroom door, which as of late has remained closed but unlocked. She says, "In here is the master bedroom." The realtor is a once-divorced, fifty-three-year-old woman with short, pepper-gray hair and unnaturally white teeth. Pristine teeth being her only vanity, her most recent Christmas card addressed to her dentist Matthew Kressel, reads: "May you have a sparkling holiday season!"

Ryan is alone in the bedroom, in the bed, with the sheets neatly turned down.

"We have fully restored hard wood floors, breezy ten-foot-high ceilings, plus a recently—five years ago, I believe—constructed master bathroom." The realtor enjoys reading cozies and collecting anything with a Dalmatian on it. Her new and doting second husband attends to and feeds this Dalmatian obsession as if it were a ravenous steamship furnace. Despite the economy, she continues to be quite successful selling properties. She's bright, diligent, affable, and has a savant-esque memory for MLS listings and the zoning definitions.

Ryan's skin turned green forty-eight hours after his death. The swampy coloration and odor were the early cues that his body had begun the putrefaction process: microbial proliferation, particularly in the intestinal tracts, produced sulfur, carbon dioxide, and methane gasses in concert with byproducts of the breakdown of his red blood cells. These gasses bloat his abdomen (his belly straining against his flannel PJs) and expel natural fluids from his nose, mouth, and other orifices. Of course, now, he is well past a few days dead, and his skin is changing color again, going purple and black.

"There's one closet, but it's a sizeable walk-in, almost seventy square feet." The realtor's oldest daughter, Melissa, is twenty-six and after years of being reckless and lost (which is how the realtor insists on describing Melissa's free-spirit, post-high school years), is a semester away from graduating pharmacy school. The realtor thinks Melissa has too many tattoos, including one on her neck that was supposed to be a solar eclipse, but looks like a black and orange octopus instead. The realtor's younger daughter Margaret is nineteen and having second and third thoughts about her biology major. Neither daughter lives with the realtor anymore, and she thinks she probably should worry about them more than she does.

Giant blisters the color of coagulated blood marble the skin of Ryan's forehead and cheeks and elsewhere on his body, most of which is still hidden under the stained PJs. His skin is loose, so much so that the top layer would peel off were the realtor (or the hopeful young couple considering making an offer) to try to move Ryan's body off the bed, no matter how gentle or careful the attempt. Ryan's nails and teeth have loosened. Internal organs and tissues have turned to liquid. Ryan's tongue has ballooned and slugs out of his open mouth. His once milk-chocolate brown eyes are soupy, cloudy, and weepy. They protrude grotesquely from their sockets.

"Do you have any questions? Is there anything else that you want to see?" Recently, the realtor has had trouble sleeping at night. She does not experience recurring nightmares, but instead suffers from insomnia, fretting over her sister-in-law, Jamie, who she truly likes and fancies as a surrogate sister. Jamie was a mortgage broker and is facing six-months to two years in prison for mortgage fraud. The realtor's gregarious younger-by-ten-years brother gets blind drunk to deal with his wife's, and by proxy, his marriage's legal crisis, which is to say he isn't dealing with it at all. The realtor is helping to pay for Jamie's outrageously expensive lawyers. She's happy to do it, but is heartbroken that Jamie claims those very same lawyers won't allow her to explain to the family, won't allow her explain to *her* what it is exactly Jamie did and why. The realtor really only cares about knowing the why. When she's lying in bed, it's *the why* that floats above her head, and she then spends those sleepless nighttime hours trying to divine a familiar shape from that particularly ominous cloud formation.

Ryan's body decomposes at the cellular level in a process called autolysis. With the cells no longer being active, the cytoplasm (cellular fluid) and mitochondria swell, the various cellular processes shut down, including the nucleus, and lysosomes release their waste digesting enzymes that dissolve and break down the individual and surrounding cells, turning muscle and tissue to liquid. There is nothing unique about what is happening to his body.

The realtor hovers in the doorway, uncomfortable in the silence of the prospective buyers. She is thankful this couple (it's out of character that the realtor has forgotten their names or what it is they do for work) has, like her, made the considerable effort to ignore the fetid smell of decay and rot, to ignore the small cloud of greedy blowflies, to ignore the spreading ink blot of the dead boy's body upon the bed. She resists the urge to ask the couple if they've ever had a Rorschach test, or if they can see shapes within clouds.

Selling a house with the dead boy on the bed (per the seller's heartbreaking instructions) will be a challenge, one that she may not be able to meet. With there being no questions from the would-be buyers, the brief house tour ends. The realtor closes the bedroom door regretfully, as if completing a ritual that has lost its cultural relevance, lost its meaning, and the dead boy is once again and forever alone.

HOME CARE

KEVIN DAVID ANDERSON

"**N**O!" ALICE SCREAMED.

Frantic, she bolted out from the seaside cottage, nearly tearing the driftwood-colored screen door from its hinges. Alice couldn't comprehend how her father had managed to wander so far in such a brief time. She had only left the elderly man alone for a minute.

Her father, a man in the final stages of dementia, stumbled along the cliffs at the end of their property, teetering on the edge of death.

Sprinting along the dirt path leading toward the cliffs, Alice continued calling to him. She knew that, even if he heard her panicked cries, it was unlikely he'd respond. His terminal condition had robbed her father of a mind that had earned two doctorates. What remained was an intermittent consciousness that moved in and out like bad TV reception.

When Alice realized how bad he was, she started the fight to bring him home, to release him from a rundown state facility, and struggled even harder to get awarded the right to manage the end of his life.

He wasn't going to perish in the care of nameless strangers that had no idea who he was. And he wasn't going to die in some stupid accident, not after Alice had navigated the bureaucracy, the courts, and scrapped everything she had together to pay attorney's fees. He was finally home and in her charge. But an instant of diverted attention allowed him to slip the veil of supervision, move off the back porch, and stagger straight for the cliffs. It was all about to end in a meaningless accident.

"No," Alice screamed. *Not like this.*

The elderly man's foot wobbled, loose gravel rolled like marbles unsteadying each step. Alice's heart leaped into her throat watching her father begin to sway.

She sprinted faster than she thought possible, closing the gap quickly. She sent thoughts forward like lifelines, trying to will her father steady. *No, please. Just hold on.*

She tried not to picture his broken body at the bottom, strewn across jagged rocks, the sea threatening at his shattered limbs. *Please let me make it.* She had to make it. She *needed* to make it.

Alice pushed the image of an unexpected end from her mind and reached out, stretching every muscle. As her father started to fall over the edge, Alice's fingers dug into his sweater like a rake churning the soil.

She wrenched back, easily righting the frail man. Spinning him around fast, his eyes went wide. For a moment he seemed confused. Then slowly, with growing awareness, recognition sparked on his face. It was a rare thing, a momentary gift, and Alice smiled as a tear traced the outline of her nose.

"Alice," he said. "What're you doing here?"

A faint chuckle escaped her lips. "What am I doing here?" she asked through heavy breaths, shaking her head. She gazed into her father's glassy eyes, feeling her relief at saving him suddenly melt away. The icy resolve that drove most of what she did froze her features as childhood memories rushed into her mind's eye. She could see by the ghost-white dread blanketing his face that those same memories were coming back to him—memories of his little girl, and what he'd done with that little girl.

Alice looked into his eyes, something she felt an unflinching need to do. They were not the eyes of a frail man near death, unable to remember his daughter's name, but of a monster, a demon that prayed on its own.

From a place of unending pain, where dark memories cast a shadow on all she had become, Alice summoned the strength to put both hands flat on his chest. She narrowed her gaze, drew in a cleansing breath, and exhaled long and hard.

Then she pushed.

TYGER

STEVE RASNIC TEM

Tyger! Tyger! burning bright
—William Blake

DANNY WOKE UP late, his alarm clock tipped over on the floor beside him. *I've spilt all my time*, he thought groggily. He never remembered falling out of bed most mornings when he woke up on the floor, but it was kind of exciting, like being in a movie.

Like most mornings, he had one picture frozen in his head from the night before: the wide mouth of the jungle cat, its fangs so bright they burned its lips away, its ribs so bright they burned stripes into its hide. Danny thought it was probably the most ferocious creature in existence, this cat, something that could live on earth and travel between stars and burn through your dreams all at the same time. It was fierce and ageless and insanely angry. In fact if you got too close to its anger you'd probably dissolve. You'd burn up so fast nobody would have a chance to see the fire. And maybe he was insane too, but sometimes Danny thought he knew just how this cat, this insane tiger, felt.

The guys would already be waiting for him. They wouldn't knock on the door, though—they were scared of his mother. There really wasn't any good reason to be scared of her except everybody could tell she was smart, and that she didn't put up with crap. She was a lot more than that, of course. The guys weren't there when he was feeling so bad that nobody but his mother could talk him through it. But that's just the way people lived their lives, he supposed. The best of you was this hidden thing most people never saw.

He could feel a new scratch across his left shoulder. It went pretty deep in places, but it didn't really hurt all that bad. Still, he was curious, and went into the bathroom where he had a second mirror set up across from the one over his sink so he could check out his back when he wanted to.

The scratch started near the middle of his lower back, ran up to just under his right shoulder blade, curved under the base of his neck, and ended in a graceful wave near the middle of his left shoulder. It looked like it had been drawn on. It was like the pinstripes on a car. He wanted to paint pinstripes on his own car someday, whenever he got one. Maybe the pinstripes would be red like this scratch.

He poured hydrogen peroxide over his back. It burned, but he liked the way it fizzed wherever there was a cut. He had lots of curvy, fancy scratches on his back, but this was the newest, and the only one that burned. Most of the others were pale, like mistakes somebody had tried to erase.

He could hear a couple of the guys calling up to his window. "Danny!" That was Tom. "Get your ass down here!" Too loud—his mom was going to hear. Tom didn't know how to do much of anything but shout. "Don't make us leave you!" That was Jer. They'd been friends a long time, but Jer was still a jerk. "Jer the Jerk," though Danny never said that to his face.

The uncomfortable part had always been that Jer did the things, and said the things, that Danny wanted to but never did. He'd be too embarrassed. And the way Jer looked a lot of the time, frowning like a kid who'd been forced to eat something really foul that was still stuck halfway down his throat, well, that was the way Danny felt.

That weird laugh in the background was definitely Charlie's, sounding like he had swallowed an angry bird.

Danny could hear the cat then, hissing, voice like a motor speeding up, crying like a baby being strangled, beginning to howl. Then screeching so loud it made Danny's ears hurt. He was pretty sure nobody else could hear that cat, or see it. That cat was just for him, and always had been. It was like Danny'd swallowed it when he was a baby and then his body had grown up around it.

He slipped into a T-shirt and jeans and ran down stairs. He exploded into the kitchen. Mom was sitting at the table drinking her coffee. "They're waiting for you outside."

"I know. Sorry. Tom—"

"Doesn't have any volume control. It's okay, honey. We all have friends like that. Try not to get into any fights with Jerry, okay? He's having a hard time."

"He's *always* having a hard time, Mom."

"I know, but he has troubles at home. His mother—"

"I know all about it, Mom. But we all have troubles, right?"

"Honey, we need to talk about your dad's visit."

"Gotta go now." He reached into the big bowl on the counter and snagged a couple of protein bars.

"You have to talk about it sometime."

"I know, Mom. The guys are waiting." He tried to be nice about it. He didn't like her pushing him. As he was running past her he gave her a quick peck on the cheek, but he must have done it too hard, because she said *ouch* and touched the spot with her fingers, covering the scratch that had just appeared. *That* had never happened before. Danny kept running and slammed out the door, his face hot, feeling bad.

"At last!" Jer yelled. "You finally done jerkin' off?"

"Quick thinking about my dick, Jer," Danny said, and the others laughed. Jer laughed too, a little late and his voice a little high in a nasty-sounding way.

They went down to the creek first because that was

closest and because that was what they always did during summer. The air was so thick with sweat bees Danny was afraid he'd get some in his mouth. He guessed he was a sissy about stuff like that, but he didn't care. He kept slapping them on his neck until he could feel gritty goo under his fingers made up of sweat and melted flat-top hair grease and insect parts. It made him get all hot and irritated. Scared by the possibility that he might get too annoyed, he made himself stop thinking, and with an explosive "Ha!" was the first one to jump into the water. The others came in behind him a little more slowly, a little more cautiously. There were a lot of shallow spots and big rocks in the stream.

He watched them land in the water one at a time, both relieved and disappointed that not one of them hit their head on the rocks and split it open.

Somebody had placed these large rocks carefully within the stream—he could tell. They'd been fitted together into a series of ledges under the water so that the stream would flow smoothly down from the hill, so that deep holes weren't formed by the churning waters, so that you could cross the stream here if you wanted without killing yourself. Without drowning.

Danny didn't know who had laid these rocks so deliberately. It might have been the old farmer who lived a few hundred yards downstream. Danny thought this fellow was probably the oldest person he knew not in a wheelchair or in bed all the time. And so strong—you could tell from his arms, so muscular.

Danny waded to the bank and found a good strong stick. The guys had been screaming and shouting and splashing each other and playing grab-ass. But now they had stopped and he could feel them watching him, waiting to see what he was going to do.

Something else was watching him both from inside himself and outside himself at the same time. That frightening cat grin in the darkest part of the woods, prowling closer, that burning smile in his brain, like a ghost with teeth trying to eat its way out of him and destroy everything he could see with his weak human eyes. In Danny's dreams it was the way devils smiled. But, far worse, it was also the smile the angels wore.

He waded back into the center of the stream and thrust the big stick down into the water between two stones, and then he wiggled it back and forth, pushing it as hard as he could first one way and then the other, straining, making a sound like he was in terrible pain.

"You takin' a shit there, Danny?" Jer called, and Frank laughed, and maybe Tom. But Danny could tell that mostly they were curious about what he was doing. Jer had a funny look on his face—as if he were eager and scared at the same time. His eyes were sunken and dark, and his throat looked swollen, like an explosion of words was about to burst out of there. And Danny thought about how much Jer looked like him at that moment, almost like they were twins, and Danny frankly couldn't have said which twin was the good one and which twin was evil.

Finally Danny got one of the rocks loose, and it tumbled, and several of the smaller rocks tore loose and followed, and one of them rolled farther, helped by the push of the stream, and almost hit Jer, but not quite—that would have been just too perfect. But at least it made him yelp and jump out of the way. At least it made the other guys laugh.

Danny really got to work then, digging the stick into the stream bed and using it as a lever, prying out more stones, and pushing them away, and tearing out the carefully-placed smaller stones behind them. After a time he threw away the stick, let it float like a spear down the creek, crouched and tore the stones out with his bare hands, lifting them and shouting, tossing them as far away as he could, not caring whether he hit one of the guys or not.

He hadn't even been thinking about the guys, just this roaring in his head, this cat scream that made the hair stand out on his arms, that made him scrunch up his neck, waiting for the cat to open him up with its claws. But then there they were, the other boys, crowding in beside him and digging through the water for stones, pulling them out and throwing them, ripping out all those handmade ledges and uncovering the mud and slime under the stones, making deep holes and broken places where he could already see the stream changing, surging into deep pools and tearing wider holes and foaming over the broken arrangement that somebody must have spent weeks building and they'd destroyed in a couple of hours.

Something was scratching him up from the inside, like a thing with sharp nails trapped deep inside his ear clawing to get out. It was screaming at him, but in that terrible torn-up language a human being couldn't understand. Then Danny was sure he could see the tiger, moving there on the bank among the stiff weeds and briars, getting ready to leap off the bank and take Danny down. So maybe it was the tiger screaming and because the tiger belonged to him, had belonged to him since he was just a kiddie, Danny was hearing it from both the inside and the out.

He could barely make the tiger out, but it looked mostly skin now, stretched so thin the bones poked through like needles when the tiger walked. Now and then it would turn its head, which was mostly teeth, toward Danny and grin.

Jer was between Danny and the cat, jumping up and down and throwing rocks and mud at everybody and Danny had never seen him so happy. He looked just like Danny felt, so excited and so scared at the same time. As Danny stared at Jer he could see the things working under his skin, insect jaws and mouthparts and antennae trying to break through his skull. It was all so ugly and familiar Danny hated to see it and turned his eyes away.

Danny reached down into the creek and picked up a stone off the bottom that filled his hand, thinking he'd finally hit that tiger and make it leave him alone. But the tiger screamed so loud just when he threw it that the rock hit Jer full in the face with a crunch and a howl and a splatter of bloody pieces.

Danny spent the next few days mostly in his room thinking about what had happened. He didn't get in trouble because nobody ever told. Jer just told his dad he fell. But Danny still wished it hadn't happened. The last thing he'd heard before he'd run away from the creek was Jer bawling and calling for his mom. Danny'd rather have smashed his own face instead.

He still woke up on the floor and each morning there were new scratches—more like carvings, like something whittling a shape out of him—some so deep and bloody he had to bandage them. He wore thick shirts even when it was hot as fire outside to hide how he'd had to wrap himself up like a mummy.

He had no idea why he'd done it, exactly. Jer annoyed him—Jer annoyed everybody—but he wouldn't have hit him for it, he didn't think. Danny had been aiming for his tiger, but somehow Jer was the one with his face smashed in.

Every living creature does what it can to guarantee its survival. That was from a nature program he'd watched just the other day, and when the narrator had said that in his deep voice it was like the word of God or something. Nature programs were boring, but for some reason Danny still watched a lot of them. When one was on he just couldn't bring himself to turn it off.

His tiger had not always been a hurtful thing. When he was little, just after Dad left, that tiger—hidden from everybody else, back in the closet or under the bed or curled up inside a big shade tree—was the only friend he had. His tiger had made it okay to go outside, to play in the sun and have adventures. Sometimes they'd tumble around in the yard together, wrestling. But back then the tiger never bit him, didn't even scratch him once. Back then they'd go sledding or swimming or sometimes they flew inside an invisible airplane that soared just above the neighborhood houses and the tree tops would tickle the belly of the plane when it flew over.

Since he'd thrown the rock into Jer's face that day the guys didn't call up to him or make it obvious that they were there, but they still came and waited for him to come out, sometimes for hours. Sometimes he'd look down from his window and see them there, hanging out under the tree where his tiger had once hidden, waiting, staring up at his window. Sometimes they'd be down there waiting long after dark. Even Jer would be there, one whole side of his face bandaged. Danny would watch them, his head there in the window so that they could all see him, but he never even waved. He wasn't ready.

Then one day he did come down, and looked at them, his scars secretly bleeding under his bandages and his thick, uncomfortable shirts. And that was when the wrestling matches began.

Danny turned around suddenly, shouted "Ha!" and tackled Tom. He could see the sudden panic in Tom's eyes and guessed he was probably wondering if this was going to be a repeat of what had happened to Jer. Although the high whine of the tiger was pulsing through his brain, he could tell this was not the same, but something more playful, something more free.

So Danny made sure he was laughing and deliberately made hooting sounds, so pretty soon Tom was laughing, too, and they rolled around in the tall grass, each pinning the other more than once, the only indication that the match was finished being that neither one was able to move anymore, and lay there panting as the others jumped and cheered and play-fought until the sun went down and the gentle, obsessive music of the katydids began.

Danny sat up and looked at the others, even at Jer who still kept his distance, and into the trees where the tiger watched back, eyes and teeth burning bright against the dark night.

The wrestling matches continued each day, Danny against Tom, Tom against Charlie, Frank trying to get Jer involved but even though Jer watched and stopped looking scared, he still shook his head at every invitation.

And the tiger was still always there, prowling the tall grass and the distant trees, prowling Danny's dreams and leaving those deep and still bleeding scars. But keeping in check, holding it together, so not once did Danny feel he needed to run away in order to protect his friends.

"Danny. Danny?" He opened his eyes and there was his mother looking down at him on the floor, her eyes travelling to the bed and the twisted wet sheets tangled around him like a nest of shredded cloth. "Your dad will be here at two, remember? You don't *have* to see him, but I think it would be better for you if you did."

He tried to pull the bedclothes up over him. "Sure, Mom. Whatever." He tried to hide what he didn't want her to see. But then he knew he was too late.

"Danny!" She dropped to her knees beside him. "What's this blood? Are you *bleeding*?"

Thankfully it was just the edge of one sleeve, which he quickly covered. "Nothing, Mom. We were playing. I scratched myself."

"I'll go get some disinfectant." She was on her feet, turning.

"It's *fine*, Mom. I've been using hydrogen peroxide."

She looked at him. He didn't think she fully believed him, but she probably didn't know what to think. "You're sure."

"Positive. I need to get dressed now. For Dad." He'd tried not to think about his dad's visit, but he figured he was stuck now.

A couple of hours later Danny was waiting out on the front steps. He fully expected his dad not to show up—he'd not shown up before, and after the first time he left, Danny didn't see him again for years. Of course Danny had been little then, and he actually didn't remember much about those years, except playing with this tiger no one else could see. His mom had tried to humor him, had asked him, "What's your tiger's name?" Even then he'd thought it a ridiculous question. Danny didn't *own* the tiger; the tiger wasn't a pet. And he had no name for the tiger, because the tiger never told it to him.

Right now Danny didn't feel the tiger or hear it, which surprised him. It surprised him that he wasn't a lot more upset than he was.

But he could *see* it there, moving beside the trash cans, and there just under the edge of the porch. It looked even worse than when he'd seen it before. Its skin had probably a hundred tears in it, and big splotches of hair were missing from its burnt and twisted head. The tiger looked like it had been in a fire maybe, or maybe some terrible accident. His mother sometimes said "worse for wear," and if anything in the world was worse for wear it was this tiger-thing. Or cat-thing, because it didn't look much tiger-like now, nothing so powerful, or special, just this torn-up, decaying thing, but which still had this mouth full of just incredible teeth when it turned and grinned.

A car pulled up at the end of the sidewalk. A sports car, low to the ground, all red and chrome and like something out of someone else's future. Although he hadn't seen him in a very long time, Danny recognized that the man climbing out of the driver's seat carrying a plastic shopping bag was his father. Their faces were similar—especially the nose and the jaw—and something about the way the man walked seemed so familiar. The only thing was, he was shorter than Danny had imagined, much shorter, and he didn't smile. For some reason even though his dad had just left him, abandoned him like that, Danny had always seen him as a friendly man, a grinning man, but the man striding up the sidewalk now didn't look as if he ever grinned at all.

Danny's mind seemed stuck back at that sports car. He kept looking at it, thinking, *it's not even a dad's car.*

Then his dad was standing right in front of him, his hand out, inviting Danny to shake it. Not saying a word to him, and looking so serious. Not knowing what else to do Danny grabbed his dad's hand, and his dad said, "Hello, son," while shaking his hand pretty firmly, and Danny didn't like that, so he was trying to give his dad back a limp, I-don't-even-care handshake, but it was pretty impossible to fight a hard handshake with a limp one—the hard handshake just kind of made the limp one disappear.

"It's been a long time, son. You've really grown." Danny wanted to tell his dad he hadn't really grown at all, not really—he still felt like a little kid. But how do you tell a grownup that? His dad sat down next to him on the step. "I'm afraid I can't stay long. I *want* to, of course. But this time I can't. I've got something I have to get to. But next time, I promise."

So this was how it was going to be. Danny wasn't really surprised. He knew his dad had another family now, another son. He looked into his dad's eyes and for a second wondered if his dad was actually blind. His eyes were little pieces of dark glass.

"So why did you leave in the first place?" Danny asked.

"Pardon?"

Danny stared at him fiercely, unblinking. He could feel a raspiness coming into his throat and a fire across his chest as the tiger opened him up again and the wound began to ooze. "I asked why you left us, abandoned us. You've never told me. You've never even apologized."

"Well, well, I'm really sorry. It was a bad thing, but life is complicated, son. And there are two sides to every story."

Danny didn't know what to do with his fists, his fingers. He started scratching himself furiously on the thigh, as if he were trying to dig through his jeans. "Mom never blamed you. She's never said one bad thing, never given her *side*. So what's yours? What's your *side*?"

His dad was staring at Danny's hand, how he was

scratching crazily at his thigh, as if it was the strangest thing he'd ever seen in his life, and maybe it was. "I use to get so angry," he said.

"What? What do you mean?" Danny's thigh was stinging. He looked down—he'd torn through his jeans and was now clawing bare skin.

"You'd be doing normal stuff, crying, making a fuss, normal kid crap. But I'd get so angry—I couldn't stand the sound you made. I think I shook you once or twice. Maybe some other things dads aren't supposed to do."

"So you're saying it was my fault."

"No, no—I don't know. Something wrong with me, something wrong with me when I was with you. I was becoming something I didn't want. So I left. I'm sorry. But I'll tell you the truth, we're all better off I did. I *am* sure of that."

His dad stopped then and started messing with that shopping bag he brought. Danny didn't think he wanted to see what was inside. He wasn't sure what he was feeling because something big and feline was tearing him up inside.

"Here." His dad handed him a brand new baseball glove. The leather smelled so strong of tanned and roasted skin Danny thought he might gag. But his dad shoved it into his hands so he pretty much had to take it. "We'll play some catch next time. How about that? I'm really sorry I can't stay today, Danny. I really am. Being an adult, it gets so *complicated.*"

His dad's goodbye was to take Danny by the shoulders and shake him back and forth a bit before jumping up and jogging toward his car. For a second Danny could feel him hesitate, no doubt wondering about the bandages he was feeling under Danny's shirt. Danny sat there until the car pulled away, then sat there a lot longer. He wasn't even aware of his mother coming out and sitting down beside him until she put her arm over his shoulders.

"He wants to be better at it, I think he always did." She

said it so softly it was almost like a voice inside his head. "But I don't think he can be. He's just . . . " she hesitated, "human."

The thought came unbidden, like an idea that floated down out of the distant burning stars. *If that's human then I don't want to be.*

Danny was remembering more and more what it had been like, how as a little boy he had wrestled for hours with this bright and ferocious tiger no one else could see. And although it felt somehow wrong that he should think of it as his, it *was* his, wasn't it, for who else's could it be?

Their wrestling matches had been surprise, fun affairs, always beginning when one tackled the other who'd hid behind a door, or a tree, or the edge of a building. No one ever got hurt. These matches ended with both of them on the ground giggling. The tiger had been a softer, more human looking thing back then. Now it was all teeth and claw and attitude, and feelings smoldering in some near-forgotten hiding place.

That night the friends gathered in the darkness under the trees. Danny didn't have to send a message—they all seemed to know where to go, and all in tune with his silent management. Even Jer showed up on time, healed and ready for battle.

Danny handed him the new glove. "It's yours," he said. "I was wrong." Jer smelled it and cast it aside.

Danny and Jer spent the next few minutes circling each other. Danny could feel himself bleeding, was ready to bleed some more. He felt the tiger enter him, felt the burning of his smile, the fire in his eyes. And across the way witnessed the change in Jer's face as the ugly insect inside him finally crawled out and covered his face, and bug and tiger at last began their terrible dance.

PANDORA'S CHILDREN

SIMON MCCAFFERY

Site 300
Tuesday
Days since Pandora Event: +10

A **LOW SOUND** in the next room draws me up from a shallow, fitful sleep—I've nodded off again seated at the interface terminal. My stomach ices over and my heart kicks faster. Acute sleep deprivation causes muscle aches, loss of coordination and memory lapses. It really fucks with the old cortex: fun stuff like audible hallucinations and shadow-things that linger on the far periphery of vision. The Army uses "chronic sleep-restricted state" to wash out sixty percent of Ranger candidates. My brother Daniel told me the stories of men built like linebackers weeping like toddlers, begging to DOR.

The rational mind denies that it has *anything* to do with the entity in the next room.

My name is Dr. Jeremy James Hall, last man standing at Site 300. Isaac's vector simulations predict I may be the last sane person in the western hemisphere, barricaded underground while monsters wearing human faces roam the cities and countryside eleven stories above us. I think Isaac is a pessimist.

I hear a low mewling from beyond the high-security steel door behind my terminal station. A thump, and scratching.

It's going to be bad.

I pour a bottle of cold water from my scavenged mini-fridge down my upturned face. The freezing water snaps me awake. I don't dare enter the makeshift sickbay while groggy.

Arranged on a lab table next to the heavy door is a pair of chemist's gloves, foam earplugs, adjustable faceshield, a jar of mentholated jelly, and a pistol-shaped military grade Taser.

"Arthur, open the A-3 door, please."

Arthur is one of three functioning supercomputers. Isaac and Ursula are nominal, but Ted is offline.

I mentally sing-song "THE RAIN IN SPAIN FALLS MAINLY ON THE PLAIN" in case the entity is trying to peep inside my mind. The door cycles and the lock bolts retract with a muffled *clunk*.

The noises on the other side cease.

My hands are shaking. I summon an image of Elena, lovely slender Elena that was, before we opened the Portal. What was inscribed on Dante's gate? Leave all hope, ye that enter.

I slip inside the room.

"To paraphrase the philosopher Robert Pirsig, demons are unscientific. They radiate no energy and contain no matter, and do not exist except in the minds of the superstitious. Of course, the laws we ascribe to the physical cosmos contain no matter and have no energy either, and exist only in the minds of scientists . . . " [*laughter from the panelists and off-camera audience*]

—*Dr. Jeremy Hall, Berkeley Physics Regents Lecture webcast series / 4 years ago / 1,927 views*

Hollywood poltergeists chill the air until your breath fogs like a wraith, but these entities prefer a pulsing, bloodstream heat. Recalibrating the environmental controls has no effect. The nested universe where *they* were trapped until ten days ago must have long ago achieved complete heat-death. Try to imagine spending *fourteen billion years* in that hyperborean deepfreeze between dead stars. Nothing to warm yourself with except an everlasting hatred and a faint memory of crushing heat generated by the singularity that imprisoned your kind as it gave birth to *our* universe. No love and light where you remain, banished, the implacable face of Creation turned away.

The creature inhabiting my lover scrabbles from a corner beyond Elena's overturned medical cot like a giant spider, torso bowed, head impossible twisted, hair hanging like black seaweed, eyes bulging with purest malice. Its shrieks drill straight through the plastic faceshield and earplugs.

I squeeze the trigger and compressed nitrogen propels the barbed electrodes through Elena's torn, soiled gown to strike home at her midriff.

The contorted Elena-thing thuds to the floor, thrashing, rictus mouth howling in fury. It's growing stronger as the human husk of Elena withers; the delivered 1,500 volts should cause an instant loss of neuromuscular control.

I fire a second charge at point-blank range.

Elena's body goes limp. The Vicks jelly doesn't block the sour smell of urine added to the rank bouquet of odors. Her breath comes in shallow, hurried pants. My father breathed that same way as he lay dying of a thunderclap heart attack on his study floor eight years ago, before I decamped from the Jesuit halls of Villanova to sunny Berkeley and agnostic atheism. If I keep subjecting Elena's desecrated body to repeated jolts I'm going to stop her weakened heart. Amnesty International says that in the past decade over three hundred Americans died after stun-gun shocks. I looked it up while the Internet was still wheezing its last packetized breath.

The de—the *entity* knows this, too. I refuse to call it by that other fucking name.

Is there anything more stubborn than a scientist?

~

I met Elena nine months ago when the Army transferred us to Site 300. Raven hair in waves and deep brown eyes to match, the daughter of a Russian physician and a Turkish hydro-engineer. We fell in love.

The emaciated scarecrow I carry to the righted cot weighs seventy pounds, ribs and clavicles jutting in hideous relief, a concentration camp victim dying of advanced meningitis. Her hips, once smooth swelling curves, are a bony horror.

Her parchment skin is cracked and soiled with excrement, pus and dried blood. She's burning up. I throw her filthy gown down the biohazard chute to be incinerated.

Her lips are shredded and tongue punctured from chewing the restraints. There's a subcutaneous crater just above the pubic bone where *it* coiled her like a serpent and attempted auto-cannibalization. The injectable antibiotics are gone so I apply Betadine and pack the wound with antibacterial jelly and gauze. I re-attach the intravenous saline and glucose lines.

Outside, I remove the faceshield and realize my face is wet. I've been silently crying the entire time. In a few short hours that pass like a delirium this nightmare scene will be replayed.

I have a day, maybe two, to devise a cure before Elena's vitals crash.

And when the creature our ancestors called *daemon* finishes batting her helpless body around like a sociopathic cat draws out the death of a wounded rodent, it will require a new host.

I'll explain about the message from the stars, but first a quick download on Site 300. Elena is mercifully asleep, so it's safe. While working to repair the damage wreaked after their arrival, I often feel the pinprick of the entity's inhuman intelligence, like the Furies, probing the edges of my mind.

Forty miles west of Oakland is a remote station affiliated with the Lawrence Livermore National Laboratory. It's an offshoot of the U of C Radiation Laboratory at Berkeley and MIT's Bits and Atoms lab, responsible for Project Sherwood (cold fusion), Project Hurdle (microwave weapons) and Project Sabre (energy-beam cannons envisioned before George Lucas popped his first pimple).

The station is equipped with living pods, self-generated power, com-lines, air handlers and the meshed supercomputers humming inside hyper-cooled shells. An undisclosed particle accelerator a quarter the size of the Large Hadron Collider curves deep beneath the green tight-knitted hills, intersecting with the Level Twelve physics lab. Soldiers patrol the surface perimeter and shoot trespassers on sight (well, they used to).

Site 300 was the logical place to mount a major classified project, like decoding a transmission we were fooled into believing emanated from an extrasolar civilization.

Wednesday
Days since Pandora Event: +11

"Tell me your name. Are you afraid to tell me?"

Gloating silence from the shape tapering away on the cot.

Putrid heat intensifies as I press for an answer. Elena's face grimaces in a rigid gorgon mask of malevolence.

I rub my stubbly face. I've stopped shaving (I don't trust myself with razors), and I avoid mirrors. I've been seeing things, and weren't mirrors once considered doorways accessible by what our forefathers believed were evil spirits?

"Is it a world like this one?

"Is it located in this galaxy?"

Teeth grind, chapped lips smack.

"It's not even this universe, right?"

The entity and its kin have escaped from the remnants of a Penrose-Hawkings singularity formed within an ancient universe extinguished as ours came into being. Watch for my article in the *Journal of Astrophysics and Astronomy*.

Elena's blackened tongue appears, wagging back and forth. Her teeth snap shut with a savage *click*, severing the tip in a cherrybomb of blood. *It* swallows the nubbin of flesh in a single gulp, gargles, and bleats shrill laughter.

I wipe the faceshield with my sleeve and only smear it.

Elena's scabbed mouth emits the voice of my dead father. Flat and faintly metallic, but recognizable.

"Jerry? Son, is that you? There's no Heaven or Hell when you die, only endless starless space. It's a matter of frequencies and geometries we don't understand."

The voice pitches higher.

"NO JESUS NO MADHI NO SHIVA NO ALLAH NO BUDDHA. JUST AN ETERNITY OF FREEZING NIGHT, OH JEREMY PLEASE HELP ME!"

I flee the room. Slumped against the outer door, I press my fists into my eye sockets and weep. For the memory of my father, our unresolved differences, the bitter arguments and my unbending stubbornness to accept his viewpoint. And for myself. The last fortifications of scientific jargon and sterile denial crumble away, and my rational mind is overrun by the greatest terror I have ever known.

The thing in the next room is a Demon.

As real as sunlight or gravity.

I am Enoch, son of Cain, that early traveler through Heaven and Hell.

Soulless laughter from the other side of the door.

Thursday?
Days since Pandora Event: +12

"What's a beauty like you doing in a top-secret government weapons lab?"

I'm watching the surveillance videos they never told us they filmed. The scene is my quarters, the night before we opened the Portal.

We're alone (we think) and tripping on the power of what we're about to achieve in the morning as cameras roll. As a species we're terminally infected by greed and addicted to accelerating technology that leaves moral judgment choking on anthrax dust, but celestial angels were offering us a chance to sidestep our self-destructive destiny.

Dr. Khanin—Elena—laughs, a bit tipsy. She gazes at the slender ring inside the small red box.

"Diamonds are nice, Jeremy, but nothing gets a modern girl's juices flowing like an underground bunker of HAL 9000 computers and atom smashers."

I lean closer to those full lips.

"How about opening a traversable wormhole? How about looking like this—" I run a fingertip down the curve of her face—"for a thousand years?"

On the video Elena and I embrace and make love. A clear breach of Army protocol, but we were never prosecuted.

We decoded an FTL transmission traced from Teller 381g, an extrasolar planet one-hundred and twenty trillion miles away. The message contained a sequence of RNA and DNA data explaining how to halt every permutation of cancer, and half of the sequence to halt collateral mitochondrial cellular damage responsible for human aging. The key to defeating Death.

The ultimate allegorical apple, wouldn't you say?

The second transmission provided instructions to construct the Portal.

So we bit into that juicy, rotten-core offering. We didn't tentatively lift the lid from Pandora's box; we *disintegrated* it.

Of course the portal didn't open onto a distant exoplanet with benevolent ETs. It tore a passage to another reality altogether, one that God, the Supreme Intelligence, the Infinite, the Cosmos—please choose the label you're comfortable with, anthropomorphic or otherwise—had sealed, but we again had been tempted to breach.

~

I dream while my eyes are open.

My mother, fifty-nine but still trim, just walked into the room and shut off the video, and told me to get some rest, I've been working too hard. Her dentures were in and bleached, but her eyes were ragged, bloody holes.

In the hours after what I'm calling the Pandora Event, soldiers went insane, butchering everyone in sight even after their rifles ran dry. Surviving personnel abandoned their posts and fled into the desert. Twelve hours later I crawled out of my hiding place and instructed Isaac to lock us down. Isaac refused, but after rummaging through cabinets of sealed codebooks I gained the proper authorization.

I called my mother in Albany, but the telecom networks were compromised. Voices answered, but they weren't human.

The video screen is dark, but I have no memory of switching it off.

In the first two days I couldn't stop watching the world being consumed by apocalypse. Military and National Guard troops tried to enforce martial law, Daniel undoubtedly among them. In New York millions poured through the streets like wild-eyed lemmings, their screams ringing off the skyscraper canyons. They appeared, well, possessed.

A new Dark Age fell across Europe, the spires and skies blackened by the levitated. Henry Sebastian D'Souza, the Archbishop of Calcutta, mobilized the Vatican's exorcists armed with incense, crucifixes, and the Church's official twenty-seven-page book of incantations.

Live from the west Sunset Strip, a TMZ crew cornered Tom Cruise outside the Viper Room. Drooling yellow bile, trapped in the flare of paparazzi floodlights, he performed his signature Jerry Maguire flip-out shuffle, no longer shtick. He bared his trademark chompers and charged the videographer. The feed jumped and dropped. Back to you, Harvey Levin!

"Isaac, does the Devil exist?"

No hesitation.

"Satan is the primitive protean symbol of physical evil and the irrational, a malevolent force responsible for natural disease and illness. In the monotheism of the Christian faith, Satan is the master of moral evil, an amalgam of the Roman Empire's discarded pagan gods and devils."

How wonderfully academic. If only I'd been born a pre-Columbian Aztec warrior weaned on diabolism, reared in a culture impregnated and shivered with elemental terror, expecting the fiery end of the world every fifty-two years . . .

Friday? Isaac, is it Friday?
Days since Pandora Event: +13

Elena is dying.

I put the single-serve cup of applesauce aside and attempt to palaver. I ignore the sounds of boot steps of murdered soldiers outside in the corridor.

"I have a bargain. Are you listening? Unlimited worlds to devour, like an endless paper-doll chain. What will you do once you've used up everyone? The ages will pass and eventually you'll be back in the galactic deepfreeze with no one to construct a new portal."

The malignant ventriloquist inhabiting Elena wires her jaws shut. Her pupils shrink to pinpricks, and then fill the corneas.

I ignore these distractions and speak in a low, reasonable tone.

"A new multiversal portal can be permanently opened, if you agree to release Elena."

Rasping breath and foul odors. Suppurating lesions bloom on Elena's cheeks and nose.

I get up, miming confidence, and leave the room.

I check on Arthur and Isaac's progress to recalibrate the particle grid, hoping my ad-jingle brainwave jamming works.

I stare at Elena's fine gold crucifix, taped to my terminal after the demon tore it from her neck.

I wait, and try to stay awake.

When I was twelve I abandoned Catechism classes. I was grooving on Fourier equations and Hilbert space interpretation. I wanted to delve into the farcical two-dimensional world of *Flatland*, not liturgy. I wanted to think about quantum foam, not Catholicism's pledge that man could forge an inner union with God.

"Look," I told my father, "an angry God that transforms sinners into salt is as superstitious as rebellious angels cast from His firmament to tempt and devour men's souls. Symbols and allegory to frighten the fearful and ignorant." If God is a label for the known physical laws that govern the universe, OK. But if God is a towering WASP-y male with cerulean eyes and a snowfall beard who sits in the sky and has preordained the spin of every electron since the moment of creation until Judgment Day—

My father raged. My mother withdrew, embarrassed.

It was the beginning of years of skirmishes.

Ted remains offline and disengaged from the array, but the remaining three Crays can finish the job. I didn't want to disconnect Ted (he pleaded and begged like HAL, then hurled the most vile curses in twelve languages), but what choice did I have after he became possessed? Demons reportedly inhabited inanimate objects, bedchambers, town square clocks, and a half-sentient ultracomputer might make a swell summer home.

I feel that prickling mind-tickle; I jerk awake.

Hot dogs! Armour Hot Dogs! The rain in fucking Spain.

The disconnected interface of the excommunicated Ted glows to life.

A wireframe shape coalesces, a noseless, sexless face with tunnels for eyes.

"We have considered your proposal." The flat, feral words are slightly out of synch with the glowing wireframe lips. "And we accept."

"Ursula, position its arms out like this."

The squat treaded robot designed to remotely disarm explosives adjusts its pipestem arms with a whine of servos. Its hands almost touch in robotic prayer; I shiver at the image and then Ursula corrects their position.

I ease Elena's unconscious body, wrapped in a blanket, into the robot's titanium grasp. I kiss her cool dirty forehead. Slung around the robot's camera mast is an overnight bag stuffed with bottled water, rations, a dead soldier's sidearm and a charged cellphone.

"Ursula, send the 'bot at max speed on a northwest track toward the highway when it reaches the surface.

"Isaac, initiate the first sequence."

The robot rolls into the elevator and the lift doors closed with a sigh.

Goodbye Elena. I'm going to try make all of this right and return for you.

I stumble back to the interface terminal.

I scan readouts, keeping an eye on the video window showing the robot's progress toward safety. I cannot see Elena's face from this distance even at max telephoto, only a pixelated sheaf of black hair peeking from the blanket.

Ten minutes drag by. Immensely powerful lasers and the particle accelerator are cycling up to full power. Forty-eight percent.

Sixty-one percent.

"Portal field initiation in six minutes," Isaac says casually, as if we are preheating the oven to bake cookies.

"Robot will reach minimum secure boundary in seven minutes," Ursula says, perhaps interpolating my expression.

"Arthur, what's the status of superconducting magnets?"

"Nominal and awaiting your cuh-*command*."
Has Arthur been compromised?
Eighty-five percent. The remaining minutes melt away.
"Portal grid at full power," Isaac says, ho-hum.
"You've got the old bitch up and running again," says my former lab partner Bill Hardler. He sits next to me and gives me a wink. The Bowie knife hilt jutting from his perforated, black-caked temple doesn't seem to bother him.
I jam my eyes shut and sing my jingles.

If I could beam love and atonement back like tachyons to the people in my life I pushed away—my father, harried mother, my Jesuit professors—I would tell them I finally *understand*.
Suddenly aware of our mortality, we wove intricate religions in every culture to answer ultimate questions. Later we embraced science and focused it like a laser to disassemble reality, to blast apart atoms and measure the heavens in our childish need to understand the fundamental forces of our existence. We penetrated the quantum world, and the more topsy-turvy doors we forced open, the more unopened doors were revealed. And some should never be breached.
Father, Mother, Daniel, there is Love and Light and unending Wonder. And there is Evil. All the laws and axioms devised by trite, foolish children are meaningless.

"Isaac, Arthur, Ursula. Fire the beams. Initiate the Portal."
It's Daniel's voice behind me that gives the order, not mine. Unmistakably his deep, calm voice but the syllables sound wet and sibilant. I forced myself not to turn and see what's become of him.
Atop the pad, time and space are raped and a bluish-white hyperspace flower unfolds in streams of stripped bosons and anti-protons. Despite its eldritch beauty it hurts the mind to gaze at its lunatic geometry.
They arrive. Muttering, chattering, gibbering. Squat

black-haired shadow forms with red jackal's eyes, black drooping ears and leering mouths bulging with canine teeth.

I speed-hum my jingles, but they perforate that pitiful barrier like a buzz saw through tissue paper.

"Do it, brother, before it's too late."

My panic spikes.

"Isaac, Arthur, Ursula. Scram the Portal."

Discorporate energy jerks me upright in the chair, a scream ripped from my mouth. They invade my mind simultaneously, pulsating in the microscopic spaces between every synapse.

Their multiversal superhighway implodes as the Portal devours itself in a cataclysmic flash of uncreation. The hovering multitude is yanked back through the event horizon, bellows and shrieks of fury instantly silenced.

But not all of them.

My left hand plucks a pen from the console, grasps it in a white-knuckled fist, and rams it into my neck. My throat floods and I begin drowning.

"Sec!"

I expel a mouthful of blood, the wine of Babylon, onto the keyboard.

"*Secon-gery!*"

"Secondary sequence initiated," Isaac says, a bit sadly?

A cyclone of voices swirls inside my mind like Hell's own harp.

I gargle and cough while my traitorous hand yanks the pen from my neck with a sickening pop, then brings it up to my left eye.

Its blood-slicked tip draws back and the turncoat muscles in my forearm flex, and I have a blink of liminal time to remember—

—at bedtime when I was a small boy, my mother read us the story of our choice before prayers from a blue compendium of children's fables and verse. *The Illustrated Treasury of Children's Literature.*

Daniel, future choirboy and Ranger, always asked to hear "The Steadfast Tin Soldier." Sometimes he requested "The History of Tom Thumb" because of the chilling death scene by spider-bite, or "The Land of Counterpane," but mainly he wanted to hear about the stalwart one-legged soldier and his pirouetting paper dancer.

I always pleaded to hear a darker story, night after night. "Pandora, The First Woman."

My mother would sigh and roll her pretty eyes, but in the end she always gave in.

I couldn't get enough of the tale of Jupiter and the vindictive Greek gods who create Pandora and deliver her to Epimetheus, Titan brother of Prometheus and emissary of mortals. Pandora is a beautiful doomsday device in female form, aglow with curiosity and avidity. And she bears a housewarming gift: a gold inlaid box stuffed with every conceivable evil and plague.

Each night I listened to the inevitable story unfold and peered through scrunched eyes at the end-piece illustration of Pandora cowering in terror as a black-smoke forest of leering demons escape up into the air. It always made my heart thump harder, and I guess I got off on that mild jolt of terror.

Soon the box was emptied, all the ills loosed upon the world, and at the bottom where the asshole pagan gods had tucked it, only Hope remained—

—and the pen rams home. Agony, and a pulsing blackness.

I *hoped* my barter of uncounted souls for poor Elena would prove irresistible. I *hoped* that disrupting the Portal at full power would suck them back to oblivion.

I also instructed Isaac to bypass evacuation protocols and detonate the limited thermonuclear failsafe device beneath the complex. Fuel-air bombs are standard these days, but Site 300 is old-school.

I hope the robot has carried Elena to a safe distance.

NIGHT TERRORS III

I hope the remnants of the exorcised human race will forgive us for our avarice and sheer stupidity.

The remaining fiends howl in unison inside my fuse-blown mind as the world goes white.

I hope—

YOU'RE A WINNER!

MATT MOORE

SQUEEZE THE PUMP again. Nothing.

The fuck?

Knocking.

Takes a second to tell it's coming from the station's convenience store. Somebody knocking on the window. Head's so goddamn—

Sorry, Lord.

So fucking fuzzy. Can't think straight.

Guy behind the counter's looking at me. A dark smudge against the yellow light inside. He's pointing at a poster in the window. Lights are so bright. Everything's got a blue-white glow. The poster's red letters waving like hot blacktop on a July day. I squint. Think it says:

PRAY INSIDE UP TO LORD

Heart thudding. Oh Lord, is this a sign? Telling me what to do after sending me to the middle of fucking nowhere. Ain't nothing out here but trees and lakes and towns smaller than the block I grew up on. But how's praying going to make it right? Mufi don't let debts go. Even if it's just two hundred bucks.

But back in rehab, Father Molina told us junkie losers you're always showing us the way if we pay attention. If we look for signs.

So it must be your will that's had me going more than a day without sleep to get me out here. Thy will be done, Lord.

Just wish I knew what the fuck it was.

All right, take a deep breath. Give my head a shake. Pull it the fuck together.

I look up again, focus this time, and read:

PRE-PAY INSIDE AFTER 10PM.

Fuck. So I *am* going inside. No pump and run. Barely had fifty bucks when Ortega lost his shit. After this, I got nothing. How am I going to keep running with no cash? Can do some stick-ups, but sooner or later they'd catch me. Then they wouldn't send me back to rehab but the joint. And Mufi's got people on the inside. After what happened with Ortega, I'd be dead for sure.

Oh, Lord have mercy. This is where it all goes down, ain't it?

Through the window, the counter jockey shrugs, like he's saying, "What's it gonna be?"

If this is your will, Lord . . .

Thy will be done.

I head for the door. Legs are heavy, feet a million miles away. Ground's shifting back and forth. Pistol's huge against my stomach.

So I gotta ask, Lord: The counter jockey, he seen my mug shot in the paper this morning? Read that shit about "armed and dangerous?" Least he's the only one inside. And I ain't seen another car for fifteen minutes. Out into the blackness, just an empty road. One way going back the way I came, the other going someplace else. A long line of streetlights light up the bottom edges of pine trees far as I can see.

Can't tell if the lights are swaying or I am.

A bell above the door tinkles. Light in here's so goddamn—

Sorry, sorry.

So fucking yellow. Tiny place. Two aisles. Ten feet end to end. Racks of chips and cookies. Motor oil. Deodorant and razors. Big cooler of drinks on one end. Coffee station next to the check out.

But there's also cameras behind the counter.

I tug my ball cap low.

Counter jockey's watching me. Greasy black hair, few days' stubble. Least he don't look the paper-reading type. Lord, why'd my photo gotta show up so quick? That your work, telling me to give it up? Or keep running? And shit, I didn't do nothing. Ortega went nuts when Mufi's people started hassling us. When 'Tega got hit, you made his gun land right at my feet. And put that rusted out car in my path when I'm hauling ass down Fuller Avenue. Some dipshit leaves it running outside a KFC in that neighborhood? Gotta be you telling me to run. Least then I knew what you wanted.

So what's it going to be now, Lord?

Coffee smells like shit, but I grab an extra large cup and pour. Need the caffeine. Besides, the extra large's got two of those peel-off game pieces instead of just one. Who knows, right?

I take a sip and wait for the kick. One of the tabs looks a little loose. What the fuck. I pull it. Got to read it twice to make sure it says: "YOU'RE A WINNER! Shoot Clerk & Empty Register!"

I drop the tab, hands trembling. My knees almost give out. The fuck is this? I ain't no killer, Lord. Doing stick-ups is one thing, but kill this man? Why you asking me to do this? If this is your will, thy will be done, but they got cameras. I won't make it too far. Then it's life in the joint for sure if Mufi's people don't get me first.

I put the coffee on the counter and drop to my knees, looking for the tab. Couldn't have said that.

Floor's covered with those things. Spilled coffee and crap from people's shoes ground into them. They all say "Sorry! Try Again!"

"Yo, man, you win something?" counter jockey asks.

I get up before he thinks I'm some psycho or something. Heart's a jackhammer. "No," I tell him, turning. "Just . . . "

Need a second to think.

Oh Lord, this is why you led me here. This man needs killing and I get the money to pay back Mufi.

Thy will be done, Lord, but the cameras.

"Um, OK," counter jockey says. He hits a few keys. "Coffee's $1.29. How much gas you gonna put in?"

I dig in my pockets. Need a second. Lord, just one more second to figure this shit out. Father Molina never said nothing about something like this. Said to trust you, talk to you, watch for signs—

"And you got 'nother chance on that cup, ya know," counter jockey says.

Oh Lord. What else you got to say? Hands shaking, I almost knock over the cup pulling the second tab. I blink a few times before I can read: "YOU'RE A WINNER! Cameras Are Broken!"

"Anything?"

The world's spinning.

"Hey, man, you okay?" counter jockey asks. He's reaching slowly to me with this right hand, like he's worried about me. But his left is moving under the counter. For a silent alarm? Or a gun?

Oh Lord, Thy will be done.

THE DEER CHASER

RACHEL NUSSBAUM

AS I PULL up in front of the kids' school and hop out of the car, I can hear birds chirping. The crisp mountain air blows the scent of pine needles past me, and the sun is bright, flickering between the swaying branches of the trees.

Just another day in the middle of bum-fuck nowhere.

It's been three months and I'm still not used to being back in my hometown. In a heartbeat I would trade the twitter of birds for the roar of the train that used to speed past the apartment, and the common scent of trees and flowers has nothing on the smell of that amazing falafel stand at the end of my old block. And yes, it's massively ungrateful of me to yearn for Seattle, for city life over a beautiful little community right next to a state park. But honestly, I couldn't help it if I tried. Being here makes me feel trapped. It reminds me of everything I was afraid of when I was eighteen. I didn't want to get stuck here with no job, living at home for the rest of my life, knocked up and tied down with a bunch of kids by my twenties. Incidentally, this is exactly what has become of the rest of my graduating class.

And then I remind myself that I'm seriously no better than any of them. That after graduating from college with a major in accounting and a minor in English, I couldn't get a single callback from any job interviews. I had to move back in with my mom, and I am now, well . . . living at home and taking care of my younger brother and sister. Now I'm just like every other hick who graduated from North Pines High, except I've got five digits worth of student loans to pay back.

With a sigh and a glance at my watch, I cross the street and start to walk to the school, feeling even shittier than I did when I parked. Good to know that even at my lowest point, I can find some way to take myself down a few extra pegs. At least helping my mom out with my siblings while she's working sixty hours a week as a lawyer keeps me from feeling completely useless, especially now that Dad's gone.

Still, it doesn't stop me from feeling like an asshole.

The front steps of the school come into view, and my heart sinks as I see Madison, plopped in the grass and sobbing her eyes out.

Son of a bitch. Not this again.

"Madie, what's wrong?" I ask, putting on my best game face. She scoots away from me, crying louder.

I sigh and put my head in my hands. Madison and I never had time to bond as sisters. She was born roughly around the same time I moved out, and now at the age of six she's suddenly got a full-time sister. I'm rarely able to comfort her when she throws these fits, and at least three times a week I bring her home sobbing to Mom. Well, I need to try at least.

"Madison, I can't fix it if I don't know what's wrong," I say.

"Another deer came into the play yard at lunch recess. She was drawing in the classroom and missed it and she won't shut up about it."

I glance up, trying to locate the source of the voice. I hear some snickering under the staircase, and I peer over to see Jasper, sitting in the grass with his friends.

"Hey, Lela." He nods over at me, grinning and playing dumb. I narrow my eyes at him.

"And why aren't you out here trying to make your little sister feel better?" I ask.

"Well I *was*," he says. "But then she pushed me and called me a poop face."

His friends laugh harder, and Madison pauses between sobs to look back at them and snarl. I sigh. I am not good at this at all, taking care of kids. Seriously, I have the maternal instincts of a pinecone.

Pinecone? Damn, I've been in this stupid forest town too long.

I look down at Madison in time to see a chunk of snot drip down her face, and Jasper and his friends yell in disgust. She sucks in more air and begins to cry louder.

"Shit," I mumble.

"I heard that!" Jasper says.

"You're twelve," I say, rolling my eyes and sitting down next to Madison. "Get over it."

He shrugs.

"Whatever. I'm going home with Ian." Jasper sighs, climbing out from under the staircase with his friends.

Well, one thing the kid's got going for him is that he's no martyr. Whenever Jasper gets into a fight or thinks he might get into one he walks away, which works pretty well for me. It might also explain why he's started walking to and from school with his friends to avoid being trapped in a car with Madison and me.

As Jasper and his friends walk away, I sigh in relief. Maybe without them to egg her on, I can get Madison to stop crying. I reach my hand out and pat her back.

"Come on, honey," I say. "There are plenty of deer coming down from the mountain these days. *Way* more than when I was a kid! You'll see one."

"Nooo," Madison whines, tears running down her chin. "I never see them! Only Jasper does."

She sucks in a deep breath in preparation for another raise of volume, and I try to think of something to fix this. Anything I can do to make her stop crying. Just one day, I want to bring her home and have her not be in tears when mom pokes her head out of her home office. One day where I can do something right. I glance up the street as Jasper disappears around the corner, and as I do my gaze lands on the mountain.

"What if I took you to the state park tonight to look for deer?" I ask.

Madison stops blubbering and glances up at me with a trembling chin.

"After dinner we'll drive up to the mountain, just you and me. We'll bring flashlights and snacks and we won't go home until we see a deer. Sound like fun?"

I silently hold my breath, hoping this will be enough to pacify her. To my relief and surprise, she smiles. She wipes the snot off her face with her sleeve and nods.

The hot coffee burns my tongue as the car winds up the rough road to the state park, and I mumble a short string of select obscenities under my breath. Catching myself, I glance back nervously at Madison. Completely oblivious, she's staring out the window at the trees, kicking her legs and bouncing lightly in her seat.

Smiling, I slow the car and pull to a stop.

"Hey, Madie," I call back. "You want to move up to the front?"

Her eyes go wide.

"Mommy doesn't let me sit in the front. She said I'm not old enough yet."

"I can keep a secret if you can." I shrug. "Let me just clear some space."

I sweep away the layer of junk from the front seat: Jasper's neglected toy robots with missing arms, crappy comic books, and his old metal baseball bat. Madison unbuckles her seatbelt and climbs up into the passenger seat, smiling up at me. I smile back and continue up the road. I guess her excitement is infectious; this is actually starting to feel a little fun.

As we enter the park, I slow down a bit and lower the windows.

"Dad, Jasper, and me used to drive up here on the weekends late at night when I was younger," I tell her. "We'd keep track of who saw the most deer, and whoever won got to decide where we'd get dessert."

"What about Mommy, Lela? Did Mommy go?" Madison asks, not looking away from the window.

"Mom was always asleep by the time we—"

"I saw something, I saw something!" Madison points out the window.

I throw the car into reverse, back up a few yards, and kill the engine in front of a small grass clearing with some dense foliage behind it. A limb snaps in the tree line, and I see the shape of an animal moving slowly between the branches. Madison sits up in her seat, straining her neck, her eyes bright and wide.

"Looks like it's going to come out," I whisper. "Just try to be really quiet so we don't scare it."

Madison bites her lip and stares with anticipation, her fingers pressed firmly against the car door. Honestly, I couldn't give a crap about a deer, but seeing Madison smile, seeing her happy for once because of something I did . . . it feels really good. Like maybe I can do this big sister thing and not just be a waste of my mom's resources. Maybe I'm not so useless.

As I watch Madison, her smile slowly begins to fade. Her face contorts with shock and she draws back. I glance out the window.

It's not a deer.

It slinks out of the forest, the moonlight outlining its figure. I squint and lean over, trying to get a closer look at it. Its fur is too dark and the proportions are all wrong for a deer. But what else could it be? A bobcat? A coyote? As it creeps closer, my jaw drops.

Its shape looks almost like a person, hunched over and

crawling on all fours. I can now see it doesn't have fur. It's covered in dark grey skin, cracked and flaking, sections of it speckled with green, moss-like patches. Its ribs and spine jut out, unnaturally sharp, and its limbs are split off at the edges where there should be feet, like tree branches. It lifts them up slowly and as it places them back down, I can make out the gleam of thick, razor claws dotting the tips of each branch-like finger.

When it crawls into the road, I feel paralyzed. With its head down, it doesn't seem to notice the car and begins to move past us, down the street.

Madison suddenly grabs my hand and I gasp.

"Lela . . . I w-w-wanna go home," she whimpers.

The creature snaps its head around, and Madison and I both jump. We're met with a vaguely human face, one with gaunt cheeks and slitted nostrils. It stares at me and I can't move. I can't look away from its terrible, bloodshot eyes. I can only open my mouth to whimper and as I do, the thing leans toward us and opens its mouth to hiss, revealing row upon row of pin-like teeth.

Somehow, my instinct for survival chips me out of my frozen terror. I turn the key, slip out of park, and floor it. The car flies down the back road, bumping sharply over the dips. The second the next exit is in view, I turn so fast my coffee cup flies out of the holder. The still scalding contents splash onto my arm, but I can hardly feel it.

"What the fuck was that thing?" I yell.

From next to me, I hear a whimper.

Oh shit. Madison.

"Madie," I whisper.

She glances up at me, her eyes wide and filled with tears. She doesn't say a word.

I need to reassure her. I need to say something, anything. But Jesus Christ, what the hell is there to say? I can't even calm myself down. This can't be happening. This can't be real.

~

The moment we get home, Madison runs into Mom's bedroom. I only wish I could be granted the same luxury.

I step into my room and peer through my open window, at the tree line bordering our dirt driveway, the swaying branches and twisting shadows. The same paralysis from back in the forest grips me. By the time I pull myself away, my legs are shaking. I practically run down the stairs.

After drawing all the curtains in the living room, I grab the thickest, heaviest quilt I can from the hall closet and wrap myself in it like a cocoon on the sofa. Three hours and two blankets later, I still feel no better. I feel hot and stuffy, and I can't breathe, but there's no way I'm uncovering myself. I toss and turn for a bit longer before I finally sit up. With shaking hands I pull my laptop off of the coffee table and boot up.

I type in a search query for unusual sightings at North Pines State Park. My heart thumps in my chest as I hit enter. After an agonizing pause, the search results pop up—and there's nothing. No strange animal sightings, not even an animal out of season reported in the last ten years. I delete the name of the park. I broaden the search to unusual animal sightings in forests.

I don't know what possesses me to click on images instead of search.

A chill runs down my spine as the images load. I scroll through picture after picture of blurred, obscured, horrific creatures hiding between trees in the darkness. Knowing that they're probably all fake does nothing to console me, because what I saw wasn't.

But if what I saw was real, who's to say these aren't? I exit the browser and slump back down in the sofa. As I do, a shadow in the hallway shifts in my peripheral vision and I jump.

"Shit!"

The hallway light goes on.

"Lela!" Mom says. "You scared me!"

As my heart settles back into my chest, I sigh in relief. She may have just given me a panic attack, but seeing her face puts me at ease. It's like that feeling you get when you're a little kid who just woke up from a bad dream and you realize everything's going to be okay.

My smile fades after a moment though, as I realize it's not going to be okay. I could tell her what I saw, and she could either believe me or not, but it wouldn't change a thing. Because that—whatever it was—is still outside somewhere. It's still real. And there's nothing Mom can do to change that.

"Sorry, hon," Mom says, flicking on the standup lamp. "Are you up late or up early?"

"Um, early," I lie.

"I'd offer to make you a pot of coffee, but I'm running on a tight schedule. Find anything good?"

I stare at her for a moment before she gestures to the computer.

"Job hunting? Any positions available in the city?" she asks, raising her eyebrows.

"*Oh*," I sigh, shaking my head and lowering my laptop screen. "Um, might have a few leads, nothing to get . . . get my hopes up over . . . "

I trail off as she walks out of the room.

"How was deer watching last night?" she asks, re-emerging with a hairbrush and walking over to the mirror that hangs over the fireplace.

"I—it was—"

"I think being out late in the dark got to Madie, she crawled into bed with me last night—sounded like she was having nightmares," Mom says, combing through her hair. It's then I realize she's wearing her suit.

"Mom, are you going somewhere?"

She stops brushing her hair and turns around, the light catching the silver buttons of her blazer.

"Don't you remember? My ride's going to be here soon,

we've got a deposition in Boise this afternoon, and I can't afford to miss my flight. You know how long it can take to drive to the airport from here. You can still watch the kids for the weekend, right? Don't have an interview?"

I have to catch myself from gasping. No. No, you can't leave now. Not after what I saw. What Madison and I both saw.

"Oh . . . um . . . y-yeah . . . "

Mom begins rattling on about the food in the fridge and extra money on the table, and I let my head sink and my vision blur.

"Hey . . . Mom?" I say. "Wh—when we were in the park earlier, Madie and I saw a weird animal."

She stops talking and turns to look at me.

"It looked . . . well, it didn't look like anything I'd ever seen before."

"That can't be good. You should try calling animal control in a few hours." She shrugs before turning back to the mirror. "To be honest, the park has always kind of given me the creeps at night. That's why I always used to go to bed early back when you kids and Dad would go on your night drives. Something about it . . . it always felt like something was watching me. You know what I mean?"

I shudder as she leaves the room and lower my laptop. I pick up the remote for the TV and turn it to the brightest cartoon I can find.

Jasper walked to school with his friends this morning as usual, leaving Madison and me alone on the drive. What's scaring me is that she's not crying. She's not even talking. I clear my throat, trying to break the tension.

"I called animal control this morning," I say to her. "Told them about what we saw. They said they were definitely going to look into it."

Half true. I knew they would think I was crazy if I told them the truth, so I described a hairless canine-like animal.

Better than doing nothing. I glance back at Madison, who's staring at the back of the car seat.

"Madie, I know what we saw last night was really strange, but there's gotta be an explanation for—"

"I had a scary dream last night," she says. I stare at her in the mirror and watch her glance up to meet my gaze. "It was in my dream."

I almost miss the turn off. Goosebumps rise on the back of my neck, and I clear my throat, trying to think of something to say. Something, anything that will reassure her. Come on . . .

But nothing comes out. I'm not just a pathetic excuse for a sister; I'm a pathetic excuse for an adult.

"It was chasing me," Madison continues. "I was in the forest and it was chasing me. It was trying to get me."

I shake my head and open my mouth, but as we turn toward the school, something catches my eye.

There's a giant crowd of kids on the front yard, and teachers are trying to usher the students inside. I can't make out what they're all looking at, but I find a parking space and spot Jasper in the growing circle. Before I can tell her to stay put, Madison opens the door and runs out to Jasper, leaving her lunchbox behind. I grab it and follow after her.

I nearly double back in horror when I see what's causing so much commotion—a deer.

A dead deer, splayed out in a pool of blood in the grass, torn asunder. From head to tail, its body is covered in massive gashes. They reveal the white gleam of bone, the fibrous webs of red muscles, and bloated organs that swelled through the slices. The deer's eyes are frozen in horror, and its tongue hangs out between its parted jaws.

As the teachers come out and begin to cover the deer with a tarp, I grab Madison and Jasper and pull them away.

"Let's go," I say, leading them back to the car.

The rest of the day is a blur. At some point, when my

thoughts become too much, I take the kids to see a movie—some 3-D cartoon our cheap theater could only show in 2-D. When the movie lets out, I'm thinking of seeing another one, but the sky is already starting to darken and the last thing I want to do is be outside at night. I drive us home and bribe Jasper to go play with Madison while I face the computer alone. This time, I know what to look for. And the idea that I may actually find something scares me shitless.

I type in "Deer attacked in North Pine State Park." And good God, do I hit the mother lode. Attacks on deer date back to when I was a kid, getting more and more frequent each year. Written off as mountain lions, coyotes, bobcats, sometimes even suspected to be the work of some sick teenagers. I click on an image and my skin crawls. The deer's been shredded, just like the one at the school—blood speckling the ground and fat maggots clinging to its flesh.

"It's the same thing that got the deer we saw, isn't it?"

"Shit!" I turn around and see Jasper.

"Where's Madie?" I ask.

"Told her it was her toys' nap time and she fell asleep with them." He shrugs as he circles around the sofa. "So you think the thing you saw in the park was the thing that killed the deer at school today?"

"How do you know about that?"

"I heard you talking about it with Mom early this morning. I asked Madie just now and she said you guys saw a monster," he says.

"She told you?" I ask.

His eyes widen.

"So it's true?"

I sigh and lean back on the sofa. Jasper sits down next to me and glances at the computer screen.

"I was thinking," he says, "about all these deer coming down from the park. What if there was a reason for it? What if something was chasing them away?"

"I'd think . . . that would make a lot of sense," I mumble.

"Did Madie tell you about the nightmare she had last night?" he asks.

"With the whatever it was? Yeah." I sigh.

"Did she tell you it talked to her?"

I freeze. I glance at Jasper, my eyes wide.

"She said it told her she wasn't supposed to see it; that people aren't supposed to see it," Jasper says, his voice beginning to shake as he continues. "I . . . I think that's why it was at the school. It knows she goes there. It was looking for her."

There's a moment of silence between us, one that feels like a lifetime. I open my mouth to speak.

And the power goes out.

Jasper and I both scream. He clings to me and I stand, yanking up my laptop to use its light. Footsteps echo down the hall and I back up. I shine the light into the blinking, horrified face of Madison.

"Lela?" Madison whispers.

Before I can say anything, there's another sound; a shatter of glass and a crash from upstairs, footsteps pattering against the floor.

"Run!" I yell, pulling the car keys out of my pocket.

Jasper and Madison take off for the door and I move behind them, the light from my laptop illuminating our way. As I get closer to the door, I turn around to glance at the staircase.

And I see it.

A pair of bloodshot eyes glare down at me from the top of the banister. Its tree-branch like limbs are growing, splintering apart into more fingers—the thick, razor claws pushing out through the skin with sickening bursts of puss and blood as they align. The monster pulls its cracked lips back, exposing thousands of teeth. I'm frozen—stunned. I feel helpless. I feel like a child. Like a deer.

"Lela, move!" Madison screams from outside the house.

I snap around and tear through the living room. Out of

the corner of my eye I see a flash of grey take off after me. I make it out the door and slam it shut behind me, only to watch five-dozen razor-sharp nails penetrate the wooden surface, sending splinters flying. Horrible, haunting shrieks coming from behind the door, a strange mix between an animal's cry and a human scream.

"The car!" I yell, turning around. "Get to the car!"

Jasper opens the door and both he and Madison jump into the front. I swing around and slide into the driver's seat just as the front door splits into pieces in the frame.

I back out of the driveway as fast as I can, but as I reverse, we see it coming, galloping forward on its massive tree limbs, fingers surrounding it like tendrils. I press down on the gas as hard as I can and for a moment, we leave it behind.

And then there's a thud on the roof of the car.

Dozens of sharp claws drill through the roof. Jasper and Madison are on the floor of the car, screaming. I close my eyes.

And somewhere between the monster's howls and Jasper and Madison's panicked cries, time stands still. Somehow when I open my eyes and glance down to look at my little brother and sister one last time, I notice Jasper's baseball bat tucked under the seat.

"Jasper! The bat!"

Jasper glances up and without a moment of hesitation, he grabs the bat and swings it at a clawed finger with all his might. With a crack, the nail splits in half. The monster screams in anguish and retracts its blades.

I hit the brakes.

It flies off the top of the car and skids to a stop in the road in front of us, writhing in pain and fury. It looks over with its reddened eyes and unhinges its jaw at me, hissing in rage.

I put my foot to the gas.

I don't know if it tried getting out of the way or if it just sat there, but we all felt the crunch and heard it shriek as I drove over it. I glance back at it in my mirror, its limbs twisted, wriggling in the road, trilling its horrible cry. I hit reverse and drive over it again. And again. And again.

I drive over it until it's nothing but a flat mass of red and grey mush.

The police come early in the morning while Madison is sleeping, along with an animal control van. They scrape what's left of the monster off the road, but the beaten pulp of the corpse is hardly distinguishable. The policeman takes our statement and pictures of the door and the top of the car. After they leave, Jasper and I go back inside to the living room.

"Why didn't they look more surprised?" Jasper asks from the sofa. "We just told them we got attacked by a monster and they acted so . . . so calm!"

"It was a monster to us," I call from the door as I sweep up splinters of wood. "To them, well, it could just as easily be a diseased wolf or mountain lion. They'll probably come back for more questions when they analyze it in the lab, but that could take months."

Jasper sighs in exasperation.

"I guess you won't even be here when they come back to ask us about it, huh?" he says.

I pause at the door.

"I don't know. I might be."

"I thought you were trying to find a job in the city?" Jasper asks. "Especially now, wouldn't you want to leave sooner than ever? I sure as hell would."

"Don't swear," I say, snapping my fingers. "And I don't know. After what happened . . . well, we beat it, didn't we? It came after us, it tried to kill us and we destroyed it, and if we can do that—if I can do that—maybe I can handle living in this hick town a bit longer."

Maybe I'm not so useless after all.

I smile at Jasper and as I do, Madison comes walking out of her room in her pajamas, rubbing her eyes.

"Hey, sleepy head," I greet her. "How you feeling? I made some scrambled eggs for breakfast and left them in the pan, they're—"

"I had another scary dream."

The broom drops from my hand.

"Madison?" I ask shakily.

Without another word she walks past me and out the mangled front door. Jasper and I exchange glances before we follow her out onto the road, where she stares down the street that curves up to the state park. It's then that I notice the steady vibrations coming from the ground. As our neighbors walk out into their driveways to discern the source of the noise, I see it, turning down the street.

Deer. Dozens of them. Ancient stags, young bucks, does and spotted fawns scampering behind their parents, their numbers enough to crowd the entire road. There must be hundreds of them.

"It's like every single deer in the forest is leaving!" Jasper says in awe.

"They are," Madison answers.

Jasper and I look down at her.

"It wasn't alone," she whispers. "He wasn't the only one. And now the others are angry."

THE STONES OF BAVDONGARDE

PETER CHARRON

SERGEANT WALTER QUINN looked over the tiny village of Bavdongarde from a nearby hill. The Kaiser's army had captured the site, nestled on the edge of the Argonne Forest, so the Americans promptly shelled it into shapeless mounds of rubble. Only the church, its steeple and roof collapsed, still stood to prove a village had existed at all. Trenches surrounded the stone walls like a labyrinthine moat filled with mud, bodies, and rusting barbed wire. The tang of burned metal and spent mustard gas lay heavy on the breeze.

It was nothing like the France of picture postcards. There were no beaches, vineyards, or burlesque dancers. Quinn was struck by the complete lack of contrast: torn and broken ground, shattered and shrapnel-raked trees, even the uniforms of his men all rendered in the same muddy brown. The overcast sky lent only a smudging light to the scene. It was like standing in a sepia toned photograph.

"They don't put this shit on postcards," said Quinn.

"Sarge?" asked one of the men.

"Nothing. Move out."

Quinn hadn't expected to meet another squad, but they ran into doughboys by a mostly intact building set away from the trenches. Their leader, a lieutenant by insignia, approached Quinn. "Monroe, Salvage Company. Where you headed, Sergeant?"

"Here, sir. I'm Quinn, First Division Sanitary Corps." Stupid name. You might think they were here to tidy up, thought Quinn. HQ should just call it what it was, grave digging.

The building was just four walls with a canvas roof. Nearby, Monroe's men rushed to pack the last of whatever useful ammunition and supplies they had scavenged.

"It's not much, Sergeant." Monroe nodded to the cottage. "But it still has a working fireplace. Regimental used it as field command during the push."

Quinn's men spread out around the back of the building. They unhitched the horses and started pulling supplies from the wagons.

A neat line of bodies lying a dozen yards off caught Quinn's attention. One, covered in a scrap of blanket, seemed out of place. Quinn went over and pulled the blanket aside. Beneath lay the body of a civilian dressed in the black cassock of a priest. He wore an odd cross; it was intertwined with a gold crescent.

A thin man with thick glasses came to stand by Quinn. "That's the symbol of the Order of St. Michael. They built a lot of the churches in this part of Europe."

Avery was the unit's bookworm and would have been a history professor by now had he not been drafted. Quinn turned to Monroe. "What the hell is this, Lieutenant?"

"We didn't have anything to do with that," Monroe's tone made it clear he didn't like the accusation.

"I didn't say you did."

"All I know is what the artillery captain told me. When the 25th got here the priest begged him not to damage the church. A few days later the Germans put snipers up in the steeple, probably sighting their mortars from there too. Captain had no choice but to order his guns to take it out.

The priest came charging over, angry and shouting. He grabbed the Captain's sidearm. In the confusion someone lost their nerve and shot the old man."

Quinn covered the priest.

"At least he wasn't around to see the church get hit. Between that and the rest of the 25th showing up Fritz must have figured they'd lost their advantage. Germans pulled out quick."

From the edge of the nearest trench one of Quinn's men swore in a steady stream of Italian.

"What's the problem, Medoni?" Quinn asked.

"They've still got both tags."

"For Christ sake," spat Quinn.

Regulations required the personal effects and one tag be collected from the dead, usually done by a unit's chaplain. Having to do it themselves, the whole process would take days longer.

Monroe swung up into his saddle. "Place is all yours, Sergeant. We've gathered all we're going to."

"What's the rush, Lieutenant?"

Monroe's eyes glanced over the trenches and for an instant Quinn thought the man looked scared.

"Something I should know?"

The lieutenant leaned forward and lowered his voice. "We usually go pretty deep into the trenches looking for ammo and other equipment. I got here with twenty men. Six went missing out in those trenches. We only found two bodies."

"Sniper?"

Monroe shook his head. "Never heard any gunshots. One had his neck broken the other had no wounds. He was just— dead. We saw something moving out there a few times, heard it too, and noticed bodies disappearing. You know how it is, you don't think of them as people, just landmarks. You have to or you couldn't do the job. You notice when they're moved or go missing."

Quinn didn't hide his skepticism. "Are you trying to sell

me on that story of shell-shocked deserters wandering the trenches?"

"I'm not selling you anything, Sergeant." Monroe sounded tired. "It's just not worth the scrap to send my men back into that bloody maze. Good luck." He tugged the reins and trotted after the wagons.

Quinn blew a piercing whistle to gather his dozen men. "All right, none of the dead were processed." This caused annoyed and angry muttering. "Hey! I don't like it any more than you do, but that's how it is. Avery, collect the tags and keep the ledger."

"How come he gets the easy job?" complained Medoni.

"Because he won't help himself to their sweethearts' lockets while he's at it," said Ben West. The big Sioux had his arms crossed and made no attempt to hide his contempt.

Medoni's pallid skin flared red around the ears along with his anger. "Fuck you, Injun Joe."

"Shut up, Medoni." Quinn was sick of the man running his mouth. It was Medoni's own fault he was on the burial squad. They'd given him a choice, this or prison. "You all know the drill. West, take a few men and see if you can find some pits deep enough. The rest of you split up and get a rough count. We'll start hauling the horses out as soon as we've got a place to dump them."

Quinn leaned on his shovel and took a long pull from his canteen before running a hand over his short, coppery hair. The afternoon wasn't much warmer than the morning. The rain had held off, but digging left him clammy with sweat. Quinn's gaze wandered in the direction of the church. He caught movement there large enough to be a man. "Who's working over by the church?"

"Nobody," said West.

"Get your weapon. Rest of you, keep working."

"What is it, Sarge?"

"I saw someone moving out there."

The most direct path to the church ran through a stretch of trenches. The wider passages were filled with knee-deep mud washed out of the unsupported walls. In those places they walked on rough planks laid over the muck. The duckboards flexed under their weight and sprang back with a sucking noise.

They climbed out where the church walls stood between them and the place Quinn had spotted movement. The building reminded Quinn of a ruined abbey he'd visited while training in England and seemed much larger than expected for a small village.

They moved silently along the wall and around the back of the cylindrical chancel. On the far side there was a gap in the curved wall torn open by a direct shell hit.

West crouched and ran his hand over a section of broken granite. "Looks like this part of the wall was made from just one massive stone."

Quinn stepped up onto the irregular block and peered into the dim interior. The altar, essentially a massive table of wooden slabs, lay overturned and badly scorched. Two more standing stones formed the sides of an archway separating the chancel from the rest of the church. The way into the hall was impassible, blocked by burned and broken roof beams.

"That wasn't the only big stone. There were six making up this back, curved wall," said Quinn.

He stepped into the fifteen-foot-wide space behind the altar. Brass vessels and candle holders cluttered the floor. Most of the painted plaster, once covering walls and ceiling, now littered the floor in chalky masses revealing the ancient stonework. Spiral carvings and those resembling skulls and a dragon-like serpent covered the face of each upright stone.

The shell blast had not only felled one of the great stones but cracked and pried up the floor closest to it. There seemed to be a space beneath, some old crypt or cellar. A German soldier lay face down, half buried in the debris. A stream of blood ran from the pool around his head to disappear into the dark below the floor.

"Must have been standing here when the wall exploded," said Quinn.

"Doesn't seem to be anyone here now." West grinned. "I don't think that German was wandering around."

"I hope not," said Quinn. He picked up a bit of broken stone and tossed it down into the hole. An odor rose from it, like long-stagnant water, strong enough to threaten nausea. The oily stench quickly filled the space. Quinn backed away before he started retching.

"What the hell?" West covered his nose with his sleeve and retreated outside. He only made it five feet before vomiting.

The polluted air brought with it a blackness that collapsed the edges of Quinn's vision threatening blindness. He backed out of the chancel where the diffuse sunlight restored his sight.

"What could be down there to smell that badly?" asked West.

"Old well maybe," Quinn offered, though the explanation felt weak. He held out his hand and pulled West to his feet. "Let's get back to work."

Shouting woke Quinn from what felt like only minutes of sleep. Adrenaline surged, allowing him to grab his weapon and be out the cottage door in one fluid motion. One of the men stood with his rifle aimed into a nearby trench, only an outline of which was visible in the firelight.

"What is it?" asked Quinn.

The soldier shook his head.

The other sentry was missing. "Where's Cother?"

The man pulled his eyes from the trench and focused on Quinn. "The horses were acting nervous so he went over to see. I caught sight of it climbing out of the transverse."

"Sight of what?"

"Something dark, like an animal or—something. It was pretty big. Cother went after it."

Shots, followed by a scream, echoed from the north.

"West, get some lanterns!" said Quinn.

Quinn ordered a tight perimeter around the cottage then took West and three others into the trenches. They advanced with caution through the narrow passage. The first junction split three ways. Nothing moved for as far as the lantern light could reach.

"We'll never find him in the dark, and this sloppy mud just fills in all the tracks," said West.

Quinn agreed. They had a better chance of being ambushed than finding anyone in the tar-black warren.

Quinn was tired and frustrated by the time they reached the cottage. "Double the watch, and from now on, no one goes out there alone."

At full light the unit split into teams and searched. West discovered blood and drag marks by the church that he was sure were not there the day before. The trail led to a dugout north of the church.

Quinn ducked to look into the small, log-walled chamber built into the trench wall. Cother's dead eyes stared back, and he wasn't alone.

Avery went pale. "My God, look at his chest."

Cother sat on the dirt, his feet straight out, with his back against the bodies of two other men forming a triangle. Cother's chest lay open and empty, his ribs spread wide like window shutters.

"I saw something like this up in the mountains once. My granddad told me it was wolves. But there's no sign of such," offered West.

"Wolves didn't do this." Avery's voice held a fragile tone. "There aren't any wolves in Europe anymore."

"I've seen packs of carrion dogs feeding on the dead. They weren't this neat though," said Quinn.

West ducked inside the structure and moved around to view the other bodies. "Shit!"

"What?" Quinn slid around the other side of Cother's

body. The other men also sat with scooped out chests. What wasn't obvious from the front was that the bent back ribs of each man had been woven together into some macabre basket with those of the body to either side. Quinn knew the leathery strips fastening the bones had to be skin.

Avery refused to move beyond the entrance. "There's got to be somebody else out here," he said finally.

"I don't want the others to see this. We'll just seal it up," said Quinn.

Avery stood aside so Quinn could exit. "Then what do we do?"

"Our job," said Quinn. "Then we can get the hell away from here."

After walling Cother inside his improvised tomb, they returned to camp. Quinn whistled in the rest of his men and called off the search.

"There's no sign of him," Quinn lied. "If he's alive he'll show up. If he's dead we'll find him along with the rest. I want to be finished with this place."

The men worked in silence with weapons close. They tried to work quickly but pulling corpses from the muck, moving and burying them wasn't an activity lending itself to speed.

Twice Quinn spotted movement about the ruined landscape. It was always in shadow or just out of the corner of his eye. As the sky dimmed one of the men suddenly fired several rounds across the open space between trench lines. Others aimed in the same direction and joined the volley.

"Cease fire!" Quinn demanded.

"There was something there," insisted the private.

"Call your targets!" Quinn barked. "The rest of you are no better. Get a handle on your nerves before one of you kills another shooting wild." Quinn's expression remained stern but fatigue kept him from holding it long. "This is the last load. It'll be too dark soon for more."

~

NIGHT TERRORS III

In the morning they discovered yesterday's graves uncovered. Bodies and parts of bodies lay strewn about. Obvious, clawed tracks dotted the area, although West could find none leading up to the grave.

Anger burned away Quinn's unease. "We're going to kill whatever's doing this. Put them back in the ground but leave the graves open. That's our bait."

"Jesus," muttered Medoni, crossing himself.

"It's not going to get any more of the dead," said Quinn. "We'll set a watch. When it comes back we'll kill it."

"I don't understand why an animal would come and root up these bodies when there are still scores of them out there," said Avery.

"It doesn't matter why. We just need to stop it." Quinn didn't want to think about Avery's question. He didn't really want to know the answer.

Half the squad went about seeing to the dead, Quinn and the rest fortified foxholes with line of sight to opened graves. At one point Medoni appeared with a German machinegun and boxes of ammunition.

"Where the hell did you find that, Medoni?" Quinn asked.

"On the German side. From the looks of the stuff lying around they pulled out fast."

West leaned on his shovel. "You're supposed to be hauling bodies, not souvenir hunting."

For once Medoni kept his mouth shut.

"We can use the extra fire power," said Quinn. "Set it up over by the trees." The darkness was near absolute after sunset. Thick clouds denied even starlight to Bavdongarde. Quinn felt his eyes straining to gather light that wasn't there. Six of them waited in the foxholes shivering under blankets and the feeble warmth of bull's eye lanterns. Medoni sat alone with his German prize. The rest were in the cottage trying to sleep.

Despite the cold and anticipation, Quinn dozed off. He woke to urgent nudging.

"Something's out there," Avery whispered.

Quinn peered over the foxhole's edge, held his breath and listened. A muddy splat and the scratching of nails on dirt were preceded by what sounded like the muffled beating of large wings. The faint breeze became foul. The sounds moved closer, on or near the open grave. Different noises followed: something heavy being dragged, then what sound like snapping.

"Lights!" shouted Quinn.

Stark cones of brilliance washed over the graves and, for an instant, revealed a black and wetly glistening form. The shape rushed out of the light—not before Quinn got the impression of great, black wings unfurling to beat the air.

Lantern beams swung wildly trying to locate the thing. Someone opened fire. Quinn caught an instant of sinuous movement. A scream came from one of the foxholes. The light of dropped lanterns illuminated two men fighting a very long, darting thing. It wove around the columns of light allowing only the flashed glimpse of an arm or obsidian talon. The second man screamed and blood sprayed across a lantern lens.

"Fire at will!"

Bullets tore through the space the beast occupied. Quinn saw the thing's long tail disappearing along the ground and into the dark beyond the foxhole.

"It's in the air!" someone shouted a moment later.

Men stood for a better aim while trying to spot with lanterns. The rest of the squad, now awake, ran from the cottage to reinforce their comrades. The thing strafed them, oblivious to the buzz of poorly aimed bullets. Men yelled, taken down both from above and by stray fire. The scene became a fragmented tableau of dead and fighting men lit at haphazard angles by discarded lanterns.

The rapid fire of Medoni's machine gun suddenly added its voice to the chaos and the creature seemed to vanish. For a moment Quinn thought they may have killed it. Then

Medoni screamed, and the machine gun's fire cut through the dirt just a foot to Quinn's right. He threw himself to the ground as the man beside him fell with multiple hits. The machine gun fell silent.

Quinn got up and ran. "Regroup at the cottage!"

Three men joined him, West, Avery, and Ross. They put their backs to the cottage's rubble stone wall.

West reloaded his pistol. "We can't fight in the open, the demon's too fast."

"There's no such thing as demons," retorted Avery, but he stood close enough for Quinn to feel him trembling.

A few minutes passed. The silence marred only by a sound like tearing leather.

Quinn's heart hammered. As the nervous rush of combat ebbed, terror seeped in. West was right, they couldn't stay here. But their chances in the woods were no better, and the trenches provided no protection against an attack from above. He thought of the ruined chancel with its intact ceiling.

But it came from there. Its stench was all over the place. No. Just from the well underneath. Someone had trapped it there a long time ago under the ring of guarding stones. They built the church over it later. Maybe they knew what was down there and wanted to make sure it stayed in the ground. Until the artillery broke the stone and let it out. Would the thing avoid its prison?

The downwash of wings overhead brought the monster's reek to Quinn's nostrils. By the sound it landed somewhere close.

"Head for the church." Quinn didn't wait to see who followed.

Quinn ran down the line retracing the path he and West had used before hoping he didn't get the turns wrong. Twice he felt the pressure of wings above their heads. On the third Ross was plucked up into the sky. Ross's initial yell of surprise was followed by a long, echoing scream ending in a thud to the left.

Quinn spotted the church. They climbed out and sprinted to the opening in the wall. Wings followed them, passing over as they ducked into the chancel.

Avery opened the hood on their single lantern. The dead German was gone.

Quinn put his hands under the edge of the altar. "Help me with this." It took all three of them to tip the eight foot altar on to its long end and shove it into the opening. In the process they exposed a one by two foot piece of marble set into its underside.

West pressed his weight against the altar. "It's not going to hold unless we brace it with something. Grab a couple of those beams."

Quinn and Avery dragged over two of the beams blocking the archway into the nave. Before they could get them into place something slammed into the barricade.

The altar shifted. Two gaunt arms shot through the gap and grabbed hold of West's uniform, lifting him off his feet. West jammed his pistol into the black flesh pressed up against the gap and fired.

The creature screamed. The sound pitched so high it went right through Quinn's head. It dropped West and retreated. They quickly wedged beams between the altar and the walls of the narrow space.

"How many rounds do you have left?" Quinn asked.

"Two," said West.

"A few more. Not that it's going to make any difference," said Avery, his tone flat and defeated.

The thing outside slammed into the barrier with enough force to dislodge the marble insert. It fell and broke open on the stones. The braces held.

"It's a reliquary," said Avery. "Every church had some sacred object set into the altar." He crouched and pulled a gold, sickle-shaped blade, the grip made of bone, from inside the broken box.

The hammering stopped.

Quinn heard a heavy crash from the blocked archway. Some of the larger bits of rubble shifted.

West aimed the lantern at the wall of debris. "It's digging its way in!"

A stout beam, one no man could possibly lift, slid rapidly away taking some of the collapsed roof with it. Much of the broken framing settled a few feet lower, providing enough space for the beast to crawl through.

West emptied his revolver before the creature's long body was clear of the hole. The beast lunged and pinned West against the wall with two of its four arms. Avery's rifle cracked a shot that grazed the monster, causing a spray of black blood. It screamed and backhanded Avery aside. The thing dug its second set of claws into West's chest just below the collar bone. It ripped downward then discarded West's ruined body.

Quinn managed a single shot before the nightmare creature reared on its legless, serpentine body, flexing muscles and beating wings. Its long tail then whipped out and struck Quinn off his feet. The back of his head cracked against the floor and his revolver slid from his grip. The creature fell on Quinn, pinning him at wrists and shoulders. The thing slowly dipped its long neck to poise an eel-like head just above Quinn's face. It opened jaws filled with backward facing, crystalline teeth. The head cocked to one side and regarded Quinn with an opaque, gelatinous eye.

"*Me Badhb wognit'ako anku ankrabudo. Marwo mene tlutsu,*" the beast spoke in a low, thick voice.

"Merciful God," whispered Quinn.

Avery came into his field of vision. There was a flash of gold. The creature roared and dug its talons reflexively into Quinn's flesh. It flung itself backward slamming Avery against the wall.

Quinn rolled to his feet. The room spun for a moment before he caught his balance. The beast's attention was fixed on Avery. It seemed hesitant to attack.

But Avery's eyes were glassy and unfocused in the lantern light. God, he's probably dead, thought Quinn. Before the creature could come to the same conclusion he jumped onto the thing's back. He wrapped his arms around its neck, beneath the gill-like ridges, and squeezed. Thick, rancid slime made it difficult for Quinn to keep his hold.

Enraged, the beast whipped its body around at an impossible angle. Quinn lost his grip and was spun off. He felt his left wrist snap as he hit the floor. He rolled away barely missing being pinned again. Now beside Avery, Quinn snatched the sickle from his unresisting hand and swung.

The arc of the blade came down across the charging creature's face. The gold tip caught one of its eyes, tearing through the membrane, and continued through the skin below. The beast's shriek drove Quinn to his knees. He covered his ears, trying to lessen the pain in his head.

The creature fled, leaving a trail of black blood marking its passage.

Quinn leaned against the wall. The room spun, blood ran from his deafened ears. Jabbing the sickle into his belt, Quinn knelt by Avery. He was still breathing, but Avery's eyes stared at nothing.

The creature did not return. Quinn managed to harness one of the horses and get Avery into a wagon. In daylight he accounted for the bodies of all his men. He left them where they lay. He had the will to do nothing else.

Quinn's hearing returned, though it stayed poor. They gave him a desk job in Paris handing out squad assignments. He supposed it was meant as a reward for managing to bring Avery back alive. The deaths of his men were officially attributed to a German sniper. Avery was alert now but didn't recognize Quinn and had yet to speak.

Quinn wondered if the wound he'd given the monster could have killed it. He couldn't stop hearing its voice. The foreign words echoed in his mind whenever his attention wandered. He wrote them down as best he could, hoping it would get them out of his head. It didn't help. It took weeks to find someone at the College de Sorbonne who could tell him anything.

"It looks and sounds like Gaulish, or something like it," said Professor Dupris. "The only words I recognize are *Me Badhb*. In myth, Badhb was a servant of the Black Goddess and considered the dead its property. Where did you hear this?"

Quinn hadn't answered. He just thanked the professor and left. Then he started seeing reports from other burial units describing mutilated bodies, disappearing corpses and open graves. Each new report came from a sight ever closer to Paris.

At night Quinn sat with the gold sickle in his lap, waiting for the sound of wings.

THE LOVE OF A TROLL ON A MID-WINTER'S NIGHT

JENNIFER BROZEK

STEVIE BROKE ONE of the cardinal rules of being an Ave Rat—show no fear or weakness. It was hard to look tough when you were trembling like a lamb in the cold of a Seattle winter night. Leather may look good, may turn knives away and blunt punches, but it did nothing for the biting wind that howled down University Avenue at three in the morning.

He was lucky, though. It wasn't snowing now, and most of the old snow had melted into dirty clumps in the gutters. That didn't stop it from being bone-chillingly cold. The rare lack of clouds made it colder. There was nothing to keep in the city's heat. Stevie huddled deeper into his scuffed jacket and thrift store scarf as he headed up the street past his favorite comic store.

At this time of night, nothing was open and busses were rare. Still his feet took him toward the Wallingford Boys and Girls Club. He knew it wasn't open either, but there might be something worth eating in the trash at Bizarro's. He couldn't remember if they locked up their trash or not, though. The cold wouldn't let him think, and his belly was willing to chance it because he had to keep walking. To stop was death. And he had no other place to go.

Stevie grinned at himself and just how melodramatic that sounded in his head. "I'm not going to die." The words were supposed to come out tough and brave. They sounded like begging to his numb ears. His brief good humor disappeared and he eyed the apartments and businesses on either side of him.

There was no welcome to be seen. No lights beyond the streetlamps. Despite the rows of buildings, he felt more alone than ever and hurried his pace back into familiar territory. None of his friends would talk to him after the fight with Joe; a fight he didn't want to think about. It was good to move fast. It warmed the blood and body. It promised success at the end of the journey.

But there was no success for Stevie. Not at the dark and cold Boys and Girls Club or Bizarro's—without a dumpster in sight. The lack of the dumpster killed what was left of his hope. His stomach growled in protest and tears stung his eyes. He rubbed the tears away with vicious swipes of his cold, shaking hands. He clenched them into fists, wanting to hit something, anything, but there was nothing safe to vent his despair on.

For a moment, Stevie didn't know what to do or where to go. He wandered until he met Stone Way and had his answer: he would go to his only real friend in this city. At least there, under the Aurora Bridge, was a chance for warmth and to get out of the wind. Maybe there'd be others and they'd share their food. He might have to pay for it in one way or another, but sometimes you did what you had to do to survive.

The decision made, Stevie stopped looking up at the rare passing car, stopped looking for an opportunity that did not exist. It was a short mile to the Fremont Troll and he knew every step by heart. The right turn onto North 36th felt like the home stretch in a race against time, and the genuine smile on Stevie's face surprised even him.

Once he arrived, a quick walk up and around the Troll told him he was alone. Stevie sighed and looked up at the tall stone figure. Under its beard, he thought the Troll was smiling. Stevie smiled back and was relieved to feel the relative heat of the area. He had been right. At least he'd be warm tonight. His stomach could deal with its hunger until the morning. He'd go begging for food then. Someone would feed him. Someone usually did. Even if it was one of the baristas out back of the coffee shop on 15th. Stale pastries were still sweet.

Sitting on the Troll's large right hand, he looked up and sighed. "I don't know what to do anymore. It's been tough lately. Too cold. Too hungry. Almost got sent to juvie. Can't go home—and you know why not." He hung his head and lied to himself. "Not that I want to go home."

Most of the time, when he talked to the Troll, it was just mundane stuff. Not this heavy shit he was carrying around. The months on the Ave had hardened him, made him appreciate what was really important. This was his first winter in Seattle and damned if he wanted to go through another one this unprepared.

"I had a fight with Joe. He said I took stuff from him . . . and maybe I did. But he didn't need it. Not like me." Stevie's words were a whisper of regret. Then his stomach grumbled loud, almost echoing under the bridge. "I'm just so fucking *hungry.*"

The words out of his mouth broke the dam holding back his emotions. He buried his face in his hands and shook, muffling his sorrow, fear, and need. The creaking of rock brought Stevie back to himself. His hands stopped in mid-wipe as he saw what made the noise: The fingers of the Troll's left hand had uncurled from their possessive grip on the VW bug.

While Stevie watched, the door of the decades-old car

swung open, inviting him in. Stevie looked up at the Troll's face and a saw a real smile where only stone had been before. The hubcap eye glistened with icy tears. The Troll nodded slowly in the direction of the car. Stevie saw that the Bug's interior was plush, warm looking, and he could smell hot food.

Stevie rubbed his eyes and wondered if he was having the weirdest acid flashback ever. He could have sworn that he'd read the VW Bug had been filled in with cement to keep "bums" from sleeping inside it and "destroying the artwork." He shoved the thought away as he stood and walked to the VW Bug, ducking under the Troll's outstretched fingers. Warmth and comfort radiated from the car's interior. He looked up at the Troll's face again. "For me?"

For you. For me. We need each other.

The voice in his head was a thousand years old. Stevie smiled wide and got into the car. The front seat bench was covered in a soft, warm fur. As a cold wind chased him into the comfort, Stevie closed the car door and listened to the Troll's fingers curl about the vehicle once more. It was warm, cozy, and safe. Next to him was stack of fast food— hamburgers, fries, hot apple pies, and a large soda.

"How?" Stevie asked as he crammed the food into his mouth.

The magic of a mid-winter's night.

Stevie had no response. Instead, he spent his time concentrating on filling his stomach until there was nothing left to eat or drink. When he was done, he gave a satisfied burp and gathered the trash into single bag. He moved that to the floorboards and laid down on the bench. Part of him wondered how he was going to get out in the morning. Part of him wondered if this was the best dream in the world. Either way, he did not want it to stop. For the first time in a long time, and for the last time, Stevie went to sleep with a full belly.

Outside, the Troll cried tears of sorrow as he, too, was fed on a cold winter's night.

SHOW AND TELL

TAYLOR GRANT

"**I**'VE BEEN KEEPING something from you," Jacob said, staring at the floor. "And I don't want to lie to you anymore."

McDaniels adjusted the wire rim glasses at the far end of his nose. "It's an admirable thing to admit that."

For the first time since he'd entered the room, Jacob met McDaniels's eyes. "You know those pictures I drew? The ones that caused all the problems?"

McDaniels offered a comforting smile. "It's not that you caused any 'problems,' Jacob. Mrs. Finelli was simply concerned that you might have some feelings that you hadn't been able to express."

"I guess she was right," Jacob said, his eyes once more cast downward.

"You can tell me whatever's on your mind. I'd like to help."

Jacob's eyes searched the tidy office. "Do you still have the pictures?"

"I do. Would you like to see them again?"

"No. I'd like *you* to see them again."

"Very well," McDaniels said. He stood up from behind his immaculate desk and reached for the student files in the metal cabinet directly behind him. He flipped through the sixth grade folders until he came upon one with the label: *Campbell, Jacob.*

Folder in hand, McDaniels sat back down in his swivel chair, which answered with a high-pitched squeak. He pulled out the series of colored pencil drawings that Mrs. Finelli had brought to his attention; Jacob had been secretly drawing them in class for several months.

McDaniels had seen a lot of disturbing drawings in his fifteen years as a school counselor, but these were particularly troubling. They were meticulously drawn and horribly *realistic*. And the specificity of the illustrations raised unsettling questions: the dark basement, hospital bed, feeding pump, oxygen tanks, suction machines, and a whole array of medical equipment that the boy had drawn in explicit detail.

The *subject* of the twenty or so drawings, however, was what had prompted Mrs. Finelli to contact McDaniels in the first place. It was a ghastly, child-like *thing* that appeared to be bedridden and perpetually propped up at a forty-five degree angle by some kind of medical apparatus. Its head was at least three times normal size, with bulging, green-colored veins covering the scalp, which seemed destined to explode from some urgent and terrible internal pressure. Its appendages were short, gnarled and incomplete.

Worst, by far, were the eyes. They looked like two translucent water balloons filled to bursting with blood, popping out beyond the normal boundaries of human eye sockets.

As McDaniels gazed upon the nightmarish drawings, it seemed as if the thing's crimson eyes were staring right *through* him. He found himself wanting to look away. While Jacob clearly had artistic talent, McDaniels hoped for the boy's sake that he would find different subject matter to explore in the future. "Are you still having the nightmares?"

"Yes," Jacob stated, matter-of-factly. "Everything I've said about the nightmares is true. The part I lied about is that they are *just* nightmares." The boy's slender fingers fidgeted nervously with each other for long seconds before he spoke. Then, in a quiet voice, "That thing in the drawings is . . . *real.*"

McDaniels raised an eyebrow.

"It's . . . my brother."

McDaniels replied with what he felt was the appropriate level of gravity, "Really."

"It's okay if you don't believe me."

"I didn't say I didn't believe you."

"Well, *I* wouldn't believe me if I were you. I mean . . . he looks like some kind of monster a kid would make up, right?"

McDaniels offered his best noncommittal look, something he'd refined to perfection over the years.

Jacob continued, "His name's Quinn. He's a few years older than me, but I'm not sure by how much. I'm not supposed to ask questions about him."

McDaniels jotted something down in his notebook. "I see. Why do you think that is?"

"It wouldn't look good."

"How so?

Jacob gave a humorless snort. "C'mon, Mr. McDaniels. You know my dad's position. He can't let the world know he hides a freak son in his basement."

McDaniels continued writing. "Can you explain what you mean by 'hides?'"

Jacob held himself as if he were sitting at a bus stop in the dead of winter. "We have this . . . basement. It's in the east wing of the house. I didn't know it was there until recently, 'cause I've never been allowed to go into the east wing. My parents have always kept it blocked off, except when we've had guests. And even then, we've never gone to that side of the house.

"I've grown up with a bunch of different gardeners, pool cleaners, housekeepers, and helpers around. It has always been off limits to them too. But one day last November I was playing hide and go seek with a friend of mine out in the back, and I noticed one of the helpers—Lucinda—go through a back door in the east wing, a door that no one was supposed to use.

"I started watching her for a few days, and I saw that she went through that door about the same time every day. So, I snuck into the east wing early one morning and hid in a closet by the back entrance, and when she came into the house I followed her. She was always talking and gossiping on her phone so she didn't notice me. I saw here go all the way to the end of the main hallway and into the very last room.

"I waited a couple of minutes, until I thought it was safe. Then I peeked inside the room and saw that she'd moved one of those . . . what do you call it . . . those big carpets from China?"

"An oriental rug?" McDaniels offered.

"Yeah, one of those. There was a big wooden door underneath it and a ramp that went all the way down to a basement. I don't think Lucinda worried about closing it, 'cause she didn't think anyone was around. I started to sneak down the ramp real quiet." Jacob paused then, his thin face pinched with distaste. "I wish . . . I'd never gone down there."

McDaniels glanced at the thing in the drawings again. He'd seen pictures of babies with massive heads that looked similar. He couldn't remember the proper medical term for it, but he knew it was sometimes referred to as "water on the brain." Jacob's interpretation, however, was more like something out of a horror film. He watched the boy squirming in his chair for a few moments, and then said, "And what did you see?"

Jacob's eyes grew wider, as if the scene were unfolding before him. "I saw Lucinda changing an IV bag. I knew what it was, 'cause I'd seen them on TV. But I couldn't see who was lying in the hospital bed from where I was standing. I tried to get a better look, but I slipped and fell on the ramp. Lucinda heard me and turned around . . . and I saw my brother for the first time. I started *screaming*. Lucinda tried to calm me down, but I couldn't stop screaming. I was still screaming after she'd carried me to the other side of the house and my parents came running.

"When my dad found out what I'd done, he wouldn't even look at me. He was so mad he punched a hole in the wall and sent me to my room. But my mom came to see me late that night, after Dad went to sleep. She'd been drinking a lot—I could always tell. She just fell on my bed and started crying and crying and crying. I'd never seen her like that before."

Jacob's eyes welled with tears, but he seemed to be doing his best to hold them back. "She told me *everything*."

McDaniels found his box of Kleenex and offered one. The boy shook his head and toughed it out. "I'm OK. It kinda feels good to talk about it—even though you probably don't believe me."

McDaniels cleared his throat. "I'm not here to judge the truth. I'm here to listen and help if I can."

The boy studied him, as if trying to discern whether or not he believed his words.

McDaniels offered a vague smile and prepared to take more notes.

"Mom told me that what I'd seen down in the basement wasn't a monster. It was her first child. Quinn. They'd built him a *special* room. He even had his own private nurse—Lucinda. She said Quinn was born with a whole bunch of stuff wrong with him—things I can't even pronounce. He couldn't see, talk, hear . . . anything. And his head is so big 'cause of his soft skull—and his brain. It's a lot bigger than normal.

"Mom said he came out that way because of a drug she took to help her get pregnant, 'cause she and dad couldn't have a baby on their own. It was an experimental drug that my dad's company made, but it caused all kinds of problems with babies."

Jacob's expression grew heavy with sorrow. "I asked her why she and Dad never told me before, and she said that they'd been waiting till I was old enough to understand. I was like, *understand what*? And that's when she told me that I was adopted . . . "

The boy's voice trailed off. Neither he nor McDaniels spoke for a full minute. The only sound in the room was the hollow *clunk* of the air conditioner as it came to life.

Finally, McDaniels broke the silence, "How did that make you feel, Jacob? Finding out that you were adopted?"

Jacob gave a quick shrug. "I don't know. Kinda mad. Kinda sad. Both at the same time, I guess. Know what I mean?"

"Of course," McDaniels said sympathetically. "That's understandable."

"I mean, I could see *why* they adopted me . . . after what happened to Quinn and all. They didn't want to take any chances, you know? What I couldn't understand was what she told me *after* that."

McDaniels took a deep breath as he flipped to the last blank page of his pad.

"Did you know that we only use about ten percent of our brains?" Jacob asked.

McDaniels nodded. "I've heard speculation to that effect . . . yes."

"Well, Mom said that Quinn can do things with his brain that we can't. But . . . he can't control it. And that's why they kept him drugged up and down in the basement. She said he did *bad things* when he was awake. I asked her how he could do bad things if he couldn't talk, hear, or move. And she couldn't answer me. All she could do was cry."

A tear dropped silently onto Jacob's cheek and a quiver crept into his voice. "She kept asking me to forgive her . . . telling me how much she loved me over and over."

Jacob wiped at his face. "The last thing she said before she left my room was: 'I'm sorry.'"

McDaniels handed the box of Kleenex to Jacob again, and this time the boy took a single tissue and wiped his eyes. "She died just a few hours later. Dad said that it was an accident, but I just *know* she took those pills on purpose."

McDaniels softened his voice, "I was very sorry to hear of your loss, Jacob. I understand how difficult that can be."

Jacob nodded, his face looking bloodless under the unflattering fluorescent lights. "I prayed that Quinn would get better. I'd always wanted a brother to play with. And every time I thought about him . . . stuck down in that cold basement alone, I would get so sad. Dad said that Quinn's brain didn't work like ours. He didn't know where he was, or what was going on. But I thought what if he was wrong? What if Quinn had known what was happening all those years but couldn't say or do anything about it? It was the worst thing I could think of.

"One night I found my dad drunk on the living room floor. It was always easy to get him to do things when he was drunk. He really wanted to sleep, but I kept bugging him about visiting Quinn and asking him for the combination to the lock on the basement door. He finally gave it to me just to get rid of me. But I didn't have the guts to go down there for a few more weeks.

"When Christmas came we didn't even put up a tree. That was something my mom was always in charge of. I searched all over the house Christmas morning, but I couldn't find my dad anywhere. I wanted to give Quinn a Christmas present so I finally went down to the basement by myself. I saw my brother just laying down there in the dark, not moving at all, but staring at me with those awful eyes. I tried not to look at him too much, because he still scared me. But I'd brought him my favorite *Batman* comic as a present, and I started to read to him.

"And then, the weirdest thing happened . . . his breathing changed. It seemed calmer, and it made me feel good to think that might be because I was there. So I started visiting him a lot, and I always brought a stack of comics with me. My dad didn't seem to mind, as long as I didn't touch anything. And Quinn . . . I think he liked the visits. But whenever Lucinda came down, I hated it 'cause she was always acting like I was in the way. But I was quiet and watched what she did, because I wanted to know how to take care of Quinn too. I mean . . . he was my brother and all."

McDaniels reached into the organizer on his desk, picked up a fresh pad of paper, flipped it open and started writing. "You talk about Lucinda in the past tense. Is she no longer with you?"

Suddenly, Jacob smashed his fist down on the arm of his chair violently, giving McDaniels a hell of a start. "It's my fault it happened—but I could never have known it would happen!"

McDaniels regained his composure and spoke reassuringly, "It's okay, Jacob. It's okay. What *happened* to Lucinda?"

Jacob gave a distraught sigh. "Remember . . . when I said they kept Quinn drugged? Well, I found out what it was. I looked it up on my computer. Doctors call it a 'morphine drip.' They use it on people when they're in lots of pain—and they use it to help people die faster."

McDaniels's mask of impassivity had begun to slip; lines of concern invaded the corners of his eyes.

Jacob raised his voice angrily, "It was like they were trying to kill him or something! So I went down into the basement and I poked a hole in the bag with a needle. I wanted to help Quinn *wake up*."

The boy's eyes darkened as he continued, "I went down the next day to check on him and the door was already open. There was this terrible smell coming out, like bleach and chemicals and stuff. As soon as I went down the stairs, I saw my dad. He'd moved Quinn and his bed to the far side of the basement and was cleaning up something off the floor with a mop. He was acting really weird, like he was sleepwalking or something. There was blood *everywhere*, and this . . . twisted-up *thing* pushed into the corner. I couldn't tell what it was, at first. It kind of looked like a body, but it was turned inside out . . . like a coat when you can see the pockets . . . all these guts and organs and stuff on the outside.

"Then I saw Lucinda's bloody shoes lying in the corner and *I knew*. The horrible thing on the ground was all that was left of her. I got dizzy and my legs went wobbly—and that's the last thing I remembered before I woke up in my room. My dad was just sitting there next to my bed, staring at me, bloodstains all over his shirt."

McDaniels was so intent on the boy's story that his pen slipped from his hands onto the desk. He quickly snatched it up and returned to his note taking.

Jacob spoke as if there were something unpalatable in his mouth, "He sat there and lied to my face; told me that Lucinda had a little *accident* with some of the medical equipment. Said he'd called an ambulance and she'd be just fine. I asked him about the bloody thing on the floor and he told me I'd hit my head—probably just imagined it. I wanted to laugh in his face. I mean, how stupid did he think I was? But I pretended to believe him 'cause I didn't like the way he kept looking at me—I just wanted to get him out of my room.

"I couldn't sleep at all that night. I kept thinking about Quinn, and how my mom said he did *bad things* when he was awake. And now I knew what she meant. Somehow Quinn had done that horrible thing to Lucinda." Light glinted off of the boy's cheeks, which were wet with tears. "And it's all my fault for waking him up."

McDaniels remained silent. He didn't want to risk Jacob shutting down again, as he had so many times in the past.

Jacob regarded his small hands as he spoke, "The next morning, I found out that Dad had fired the house staff: the housekeepers, gardeners, pool cleaners—everyone. He said it was just going to be him, Quinn, and me from now on, *one big happy family*. And when he said it, there was this *smile* on his face that didn't look right.

"Things only got worse after that. My dad moved Quinn's hospital bed into the family room, close to one of the windows—probably the first time he'd ever been near the sun. It was also the first time I'd seen Quinn fully awake. He looked even scarier in the daylight. The veins in his head had gotten thicker. His eyes were redder, and they bulged even more. His face—it twitched a lot, like he was always in pain.

"And my dad . . . he became a completely different person. He'd never been interested in anything except his job before, but now his whole life was about my brother. He took personal leave from work so he could take care of Quinn. He cleaned him, fed him, and took care of whatever he needed.

"That's when it hit me. Quinn had to be controlling him—*with his mind*. That was why they'd kept Quinn drugged up all the time: to keep him from doing bad things with his mind! It was my brother that made dad clean up that mess with Lucinda. That's why he was acting like he was sleepwalking when he did it. He also forced my dad to fire the house staff—and bring him out of the basement too. I know my dad never would've done any of that stuff on his own—especially take leave from his job.

"It was right around then that my nightmares started too. The ones I told you about—where Quinn's thoughts are in mine." Jacob suddenly stood up. His eyes were scrunched shut, as if a sharp pain were lancing through his head.

"What is it?" McDaniels said with genuine concern.

The boy pounded his fist against his head. Once. Twice. Three times. "He's in my head right now. I can't get him out of my head!"

McDaniels tried calming words, but they felt hollow even as he said them. "It's okay, Jacob. Everything's going to be okay—"

The boy's eyes snapped open and he gave McDaniels a look that stopped him cold. "No, it's *not*. It's not gonna be okay *at all*."

McDaniels raised his hands. "I can see you're upset. And I'm here to listen. But I need you to relax and take a seat. Can you do that for me?"

Jacob met his gaze defiantly for a long and uncomfortable moment. Finally, he plopped back down in his chair, rubbing his temples; his face a taut mask of resistance.

"Maybe we should continue this later, Jacob."

"No!" Jacob snapped. "I still have to tell you the most important part—the whole reason I'm here."

McDaniels exhaled loudly. "Okay. I'm listening."

"Quinn . . . he tells me things. Not in words. It's more like . . . I can *feel* what he feels. And all he seems to feel is *hate*—especially for what my parents did to him. He wants to do terrible things to my dad—even worse than what he did to Lucinda. But I won't let him. I had to explain that killing him would be bad for both of us. We need a grownup for money, food, electricity and stuff. But in some ways, it's as if my dad is already gone. Quinn's turned him into this *thing*—like a zombie that only looks like my dad. It's awful to see."

McDaniels's hand was cramping up from all the writing, but he didn't dare stop. He wanted to make sure he got everything down.

Jacob's fingers unconsciously probed the area around his eyes. "When Quinn is in my head, he can see and learn about the world through me; like when I'm watching TV or using my computer. But his brain doesn't work the same—he learns way faster. He can scan a whole webpage in a few seconds. He wants me to keep clicking page after page . . . I can barely keep up with him.

"And then a few weeks ago he started having me bookmark all of these terrible news stories. The news people call them 'freak accidents.' Like a few weeks ago when all of those kindergarten kids on that school bus stopped breathing for no reason. And then there was a gas explosion that destroyed a bunch of warehouses that my dad's company owns. Killed over a hundred employees. And everyone on the news is talking about these crazy fires that keep happening all over the city. I have over fifty bookmarks of things like that.

"I don't know how, but I think Quinn makes these things happen.

"But what scared me more than anything, were the two bookmarks from yesterday. The first one was a website about meltdowns at nuclear power plants and how they happen. And the second one was about the nuclear plant in our town."

Jacob paused for a moment and studied McDaniels's face. "I can tell that you don't believe me."

McDaniels reached under his glasses and rubbed his eyes before answering. "What's important here is that *you* believe it, Jacob. And I'm glad that you trusted me enough to tell me what's been troubling you."

Jacob reached for his backpack, which was sitting near his feet on the floor. It was faded black with a yellow Batman logo emblazoned upon on it, and it appeared to be filled to the bursting point.

"You remember 'Show and Tell,' don't you, Mr. McDaniels?"

McDaniels nodded as he reached for the small bottle of water on his desk. He unscrewed the cap and began to drink. His throat was so constricted and dry that it actually hurt.

Jacob said, "You're probably wondering why I would tell you all of this—stuff that could get my family in trouble." He unzipped his backpack and stepped closer to McDaniels's desk. "It's because I knew you wouldn't believe me. And even if you *did*, it wouldn't matter . . . 'cause you're not leaving this room alive."

McDaniels choked on his water.

Jacob's face transformed then. His features took on a hateful, savage quality. "You told me everything I said in this room was confidential, Mr. McDaniels. But you *lied*. When you and Mrs. Finelli called my dad about those drawings, you broke your promise. I trusted you."

McDaniels wiped water from his chin with a trembling hand. "Listen . . . Jacob. It's true that our conversations are confidential. But teachers and counselors have the right to contact parents under certain circumstances."

Jacob moved awkwardly—as if he weren't in complete control of his body. "You thought you were talking to my dad, but you were *wrong*."

McDaniels started to respond, but he could only muster a weak gurgling sound.

Jacob reached into his backpack. "Mrs. Finelli didn't show up for school today because I visited her at her home last night—and I told her the same story I told you."

McDaniels stood up, struggling for his next breath, and then doubled over from a severe jolt of pain to his abdomen.

Jacob yanked Mrs. Finelli's severed head from his backpack. There were two gaping holes where her eyes had been, and her blood-streaked face was stretched into a hideous, eternal scream.

McDaniels dropped to the floor in agony as his internal organs began to shift and twist, like a pit of snakes had been unleashed inside his body.

The boy McDaniels knew as Jacob Campbell stood over him, his face twitching, as if he was in pain. At that moment, the school counselor realized that everything the boy had said was true.

The last thing McDaniels saw, as his torso split open and his insides began to push their way out, was the boy staring down at him with familiar, bulging red eyes.

WHISPERS OF THE EARTH

ERIC J. GUIGNARD

THE DAY WAS March 25, and it was the tenth anniversary of his wife's death.

That day—today—was etched into his mind as permanently as the letters that spelled Hannah's name on the slab of stone in Franklin Cemetery. Her memory would never leave him, but most days he could push it behind him like a signpost he'd driven past and could only faintly make out in the receding distance. Of course, as this day drew nearer, the distance he travelled from that signpost seemed to reverse and he watched it, like a thing in the rearview mirror, as it returned closer and closer.

Lyle knew today would be worse than her other death anniversaries, and that knowledge did not deceive. Ten years, after all, was the same amount of time they had been wed. Tomorrow, she would be dead longer than they were together. Married at thirty. Dead at forty. Alone at fifty.

For none of us liveth to himself, and no man dieth to himself.

The words of Pastor Scott, who then found it necessary to repeat the passage in simplified terms: *Hannah's love will continue on in the memories of those she touched.*

If Lyle were a vessel for the Lord—as Pastor Scott said he was—then it was true she would live forever in him, hovering in the back of his thoughts, sharing his intimate struggles, whispering sweet memories of their life together.

Whispering his name.

Lyle, she said. *I miss you so much . . .*

He knew she did miss him, as he missed her. She said as much in his thoughts. Hannah's death was never reconciled, never explained. Pastor Scott spoke of his grief, warned him not to question God's will, to have faith in her absence, to accept that her body was taken back to the earth.

I'm all alone . . . somewhere, lost in the earth . . .

Another reason he could never lay her memory entirely to rest was knowing that stone slab at Franklin Cemetery was a formality, an afterthought. It jutted from a grave filled only with roots and dirt and a lie. Hannah's body had never been found.

The Lord giveth and the Lord taketh away . . .

Her voice sounded stronger today, and he almost spoke out loud in reply. Almost caught himself chatting like a madman to the blue sky above. No one would blame him, of course, but speaking to your dead wife after ten years was a slippery slope. Once you started, it became ordinary, and he knew men that turned odd from lesser causes.

The morning was bright and clear, and Lyle walked the acres of his property recalling good memories. He smelled vanilla in the air, and it was as if her voice became an aroma, filling his nostrils. Every morning she had placed a drop of vanilla oil on the sides of her neck which he breathed in deep whenever he leaned in to kiss her.

He passed through rows of apple trees and out the other side, and the green pasture land before him shone with sparkles of light as if the world reflected through an emerald. The land was beautiful, and he thought again of Hannah.

The great black hole that lay open in the earth before him was so unexpected he did not immediately register it. Lyle almost walked right in as if that was his plan all along, before yelping and jumping away from the sinking edge.

"God Almighty," he said, and his face turned pale as ice. He apologized in silence for taking the Lord's name in vain and stared until his mouth nearly fell open as wide as the chasm in the ground.

It was a giant sinkhole, a dozen feet across, and appearing as an elevator shaft that dropped so far down that the sun above would never penetrate the darkness of its black depths.

Lyle occasionally read in the newspapers about sinkholes opening up, some so large a city block could fall into them. Most, though, only dropped ten or twenty feet, as if that part of the earth's mantle was just the skin of a popped, shallow bubble. He thought he might go mad staring into this hole that, somehow, he discerned as bottomless. The rim of the sinkhole was smooth, too, like a cartoon hole lacking the rough edges that are expected by the ground's occasional movements.

He heard her whisper again, but this time could not be sure if it truly was in his mind, or somehow floated up from the descent of the hole.

I'm here . . .

Lyle called into Dunbar City Hall and waited on hold nearly twenty minutes before the clerk finally answered.

"This is Marty Simmons. Sorry for the wait."

"I was startin' to think the city forgot I pay taxes to keep it running."

"Hey, Lyle, it's been a lunatic morning, here. Folks calling in since we opened, until I thought the city woke up with a case of the bat-shit crazies. Anyway, I can guess what you're calling about."

"It's some fright when you're strolling along and nearly fall down a pit that decided to open shop on your land."

"I understand. You're not the only one this happened to."

"There are others?"

"We've been getting calls from all over the city. A sinkhole opened next to Tom Grady's house, and another on Liz Townsend's farm. Got reports from Charles Halloway, John Clark, and a handful of others. One sinkhole opened up on Stephen Brown's land that three of his heifers fell into. He can't hear a cry from any of them, they fell so deep. Hell, one hole even opened up right behind Cornerstone Baptist Church."

"I never heard of the ground turning to Swiss cheese before," Lyle said.

"Nor I. Now you know why it took so long to get your call. Liz Townsend's in hysterics, she even says she heard a voice from the hole on her farm, like maybe someone tumbled in."

"City have any plans about what'll be done to fix this, or should I just build an outhouse over it?"

Marty chuckled, then paused. "I'll make a report for you. Suppose we can hold a meeting tomorrow for everyone affected. Find out who's got it worse and go from there. The news already reached Pittsburg, and some reporters are coming in today."

"And so the vultures found a new scrap to feed on."

"They love to rub salt in our wounds. Never come around when we're prospering, but if there's an accident, suddenly the news crews appear, calling us superstitious on one hand and cursed on the other."

"Any thoughts as to what may have caused these holes?" Lyle asked.

"Dunno. Maybe an earthquake. Maybe groundwater eating away at the bedrock beneath us. Remember the sinkhole in Allentown last year? Half the city was evacuated for fear the earth was caving in. That's what's going to happen here, mark my words."

"It'll take more than a hole on my property to make me pack it up."

"We'll see. Anyway, pal, I've got the next call waiting on hold. Stop by tomorrow and we'll chat."

After Lyle hung up, the morning didn't seem as bright and clear as earlier, before he nearly walked into the sinkhole. The sky was still blue, as it so often is in southern Pennsylvania, but he discerned a fine veil seeming to drape over his corner of the land. There were murmurs in his thoughts that didn't resemble his own, and a chill touched his skin.

He didn't want to be alone in the house today, amongst the dusty memories and sense of foreboding. As empty as it was, he would pay his respects at Hannah's grave, then fill the day with chores and errands to keep his mind from dwelling on troubles.

And that's what he did.

The bed seemed larger than ever that night, a great expanse of stuffing and blankets that, instead of providing comfort, only accentuated the emptiness. Lyle lay with his hands crossed behind his head, resting on the same side he had always lain, him on the right and Hannah on the left. On the far wall, past the void she once filled, a window gaped open, and he heard the late-night critters of the land, the crickets and owls and coyotes.

He heard, too, a woman's voice, like the drifting shreds of a kite, torn and blowing without direction between the tree branches.

No man dieth to himself, she said.

He sat up and cocked his head, trying to filter out that voice amongst the other nighttime noises. Hannah's memory had nestled up cozy in the back of his head today, whispering to him louder and louder, and he began to doubt the distinction between what intoned amongst his thoughts and what sounded in reality. A distant dog barked at some unseen foe and rustling tree limbs pushed against each other. A gust of wind scattered dry leaves against the window, some floating through to land on the floor, like discarded broken relics. Lyle found himself wondering what existed in the night, what rose while men slept and moved amongst the mountain's enigmas.

He had lived in Dunbar all his life, the city nestled far into the base of the Allegheny Mountains' green-and-silver range. There were things in those mountains that the rest of the world never heard about, but Lyle knew since boyhood. There was a man of green light who lived inside Dante's cave, and if you saw him you went blind. A pair of creatures that were half-horse, half-bear lived in the woods on the far end of Hunter's Loop and if you strayed into their lair under a full moon, you'd never stray back out. Goblins and shades and talking beasts all lived within a day's hike of Dunbar, and Lyle knew all their exploits. Anything could exist in that territory where Indians once fought using dinosaur bones. Of course, some of those things were mired in superstition, while only one or two were hard-truth, but figuring where myth ended and fact began was like trying to measure the distance of a fart in a whirlwind.

Great are the mysteries of the world, he thought. *But know, too, that God has a place for all things and though we may not understand, it is not for us to question his reasons.*

He closed his eyes, inducing the ritual of memories that preceded sleep.

The woman's voice sounded again, louder this time, more clear. *And to Earth we shall return . . .*

Lyle scrambled to the window and leaned out. "Someone out there?"

The moon cast long shadows pulling each tree into a stick giant. Things pattered and moved in the night, and he smelled the slightest fragrance of vanilla.

Lyle . . .

He got into his trousers and shirt quick as a whistle and dashed outside with his Coleman lantern.

"This is private property," he called out to the stars. "If you need something, you'd best name yourself."

I've been waiting . . .

This time the voice sounded muffled, as if sinking. It drifted from the apple orchards or, perhaps, what lay on the other side of the orchards. He swung the lantern across the path of trampled grass that led into the trees.

"If you're ribbin' me, I'll knock you into Tuesday," he shouted.

The voice did not reply, and that worried him more than if it continued speaking from the gloom. Was it Hannah's voice in his head, getting louder as if finding a way to break through the aural barrier of his consciousness into the real world?

Something moved in the darkness, a leathery whisk of flight and a shaking branch. Lyle crossed between the apple trees and it flew past with a whoosh. He waved the Coleman and spotted a small bat darting after the glowing tails of fireflies.

The scent of vanilla grew stronger. It was a hypnotic fragrance, an alluring tug that suggested he close his eyes and float along the stream of memories. He kept walking, following it past the apple orchards.

Lyle . . .

He found himself standing again at the lip of the sinkhole. The lantern shone past its smooth edges into a darkness that somehow was twice as black as the midnight sky above.

Come to me, as we are one . . .

The misery and loneliness of ten years felt as if it sloughed off like caked dirt under a hot shower. He felt lighter, calmer, as if he had a purpose, a destination.

I've missed you . . .

The voice was real, was Hannah's, and he wondered at his sanity, if he had, perhaps, even gone crazy long ago, and the sinkhole was really a tunnel dug through his own brain by grief. He stepped nearer to its edge, so close a tap from behind might propel him forward, and he searched for her face within the ebony nothingness.

How long did it take a body to decompose back into the elements it sprang from? How long for a body crushed and buried to dissolve under the moving earth until its bones became soft as soot and guts the fertilizer for plants.

What did Pastor Scott say? *Earth to earth, ashes to ashes, dust to dust . . .*

She was the earth now, and she called to him.

He leaned forward.

Lyle . . .

The voice seemed to pull him in but, on the brink of surrender, he threw himself backward, landing on his keister in the cold grass. The Coleman clattered aside, pointing a beam across the sinkhole.

What am I doing? he thought, and scrambled further away. *She ain't down there, it's been ten years.*

He looked up to the crescent moon and sprawl of stars, as if searching for a sign.

Lyle retrieved the lantern and rushed back to his house. He thought her voice chased him from behind the apple orchards, like a child's game of tag, but he willed himself to stop listening. Once inside, he locked the doors and closed the windows and opened his Bible for answers, wondering if he fled from the one thing he regularly begged God to return.

Late the next morning, Lyle drove around the winding mountain roads and into Dunbar. Parking was crowded in front of city hall's red brick facade, most of the spaces filled by out-of-town cars and a couple large news vans decorated with satellite dishes and tall antennas.

He parked and got out and walked to the building's glass front doors. Marty Simmons approached from behind, smoking a Marlboro.

"Don't let those reporters know you've got a hole on your land," he said.

"They makin' a big deal of it?" Lyle asked.

"Bigger than you know." He took a drag and exhaled in a blue-gray cloud. "Walk with me."

They turned away from city hall and strode down the sidewalk toward the gazebo next to Dunbar's library.

"Where's everyone else?" Lyle asked. "Thought we were going to have a meeting."

"Most folks are staying away while the media's sittin' here."

"They sure know how to turn bad into worse."

Marty nodded, and a sprinkle of cigarette ash fell onto his collared shirt. "Remember I told you a sinkhole opened up right behind the church?"

"I do."

"It was a big hole, Lyle, big enough to drive a full-size truck into, and I don't know how deep it went. I was out there yesterday morning after I talked with you. I tossed a rock down and never heard it hit bottom."

"Sounds like what I've got."

"The hole is gone."

"Gone, like filled in?"

"Filled in, closed up, whatever you want to call it. It's gone, and there ain't even a hint there ever was a hole. No depression in the land, no cracks in the earth. The grass is growing green and cut short like a lawnmower just went over it last week."

"That don't make sense."

"Exactly. I went back out there this morning with the sheriff and the news crews. They wanted to film one of our sinkholes, and what better for sensationalism than showing Cornerstone Baptist Church as the backdrop?"

"Of course, so they can remind us of ten years ago."

"Pastor Scott was going to meet us by the hole, too, but never showed. I asked around and nobody's caught a trace of him since yesterday. He was supposed to have dinner last night with the mayor but never arrived. It's like he vanished."

"You think something happened to him?"

"I don't know, but the sheriff sent a couple men to look around. The reporters started questioning the sinkholes as a hoax, but I'm taking them out to investigate Liz Townsend's farm next. They're talking with some council members right now. Anyway, I'd suggest steering clear of the pack—the media's like a sick dog, and you never know who they're going to crap on."

"Thanks for the advice."

Marty stubbed out the Marlboro on the banister rail of the gazebo. He looked around to make sure no one was watching, then flicked the butt into the street.

"Sweeper's coming by tomorrow," he said.

Lyle shrugged.

"Another thing," Marty said. "And you might think my screw is turning loose, but it hasn't gotten past me that mudslide disaster was ten years ago to the day."

"Nature's got cruel timing."

"I don't think it's a coincidence."

"The sinkholes?"

"Lyle, it ain't just the hole on *your* land. It's all the sinkholes. Remember, I'm the one logging the reports. I told you some of who were affected . . . it's the families of those who were carried away."

"Go on."

Marty lifted a hand and began ticking away fingers. "Tom Grady's got a hole alongside his house. Like you, he lost his wife at that picnic. I catch him crying sometimes, when he's sitting alone at the diner. Then there's Liz Townsend, whose husband, Eddie, was taken. She holds onto the past like a girl clutches her toy doll; they're inseparable. Remember that no trace of Stephen and Ruth Brown's two sons was ever found, 'cept a penny loafer caught on a tree limb. Charles Halloway lost his sister and John Clark lost his parents. Ain't a one of them ever fully recovered. And a dozen others from that day—they've all got sinkholes on their land."

"That's a heavy load. But what does it mean?"

"I don't know. Think about Pastor Scott who put the picnic together. If the Lord was assessing faith that day, Scott was tested the greatest. He lost his wife and all three daughters to that mudslide. A sinkhole appeared alongside his church."

"And now it's gone."

"And so is he," Marty said. "All these years he preached to us, saying those killed were in a better place. But I know it was eating him up inside. It's a Catch-22: He couldn't curse the Lord or question His almighty will for their deaths, otherwise he won't end up in the Heaven he believes his family is waiting at."

Lyle shook his head.

Marty continued. "So Pastor Scott kept preaching at the pulpit, smiling and saying it's all part of a grand plan, everything happens for a reason and it's not our place to question why. If Scott believed that, perhaps he saw the sinkhole as a message, another test of his faith."

"That's a big leap you're suggesting."

"And maybe it brought him back to his family in some way. Or, maybe, I'm just making too much of this, framing crazy assumptions like the reporters."

"Nothing sounds too crazy to me," Lyle said. "That pit on my land isn't natural."

Up the street, people began to exit city hall, milling around cars and talking on cell phones.

"Looks like it's time to get back," Marty said. "I'll see what happens at Liz Townsend's farm."

"Let me know. In the meantime, think I'll check on the Browns myself."

Ten years ago, he heard her after the mudslide hit, after the crashing thunder of earth silenced and shock passed like a crack of lightning. In that spare second before the others started screaming, he heard her voice from the mud and debris.

"Lyle!"

Then the shrieks sounded, and the pleas, and people scrambling to unbury themselves or their loved ones. It was a dervish of neighbors and fellow parishioners digging through the sludge, shouting for help, ordering commands, moaning, crying.

And he tried to tell everyone to shut up. He nearly wished the panicked and wounded were all dead, so in their silence he could hear Hannah, follow her voice to where the avalanche took her. But the wailing around him increased, and the others thought they heard their own parents and spouses and children crying from under the mud and everyone then shouted louder, trying to bellow over the others, so that Lyle never heard her voice again.

The morning before the disaster was good, such as days can be when begun with turquoise skies and the whistle of wrens and a plate of pancakes steaming in the cold spring dawn. Her smell of vanilla oil broke through the warm maple syrup and they ate together commenting on what they did yesterday and what they would do today.

That afternoon was Cornerstone Baptist Church's annual picnic, set on the shore of McGowan's Lake under the shade of the Allegheny Mountains. Lyle and Hannah almost didn't go, as it was a Saturday afternoon and Lyle wanted to plant and Hannah needed to pick up some camera equipment from Pittsburgh. But the absence from church events is conspicuous in small towns and they knew what sort of comments might be made from behind-the-hand mutters.

So they arrived at the picnic early, in order to stake a location overlooking the cold lake's cyan face. There may have been a hundred people in attendance that bright afternoon. Kites came out and children ran amongst trees. Tables were set with red-and-white gingham and platters shared of fried chicken, coleslaw, baked beans, and cobbler. Lyle and Hannah sat with Stephen and Ruth Brown and laughed at long-running jokes. Pastor Scott spoke to each in attendance, commenting on the chicken's flavor or a mother's pretty dress. Scott's wife picked flowers with a group of children.

Then a rumble sounded and the earth shook, and the world seemed to crack in half. It was early spring and the snow runoff had loosened the slope of Hardy Hill. With a shattering detonation, the slope slid down in a great wave of mud and rock and swept away the picnickers.

In that spare second after the earth settled and before the survivors started screaming, he heard her voice from the sludge and debris.

"Lyle!"

Lyle stood with Stephen and Ruth Brown and looked deep into the sinkhole on their pastureland. The hole was identical to his own, as if the chasms were born as twins, each about twelve feet across and cut perfectly into the earth like someone drilled cylinders straight into the ground.

"Can you hear them?" Stephen Brown asked in a voice so tiny, mice could have roared louder.

Lyle shook his head. The hole may have led to another universe for the depth it appeared to fall.

"They're our sons," Ruth said. "They're callin' to us from down there."

He looked at each of the Browns, then back into the hole. Lyle didn't know if coming here was a mistake or a vindication of his sanity. At least he knew he wasn't the only one listening to voices that weren't there. He shook his head again. "I don't hear anything."

Ruth sobbed and Stephen almost did too. "We've still got his shoe, Jeremy's little shoe. He's down there with a bare foot."

"What do your boys say?"

"They're looking for us. They miss us. They say, 'Where are you, Mommy and Daddy?'"

Stephen reached around his wife's shoulders, and she turned her head against his chest and held him tight.

"I can't say whether you're imagining it or not," Lyle said. "I hear Hannah on my own land."

Ruth spoke into her husband's chest. "Pastor Scott said the same about his own family."

Stephen nodded. "I was at the church yesterday afternoon. I saw the sinkhole, and Pastor Scott stood so close on its edge his toes hung over. He told me they were down there, all of them, his wife and three daughters. He said, 'The Lord was giving them back. The earth would make them a family again.'"

"Pastor Scott's disappeared," Lyle said.

"I know. A deputy came by a bit ago, asking when I saw him last. He tried to tell me there wasn't any hole on the church grounds at all, but it was there. I saw it."

"I believe you. Marty Simmons saw it too."

"Maybe they weren't supposed to have been taken from us that day. Or maybe we were supposed to have joined them. Maybe whoever plans these things made a mistake. But that hole is speaking to us. It's telling us our boys are down there," Lyle said. "I'm going in. I'm going to find our sons, no matter how far down they've fallen."

Lyle thought obligation should compel him to convince Stephen otherwise, tell him it was madness to climb into that pit looking for people who were missing—surely dead—for ten years. It was duty to talk a friend out of doing something that would likely lead to injury or worse.

But, at the same time, he believed them to be right. And what he wanted most that moment was to return home, because he now believed Hannah really was there, calling for him from the darkness of *his* sinkhole. He decided such, because she didn't call for him on the Browns's land—here, her voice was silent. Here, it was the sinkhole only for the Browns's sons. This was no trick of his brain, no phenomena of his surroundings. She called for him from one place only, that place she was taken, as she had called for him the day of the picnic . . .

~

Night fell, and Lyle sat on his porch listening. She was out there, whispering to him.

Come to me, Lyle.

He had a decision to make, but he let it stretch out before him, allowing the moment to simmer, listening to Hannah's words as if she sat on the porch alongside him.

I've been waiting such a long time . . .

If he decided her return was a transgression against natural order, he could simply leave and didn't think she would follow. Lyle considered that whatever caused the earth to open up its secrets for him was a one-time offer. Whether it was the Lord's choice or a trick, she was here and here only. If he left, he would never hear her voice again.

Or he could find her. She *was* down there, like all the other people killed that afternoon by McGowan's Lake, returned to collect their loved ones. Without Hannah, there wasn't much in the world that kept him going, no other family or opportunities; just gray age and loneliness. Was it different for any of the others from that church picnic? Had they ever stopped grieving, or did it matter? Maybe it wasn't just the survivors who grieved all these years, maybe it was the dead, too, stolen from the sunshine and arms of their loved ones, buried under the mud and never found.

Until now.

Lyle . . .

The Lord giveth and the Lord taketh away, he thought.

He thought also of the message saved on his phone. Lyle had arrived home from the Browns's farm and saw the blinking green light on his answering machine. It was Marty Simmons: "Stay away from the sinkhole, Lyle. Whatever it is you think you hear, stay away. Liz Townsend is missing, the hole behind her farm is gone. I saw her earlier today with the reporters, and she swore her dead husband was calling. Now John Clark is missing and Charles Halloway. The holes on their grounds are closed up, too, like they never existed.

Something took them away. It ain't natural, Lyle, not to hear someone who's been buried ten years. Listen to me, call me, come back to town. Just stay away from that hole."

But Marty was only another voice now, like Hannah, a murmur without physical form, a ventriloquism speaking from the chasm of his mind.

We're all just earth, after all . . .

He found it took less time than ever to make his way across the yard, through the apple trees, and out the other side into the pasture. He brought the Coleman to light his way, though he didn't need it. He could close his eyes and she would lead him to the brink of reunion. Vanilla curled around his limbs and the moon split in two.

When Lyle again looked upon the black sinkhole, he realized it wasn't a sinkhole at all, and he wondered how he ever thought different. It was a mouth, and her lips began to rise from the edges of its opening, parting slightly to show the curve of a coral-pink tongue.

The contours of the ground flexed and eddied as if made of soft mud, and Hannah's mouth moved, opening wider. Her lips pursed, bulging from the land in prodigious mass, and she spoke.

Come to me.

The night critters were silent. He no longer heard their chirps or howls or croaks.

Earth to earth, ashes to ashes, dust to dust.

He saw a vision of himself sitting on the porch, contemplating the years since Hannah's death, when a crash sounded, and a mudslide roared from the night stars to carry him away. He was wrong to think he would be allowed to leave; he could never escape the earth.

So he leaned in to kiss her lips the way he did every morning after she placed a drop of vanilla oil on the sides of her neck.

I've missed you . . .

Lyle knelt, and vanilla-scented mud gathered at his feet.

He was sucked into the hole before he could say goodbye. He fell through memories and dreams and thought he heard Stephen Brown calling for his sons.

Whether he was dead or insane, touched by God or called by Hannah, he couldn't say. He wondered why the voice in his head turned silent.

The faraway sky vanished and the sinkhole closed its lips and Lyle was swallowed into the earth.

THE NEXT IN LINE

RICHARD FARREN BARBER

HE BOY AT the front of the line shivered. Droplets of water stood out on his bare skin. He wrapped his arms around his shoulders as if he could hug himself warm but, as far as Barney could tell, it wasn't working. He thought the boy was beginning to turn blue with the cold.

Barney watched the lifeguard who sat nestled in his high chair with a silver whistle tied around his neck. When a gangly arrangement of legs and arms emerged from the flume the lifeguard nodded almost imperceptibly.

The boy at the front of the line shuffled forward. Barney wanted to tell him to hurry up, but he was silent as the small boy trudged past the lifeguard and stepped onto the staircase. A moment later he was out of sight.

"You know why he's sitting there, don't you?"

Barney turned. He hadn't heard anyone come up behind him. Now there were two boys: towering, skinny things with red pimples across their faces and white ribs pushing through their chests.

Older boys. Fifteen at least, maybe more.

"You dumb?" the boy in the red swimming shorts asked. His friend laughed. "You stoo-pid?"

Barney stared at both of them. He felt vulnerable standing in the queue wearing only his ragged swimming shorts. He wrapped his hands around his shoulders, but that reminded him too much of the boy who had just disappeared up the staircase, and so he brought them down by his side and stood in stiff formality in front of the boys.

"The lifeguard. You know why he sits there?" the boy asked.

Barney said nothing. Of course he knew. The lifeguard made sure that only one person went up to the top of the flume at any time. To avoid accidents. He didn't remember when he had learned this, and he couldn't remember anyone ever explaining it to him. It was just something he knew.

Barney looked at the pimple-faced boy and knew that this wasn't the answer he wanted.

"He's counting children," the boy said. "He counts them as they go up and he counts them when they come back down."

His friend laughed, but Barney couldn't see what was so funny.

"Because they don't always come down."

Barney shivered.

Over his shoulder the splash pool erupted as the boy from the front of the queue arrived at the bottom of the slide. For a moment the sound of rushing water filled the small space. Barney turned to watch the small boy emerge from the boiling churn of water. His eyes were wide and his hands were cast out in front of his face as if he was warding something away.

The boy staggered out of the pool and stood for a moment in front of the slide, staring back up into the cavernous mouth of the flume. The curved blue sides twisted up so that there was nothing to see but darkness.

"He knows," the pimpled boy whispered into Barney's ear. "He made it out alive and he knows that he should consider himself lucky."

"You're lying."

"Am I?" the boy asked. "Am I really? Look at him. Look at him properly. Do you think he enjoyed that?"

The boy walked along the side of the queue, passing close enough that Barney could reach out and touch him. The boy looked at Barney and then immediately looked away, as if even acknowledging each other was not safe.

No, Barney thought. He didn't look like he was having fun. He looked like he was terrified.

"He knows," the pimpled boy whispered to Barney again. "He knows why there always has to be a lifeguard sitting in the chair when they open the flumes. And he knows why the flumes are usually closed when he comes swimming."

Barney turned back, stared up into the light grey eyes of the boy.

"Why?" Barney asked, his voice quiet, almost a whisper, and yet the other boy heard him and grinned.

"Because *it* lives in the flumes. And sometimes when a child goes up to the top of the slide, they don't come down. And it doesn't matter how many people they send up to look for them, they're never seen again. *Never.*"

The pimpled boy grinned, and his pale white teeth looked like a row of nuggety bones.

Barney tried to laugh but his mouth was dry. Of course it wasn't true. The lifeguard sat in his chair to make sure that two people didn't go down the slide at once. That they didn't collide inside the chute and wrap together in a muddle of broken ankles and wrists. That was why. *Wasn't it?*

"It happened to a boy I knew," the other boy said. Barney switched his attention between them. This second boy looked as if he had not spoken, as if the words had been part of some magic trick. He nodded to Barney and then drew his finger across his chest. "Cross my heart, hope to die. He was in the same class as me. My friends told me. They came to the pool in summer and he went up the flumes even though they all told him not to, even though everyone warned him that *it* lives in the flumes."

"I think I heard about him," the first boy said to his friend. "Was he from the estate?"

The second boy nodded. "That's the one. His name was . . . John or Jack or Jimmy. I didn't know him that well. When he didn't come into school the following Monday no one said a word about him. It was as if he had never existed."

"Because it lives in the flumes. They all know that—the lifeguards, the teachers, the police—they all know, but none of them can do anything about it and so they try to pretend it isn't there."

"Move up."

Barney turned around. There were two boys in the queue ahead of him, but a space had grown between him and the next person. He stared at the two pale bodies and shuffled forward to close the gap in the line.

"That's better," the first boy said. He smiled to show his teeth once more.

"I don't believe you," Barney said. He waited for one of the boys—or maybe both of them—to laugh at him, but as terrible as that would have been, it was so much worse when they didn't, when they simply stood in front of him, nodding slightly to themselves.

"That's what they all say, until the next boy goes missing."

"Or girl," the second boy suggested. "I hear it takes girls too."

The first boy nodded. "That's true. But mostly boys. Mostly young boys." The pair of them nodded to each other, as if they were glad they had managed to sort out that misunderstanding.

Barney shook his head. "If there was something up there, and if people knew it was up there, then they wouldn't let us up. Not until . . . Not until it was gone."

The first pimple-faced boy clapped Barney hard on the shoulder, the blow strong enough to cause him to stagger forward a couple of steps. "You'd think so," he said. "You'd think exactly that. Except they can't."

"Why?"

"Because . . . " he started, and then hesitated.

"Because they can't get it out of there," the second boy picked up. "They tried once before. They sent up police and then the army. With guns."

"With guns," the first boy agreed.

"But they couldn't get it out. Because the staircase is too thin—they could only go up one at a time and then they could only go down the flume individually. And when they did it got them."

"So why don't they just board it up?" Barney said. He thought about the number of times he'd come to the swimming pool to find the gateway into the flumes blocked by thick blue floats.

The first boy nodded. "Once they blocked up this entrance with old inflatables and toys and all that crap. But it wasn't enough. One night, weeks and weeks after they had closed up the flumes, when they had almost begun to forget that it was in there, it came out."

"It was *hungry*," the second boy said.

"It was *starving*," the first boy said. "It hadn't eaten in weeks. It came out of the flumes in the middle of the night, when everyone in town was asleep. The following morning they found the remains of a small girl in her own bedroom . . . "

"Surrounded by a puddle of water," the second boy said. "My friend said that you could smell the chlorine as soon as you walked into the house."

The two older boys looked at each other, and then the second boy continued. "So they decided that it was safer to make sure it stayed inside the flumes rather than roving around the town, because once it got out it might carry on eating and eating until there was no one left. At least while it's in the flumes it only eats someone every couple of weeks."

"Hey!"

The shout came from behind Barney's shoulder and he twisted round.

"You're up next," the lifeguard shouted down from his chair.

Barney looked at him, and the space where the rest of the queue had been.

"But . . . But . . . " he stammered. "Where did the others go?"

"You're next," the lifeguard repeated. "You going or what?"

"But the two boys in front of me—they haven't come down yet."

The lifeguard raised an eyebrow. It was a look that said, *What are you going to do about it?*

"I would have noticed them. They would have had to walk past me," Barney said.

Over his shoulder the two pimpled youths laughed. Barney whirled again. "You saw them, didn't you?" he asked. "There were two others in front of me. A boy in a—a—" he tried to remember what the boy had been wearing, but all that came to mind was the way the very first boy had stood at the front of the queue, his teeth chattering with cold or fear. "There were two of them," Barney said.

"Maybe you're in luck then," the boy said. "Maybe it's already had enough to eat today. *Two* boys. I've never heard of it taking two at once before."

"Two?" the other boy said. "You're right. That hasn't happened before, at least not that I've ever heard. So maybe it will have had enough . . . but why stop at two? Why not three? Or four?"

"Stop it," Barney said. His voice slapped against the harsh tiled walls of the chamber. "I know you're only saying this to scare me."

The boy grinned.

"Oy!" the lifeguard shouted. "No holding up the queue."

Barney peered up at him. The man in the lifeguard chair looked frightened. Which didn't make any sense at all. Why would he be frightened by the idea that someone would not go up the stairs to the flume? Why would it make any difference to him?

Barney took a step backward; away from the flight of blue steps. He brushed against the two boys behind him. Their cold, wet hands fell on his bare shoulders and he nearly screamed.

"You gotta go," the first boy whispered to him. "If you don't go the lifeguard might come down from his chair and drag you up the stairs."

"And you'd be *doomed*," his friend said, the word cannoning off the walls. *Dooooooomed.*

"If you go up the stairs kicking and screaming then it's bound to notice you. It'll be waiting for you in the dark and as soon as the lifeguard pushes you into the mouth of the slide ..."

"And he *will* push you . . . " his friend chipped in.

"As soon as he pushes you into the slide it will come for you." He said this with such relish that Barney thought they were actually looking forward to the moment when the water at the bottom of the slide would turn pink with his blood.

"You gotta do it."

Barney felt their hands press against his shoulders.

He took one hesitant step forward. Another step. With the third, the two boys were no longer holding onto his shoulders and with the fourth he was beyond the lifeguard's chair and had almost reached the bottom step of the staircase. He looked behind him—a line of small children snaked out of the tunnel and back to the main pool.

Barney placed his foot on the bottom step of the staircase. The hard plastic scraped the skin of his foot. He reached out his hand to grasp the side of the staircase and he saw that it was shaking.

Just the cold, he told himself. *There's nothing up there. They just made up that story to scare me.*

He glanced over his shoulder. The two boys waved at him. Barney felt a flare of hate rise within him, bright and hot.

He took another step and the two boys were out of sight. He could see the crown of the lifeguard's head: a tuft of brown hair. He turned the corner and he was in the barrel of the plastic staircase, completely alone.

The next step seemed to take him an age to make. He could feel his legs wilting beneath him. It was like trying to walk up the staircase on rubber stilts, and Barney wanted to do nothing except sit down on the step and cry, but he knew that if he did then eventually they would come for him and they would drag him to the top of the staircase, and it didn't matter how much he kicked or screamed, they would cast him into the wide, black mouth at the top of the slide where *it* would be waiting for him.

And so he took another step. And another. The stairs shuddered beneath him.

There was a small platform at the top of the slide. Three entrances, one of which was barred with broken chairs and damaged inflatables. Barney thought that the scratches on some of the inflatables looked like teeth marks, and then he wished he had not looked so closely.

He shivered. *The cold.*

The sound of running water echoed around the small chamber. But he thought he could hear another sound below that. A deep, low voice. Like an animal growling in pain. Or anticipation.

Water ran down each of the two working slides.

Barney looked over his shoulder. He wondered how long it would be before someone came looking for him.

"It's just a story," he whispered. His words slipped down the open mouth of the flume and he heard a faint echo returned to him. Taunting.

The low rumble of the water continued.

He put a hand on either side of the flume. Water rinsed over his bare feet, tugging against his ankles, urging him forward.

"Just a story," he said. It sounded more confident then he felt.

He leaned back, and threw himself forward. Into the hole.

WHITE MOON RISING

DENNIS ETCHISON

IT **WENT LIKE** this: in her room at the top of the stairs in the empty sorority house she lay warm and rumpled in her bed, trying hard to sleep some more. It was now near noon and the light streaming through the open curtains had forced her awake again. She did not seem to care if she ever got up; she had no classes, not for a week. Still she could not make herself relax. The late morning flashed a granular red through her eyelids. Then she heard the front door down below open and close, the click echoing through the abandoned house like a garbage can dropped in an alley at dawn. Probably it was one of the few remaining girls returning from an overnight date or to pick up books before leaving for vacation. Lissa hoped so. Now she could hear footsteps treading up the stairs. She tried to imagine who it was. The footsteps reached the top of the stairs and stopped. Firmly, deliberately the footfalls turned and came down the hall, toward her room. Maybe it was Sharon. She wanted it to be Sharon. She kept her eyes tightly closed. The shoes thumped deep into the rug; the loose board in the middle of the hail creaked. Finally whoever it was reached her room—there, just on the other side of the door. Lissa felt ice crystals forming in her blood. She waited for the knock, for the clearing of a familiar throat, for the sound of her own name to come muffled through the door. But there was no sound.

Still she waited. She held a breath. The blood pulsed coldly in her ears like a drum beaten underwater. She wanted to speak out. Then the sound of a hand on the loose door-knob. And the almost imperceptible wingbeat of the door gliding open. I know, she thought, I'll lie perfectly still, I won't let anything move in my body and I'll be safe, whoever it is won't see me and will go away. Yes, she thought, that's what I will have to do. Now she clearly felt a presence next to her bed. She was sure that someone was standing there in the doorway to her right, a hand probably still on the knob. She had not heard it rattle a second time. Time passed. She counted her heartbeats. At last she knew she could hold her breath no longer. She would have to do something very brave. With a rush that screamed adrenaline into her body she sat bolt upright, at the same instant snapping her head to the right and unsticking her eyes with a pop. There was no one there. The door was still closed and locked. The room was empty. Suddenly she realized that her kidneys were throbbing in dull pain. She knew what that was. It was fear.

The sunlight washed in through the window.

"Oh Joe," said his wife, "it makes me sick, just physically ill. And I know it gets to you, too."

Joe Mallory cleaned up the steak and eggs on his plate with a last swipe, then hesitated and let his fork mark a slow pattern through the smear of yolk that remained.

"No." He cleared his throat. "No, honey. Just a job." Gently he removed the newspaper from her side, poked it in half and tried to find something else to read.

"Joey," she said. She reached across the tablecloth suddenly and covered his hand. "I know you. And I know I shouldn't have let you take this job, not this one."

He looked up and was surprised and strangely moved to see her clear brown eyes glistening. As he forced his shoulders to shrug and his mouth to smile, she placed her other hand as well over his. From the open kitchen window sprang the sounds of bright chains of children on their way to the elementary school. He could almost see their black bowl haircuts and dirty feet. He wished he could help them, but it was already too late. He blinked, trying to concentrate.

"Babe," he said calmly, resurrecting a pet name they had abandoned before he went overseas. "One more semester and I'm finished with night classes. Look. You know the size of the government checks, and you know they aren't going to get any bigger. We both know Ray can't take me on without a degree—"

"You know he would, Joey, if you ask him again. What's a brother for?" Instantly she darkened, regretting the last. She held to his hand, hoping that he would let it pass.

"Now let me finish," he said slowly. "I can't handle a position like that yet, not without leaning on someone half the time. I have to do it right. This damned uniform is just a job until I'm ready. Till then, well, what else do I know? Really, now?" He flipped her hands over and warmed them with his. "I have to make things right before I go ahead, to feel like I'm my own man. I thought you understood that."

"Oh, I know all that. I'm sorry. I know. It was just all the details, the whole horrible thing, these last few weeks. It sounds so awful."

She rested her forehead on her arm and cried for a few seconds. Then she pressed her nose and stood up, stacking the dishes. "Come on, you big jock. You'll be late."

He pushed away from the table and crossed the kitchen in three steps. He took his wife in his arms and held her close for a long minute, while the electric clock hummed high and white on the wall.

She rocked back and forth with his body. Finally she began to laugh.

"Get out of here," she said, trying hard.

"Meet me at work," he said. "I'll take you to Fernando's for dinner."

The tears settled diamond-bright in her eyes. She kissed him noisily and pushed him out the door.

She watched him through the window.

He came back in.

"Forgot something," he said. He walked briskly to the breakfast nook, picked up the morning paper and dropped it in the waste can. "Give my love to the ice cream man," he said before he shut the door again.

"Hey, I don't even know the . . . "

He was gone and she stopped laughing. She went to the can and picked out the paper. She spread it on the table and stared down at it.

"Shit," she said very seriously. "Oh shit, Joe . . . "

The latest headline read:

Security Doubled
ANOTHER BRUTAL COED SLAYING

Lissa, now in tank top and embroidered Levi's, toed into her sandals and slipped down the stairs, her thin fingers playing lightly over the handrail.

"Sharon?" On the wall at the foot of the stairs she noticed the poster Sharon had brought with her from New York. It was one of those old *You Don't Have To Be Jewish To Love Levy's* advertisements, showing an Indian biting into a slice of rye bread; Sharon had replaced the Indian with the horribly burned face of an Asian child, and now she saw that someone had written across the face with a red marking pen the words *You Don't Have To Be A Unicorn To Enjoy The Tapestry* in an unmistakably feminine hand. She wondered what *that* meant. "Has anybody seen Sharon?" she called, tapping her nails on the railing. Then, "Is anybody here?"

She thought she heard voices and stepped off the stairs. But she saw only the bright, still day outside the open front door, and the two familiar Security guards at the edge of the dry lawn. They stood with their hands behind their backs and, Lissa thought, peculiar smiles on their faces; as they rocked on their heels their billy clubs swung tautly from wide, black belts.

Something about them gave her the creeps.

Her eyes listlessly scanned the living room, finding nothing to settle on.

She stepped away from the open front door. Sharon must have left it open. On the way out, probably to see Eliot.

She could call Eliot and find out, couldn't she?

She took two steps toward the phone. She stopped. The thought of the newly-installed tap put her off again. Damn it, she thought. It irks me, just the idea of it. It really does.

She sighed. She stood in the middle of the rug, her left hand resting on the back of the sofa and her right hand fingering her left elbow. She took a breath, held it, let it out. Then she went over to the big front door and nudged it shut. With her back. She didn't particularly want to look outside.

Officer William W. Williams was doing push-ups on the grass.

"How many I got, John?"

"Uh, forty-seven by my count, Bill."

"You lyin'!"

"You're not going to break no record today, Williams," said Officer Hall around a lumpy chili dog from the food service machines.

"You shut up, Hal." Williams spat to one side and pumped three more times. The muscles on his shining arms inflated with each stroke.

"Fifty," said Joe matter-of-factly, "and still counting."

Williams quivered high on his corded arms for a beat, then dipped again.

"Mother," he breathed.

The sun, setting some kind of record for April, beat down in shimmering waves, now mercifully on the tin roof of the pergola so that the officers were able to remove their spongy hats, at least for half an hour. Joe felt not quite a breeze but at least a shift in the hovering air layers here in the shade; the sweat in his short black hair was beginning to evaporate, cooling and contracting his scalp. It was, he thought without knowing why, a day for ice cream. Williams, however, chose to remain under the sun, bridging again and again over the blanched grass.

"What did the Chief have to say this morning?" asked Joe. "Sorry I missed the briefing."

The men did not answer.

As far as Joe could see the campus was deserted, the gray buildings flat and silent, the sparsely-sown trees moving not at all in the noonday heat. Though he knew better, Joe wondered idly if anyone other than Security was on the grounds today.

Old John, white-haired and better suited to a Santa Claus costume than a black uniform, folded his hands unsteadily.

"It was another one of his pep talks, Joe. You know Withers." Joe didn't very well, but it didn't matter. "I guess you didn't miss anything."

Hall resumed chewing.

Joe realized that Williams had suspended over the lawn. Finally he moved. *Down.*

"Well, I hope we get him," offered Joe, "and soon. A guy like that has got to be sick, and needs help."

Up. Williams stopped.

Hall stopped eating.

Joe felt odd. He repeated to himself what he had said, trying to figure why they were uptight. Something about Withers, maybe. Except for Old John, they didn't seem to like the Chief. That must be it.

"Hell," said Hall, "this is the easiest job in the world. We don't have to do anything. A person commits a violation, he does himself in." He spoke carefully, as if laying out a scientific fact. "Because if he's human, he's ashamed of the act. That's all the lever we need." Barely changing his tone he said, "Look at that one, will you?"

They looked. A young girl, slender and poised, was crossing the parking lot in old Levi's, very tight, and a form-fitting top.

Down. "Hoo. That one is sweet and tough," said Williams. *Up.*

"You take girls like that," Hall went on. "They don't have any sense of shame. Man, somebody's got to teach her a lesson."

"I'm not sure I follow you," said Joe.

Down. Williams rolled over onto his back. "Gimme some of that Dr. Pepper."

Hall cackled and took the bottle over to Williams. He knelt and whispered something. Williams nodded, then drained the bottle and lay back, gazing dreamily through the low trees by the pergola. "Somebody gimme my shirt an' gun." He sang a few notes to himself. "You know what we need around here?" he asked. "Bows an' arrows. That's what we had in 'Nam. Pick a sentry out of a tree at a hundred yards. *Whoosh.* Simple as that. Don't make no noise."

The girl was disappearing from sight.

"What time's it getting to be?" asked Joe. He reached for his walkie-talkie. "We'd better check in with the command post."

"No reason to hurry," said Hall.

Williams rolled over onto his belly. *Up.* He started counting again. *Down.*

Up.

Down.

"Hey, you can knock it off," Hall said to him. "She's gone." They all had a good laugh over that.

Lissa walking across the grass: What were they laughing about?

Beyond the glimmering parking lot she glanced over her shoulder at the pergola, blurry without her glasses, bouncing behind her with each step. She shrugged and went on.

She looked down. She slipped her shoes off and felt the warm grass, following her feet past the Library and the new Student Union, staying on the shade. At the far side of the campus she climbed the cool steps to the lab.

"Knock-knock?"

She slid around the open door.

The stink from the tiered cages was overpowering; she knew at once that it would be too much for her.

She heard someone clear his throat. She held her breath, tucked in her top, and walked forward between the skittering enclosures.

"Oh!"

An elecric buzz rattled the cages.

The rats scrambled over one another, hundreds and hundreds of rats. She almost screamed. The buzzing stopped. The rats subsided.

A hand, cold and clammy as sweating brass, touched her neck. She stiffened. It seemed to be trying to press her straight down into the floor.

"Ah, but you're not Sherrie, are you." It was a statement. "Apologies."

She was released. She turned. She saw a moist left hand recently relieved of its rubber glove; as she faced it, an acrid fume sliced up her nostrils. Formaldehyde.

She stumbled back. "W'll, hi, Eliot. I was looking for Sharon." She rubbed at her watering eyes. "I was on my way to your apartment, but I thought I'd stop by here first." She looked up into his pallid, implacable face. And shuddered. "You haven't seen her?"

"Afraid not, Lissa."

He simply observed her, waiting.

She wanted out, but she said, "Well, what are you up to in here, anyway? I never saw all these—these *mice* the last time I was here."

He snapped off his right glove and moved to the sink, applied talc. He pocketed his pale hands in his white coat and leaned against a supply cabinet.

"A low voltage is discharged through the bottom of each cage," said Eliot, "every two minutes, twenty-four hours a day. At various stages I remove typical specimens and dissect the adrenal cortex, the thymus, the spleen, the lymph nodes and so forth, and of course the stomach. There is a definite syndrome, you know."

Are you for real? she wondered, drifting to the window. Below, a fat, greasy-looking mama's boy with horn-rimmed glasses gazed up at the window. She had seen him hanging around a number of times lately. Too many times. She stepped away from the window.

"The adrenal cortex," continued Eliot conversationally, "is always enlarged. All the lymphatic structures are shrunken. And there are deep ulcers, usually in the stomach and upper gut."

He's not kidding, she thought. She looked outside again. The young man was gone. She felt relieved. "What do you call it?" she said, almost reflexly.

"A stress rig," said Eliot. Cheerfully, she thought. Then, "Sherrie's probably back at the House by now. Be careful going home, will you? I know I don't need to remind you." When she did not say anything, "About what happened to the others. It was a combination, a choke hold from behind, forearm across the throat, under the chin, one arm in a hammerlock. Fractures of the larynx, internal hemorrhaging. And this vertebra, this one right here, at the base of the neck. That's what finished them. He had to lift them off their feet. Here." He reached out to show her.

Suddenly, jarringly, the cages buzzed.

Let me out of here! She felt sick.

"Well, I'll see you later, Eliot." She did not wait for an answer.

Outside and down the stairs, a breeze was coming in with the dusk. It's really summer, she thought. She wanted desperately to be at the beach. She could almost smell the Sea & Ski basting her skin. A bird sang high on a telephone wire. O let there always be summers, she thought. A hundred, a thousand of them. That was what she wanted. She wanted there to be a thousand summers.

Joe trod blankly along University Drive. Off duty at last, he was on his way back to the campus, where his wife would be waiting.

"How long has this been happening?" he asked, a little dazed.

"Ed Withers's been paying off Hall to keep him quiet ever since, Lord, seven-eight months," said Old John, strolling with his hands behind his back, his voice low as a moribund bulldog's. "Anyway, Joey"—he had never called him that before—"I figured you ought to know. What I mean to get across is, try to keep to yourself as much as you can while you're here. They're a kind of—oh, they're a bunch of what you would call motivated young officers. Highly motivated."

"What I can't understand," Joe persisted, "is why everyone is keeping his mouth shut."

Old John averted his eyes and took an unexpected number of steps to answer. He fingered his handcuffs nervously; they glinted in the day's dying rays of sunlight. "Job's a job, you know what I mean," muttered Old John.

Joe turned those words over and over as they came to Portola Place.

What in the world did that have to do with it? He stopped at the curb. "What does that have to do with it?" he asked.

But Old John was trekking on down Portola Place. He continued to keep an eye on Joe, however. Joe saw him put a hand behind his ear.

"Nothing," Joe shouted. Nothing at all. "See you Friday."

He shook his head. Even here, he thought. He took a too-deep breath of the lukewarm air, squinting as the setting sun peeped its staring red eye from between the buildings. He started walking again. He lowered his head and watched his feet move, crossing the street at a fast clip.

So Hall's wife was getting pumped by the Chief of Security. And Chief Withers was being—was there a less melodramatic word for it?—blackmailed by Hall. With a promotion thrown in. Joe throttled a bitter laugh. He wondered whether Hall's wife knew that end of it. And whether she was smugly enjoying the benefits with her husband. What the hell, what the hell, what the hell, Joe thought aimlessly. And heard a rustling in the bushes.

"Where's the cook?"

"She's not coming in again till after vacation."

"Well, where's the House Mother?" said Kathy. "I know, I know, there's no House Mother here. Ooh, I wish I was still at PT!"

"Better not let Madam President hear you bitching," said Sharon. "She'll kick you out on your lily-white ass."

Kathy groaned and went upstairs.

Lissa laughed. She had seen the House Mother for the Pi Taus; her face had more lines in it than *War and Peace*, which she had been reading for English 260. Trying to read. Part I had been on *The Six O'Clock Movie* Monday. Dutifully she had watched it, but for some reason she missed Part II. Part III had been on for a few minutes now.

"Henry Fonda's the only one who acts like he read the book," said Sharon, giving up on the color controls and laying her legs over the arms of the couch again. The set, which rendered everything the color of bile, did look, as Sharon had once remarked, "like somebody took a whiz on it." Lissa tried to follow the plot, but by now it made no sense at all to her.

"Who's been leeching my Marlboros, anyway?" said Sharon, digging under the cushions.

Lissa flipped over to Channel 11. "Hey, *Chiller*'s on."

"Right arm," said Sharon.

"Is that *Frank*enstein?"

"Fuck yes," said Sharon. "I've seen this flick so many—"

"You know, I've never seen it all the way through," said Lissa. "My folks would never let me."

"Ha!"

"No, really."

"Well, go ahead, knock yourself out."

Fascinated, Lissa watched the scene in which little Maria so innocently shared her flowers with the Monster on the riverbank. One by delicate one they cast daisies on the water. Then, very slowly, the Monster's expression began to change, as the child ran out of flowers, as the scene began to fade out.

"That's the part they always cut," said Sharon. "You should see his face right after this, before they find her with her neck broken. You know what I think? I don't believe he ever meant to kill her at all. I think he just sort of, you know, crushed her to him. You know what I mean? I don't think there was anything evil about it. They were both innocents. Neither one of them knew anything about it."

A bald-headed used-car salesman appeared on the screen, his face a sneer of chartreuse.

Joe stood stock-still and waited for the next sound.

It did not come.

He stepped onto the blue-shadowed lawn. His hand steadied on his flashlight.

He heard footfalls on the other side of the hedge, close to a house.

He let himself into the foliage, deciding to follow it up. Leaves, small and shiny, tracked past him on either side, hard branches skidding off his head, almost knocking his hat to the ground.

Close to the other side, he saw a man's back moving quickly away from him along the side of the house, toward the front sidewalk. The house was dark, probably empty; he hoped so. He felt disoriented for a fraction of a second, almost as if he were not really here but somewhere else entirely. Then he saw the figure stand straight and slow to a normal gait, crossing under the street lamp. Then the figure returned to a crouch and headed into the trees on the other side. Peeping Tom? Or the one he had been hired to catch? Well, if this is the one, he must be one poor scared son of a bitch right now, even if he doesn't know he's being watched. In fact, Joe realized, his own heart hammering at the back of his badge, that part wouldn't really have anything to do with the feeling, not anything at all.

Joe pulled free of the hedge and backed up. He moved down behind the next four houses in line and then continued forward to the street and crossed at the end of the block. He cut into the alley just past the houses.

He stayed close to the wooden fence, navigating around trash barrels—empty, they would drum an alarm down the whole of Sorority Row.

He heard tennis shoes grinding into the gravel.

A young man crossed the alley not fifty feet in front of him.

They heard Kathy put a record on the turntable upstairs.

The TV screen receded into the deepening shadows of the living room. A cricket started up, sounding so close that Lissa glanced nervously about to see if it was in the house with them. Outside, an elderly officer paced past the hedge, hands behind his back.

"Look at that old codger." Sharon's ash flared and hissed before her face, then arced down. "I'll bet they still don't give them real bullets to use. Yeah, I saw his gun one time. The barrel was plugged up with wood or bubble gum or something. I wonder if they're going to do any good now that we need them? Somebody needs them. The only thing they've been good for so far is to *remind* us all. D'you see what I mean?" She sat forward. "God, I've got to get away from here for a while. I'm starting to vegetate. When's Eliot coming over?"

"He didn't say."

"He always takes his time. I don't know what he does on his way over here, wandering around jacking his brain off with some new pet theory."

"Sharon!"

"Well, it's the truth."

They sat with the sound turned down. The cricket synched with the record for a few bars, then continued on its own again.

"Can I have one of those, please?"

"I didn't know you were smoking now, Lees."

"I'm not. Not really."

The young man crossed the alley.

Joe froze.

Then he followed.

Passing between two houses, he stopped again and dropped to one knee.

He saw ahead to the next street. The young man had already crossed over and was now hesitating by one of the huts on the other side. Houses, he told himself. Now Joe looked between the trees and houses as down a tunnel: as the street lamp flicked on, the pavement mottled under the new light, his eyes focused through to a square of still-bright sky visible now above the long campus parking lot.

He waited.

Another figure, nearly a silhouette, appeared against the sky.

It was a woman.

He snapped to, aware that he had lost track of his prey. The young man was gone. He had slipped through, probably to the lot. But—*had* he gone through, or was he still somewhere on the block between, sidestepping from house to house?

He had blown it.

He started to move anyway.

Then it hit him. The woman. The woman waiting in the lot.

It had to be his wife.

"Eliot," said Sharon, "is very into it. And therefore out of it. If you know what I mean. There are moments with us. Not many, but there are. You were right, though. Sometimes I do wonder if it's worth it. God, I've been staring into this box too long. Now it's beginning to stare back." She clicked off the TV with her toes. "I don't need to turn on the tube to see rape, murder and perversion. I can get all that right here at school."

Lissa heard a record droning upstairs. It sounded like Dylan.

turn, turn, turn again

"Tell her to turn it over, will you?" said Sharon. "That song's bumming me out."

Lissa felt her way to the top of the first landing.

"Lis-sa? Bring down something to scarf, will you? Um,

Screaming Yellow Zonkers. Whatever she's got hidden up there. An-y-thing!"

Lissa smiled.

turn, turn to the rain and the wind

She walked on down the hail.

Joe had squatted so long that his gaze was fixed, almost as if the rectangle of light sky had somehow been looking back down into him instead. His eyes stung.

Fatigue. He hoped. Four days a week had seemed fine at first. Enough time to do some good, maybe, but not enough to—but it was late now, much later than he had thought, judging from the color of the sky. Marlene, he realized, blinking alert, had been waiting—how long? How long had he crouched here? And how long before, at the other village? Block, he reminded himself, block.

He crossed the street, his breath jangling in his ears like dog tags.

He shot a glance at the patch of sky and the dark figure of his wife.

His pace quickened.

As he headed over a lawn, a young man bolted out of the shrubs, a pair of horn-rimmed glasses clattering from his face.

With Ritz crackers and a five-pack of Hydrox cookies in one hand, she drew the knob toward her, cutting the sliver of light from Kathy's room, and made for the stairs.

There was a knock on the front door.

The stairway was an unknown in the dark. She waited.

Finally, "Sharon? Can you get that?"

The knock again.

She descended, pressing against the wall.

"Just a—" She felt a catch in her throat. Why?

The door swung open.

The kid was squirming on the lawn, his face jumping.

"Whatsa matter? I'm on my way home from a study date! Whatsa *matter?*"

Joe closed the cuffs, pressed the key into the notch and set the lock.

Something in the young man's face, swarming in a film of sweat, refused to let Joe relax. He shoved the glasses at him and pulled him to his feet. He glanced ahead. The sky was dark, too dark to see her.

He whipped the antenna up on his walkie-talkie. It shook in his hands, waving back and forth in the night air.

She saw a woman, backlighted in the open doorway.

"I'm sorry," said the woman. "But I wonder if you've seen my husband. He was supposed to meet—"

"No, I—" stammered Lissa. "Do you mean he was outside?" Where was Sharon? *Where?* She left the doorway. "Just a minute, okay?"

She felt around the room. "Share?" she called. I know, she thought. She said she was hungry. I'll check the kitchen. If I can only find the light!

"Sha-ron!" she called, and wondered why her voice was breaking.

"We don't want to hurt you," Joe said. "Believe that."

He drew his prisoner through the shrubs, crushing twigs and unseen garden creatures in his path.

He turned up the gain and depressed the call button. He needed back-up. His throat was dry and the back of his tongue hurt.

A shrill electronic sound whined close by. Instantly he recognized it. It was feedback—his own signal being picked up on another receiver.

"I guess you wouldn't know who I mean," the woman said from the doorway. "But he's one of the Security..."

It's so dark, thought Lissa at the door to the kitchen. She forced herself across the chill linoleum, her arms outstretched like antennae.

She heard a sound—a low voice. It was singing:
some folks like t' talk about it
some don't
A wind from nowhere blew through her chest.

He pushed the kid ahead of him, following the sound.

Louder. Joe was relieved. Reinforcements were near.

Then he noticed his prisoner's stare.

At the rear of the last house by the parking lot, dark shapes were moving.

She seemed to swim through darkness past the smooth pulsating refrigerator where there were always tooth marks in the cheese, to the drawer from which the tools had been quietly disappearing for weeks, clamoring for something, anything with which to protect herself. It was silly, she knew, but—there. A butcher knife.

Joe released his own wrist and locked the kid to the branch of what might have been a rubber tree.

"We'll be back for you, Charlie," he said.

She felt herself drawn down the short stone steps from the kitchen to the storage porch, to the low singing and other voices and what sounded like a scratching close to the screen door that opened into the back yard.

The officer plunges through the shrubbery. At that someone slams out the back door, sees dark forms and the girl held to the dirt and reflexly cocks back an arm, white moons rising on the nails that clench the knife. The officer sees the downed girl, uniforms, another figure lunging into it. There is no time to question, not now while there is still time to stop it before it happens again. He remembers them sitting there dumbly in their baggy pajamas, their wooden bowls empty of the ice cream a few minutes before it happened, and how he had gone away and done nothing, not even when he heard the laughter and the grunting and the automatic fire. And the screams. But not this time. He dodges and grabs the empty hand, wrenching it into a hammerlock as he encircles the waist with his left arm, releasing the wrist with his right and setting his forearm under the chin. The back arches and the legs kick madly, but the hand refuses to let go the knife. Faces turn up. One of the officers stays atop their victim. It is Williams who closes in from the front, spreading his milky palm across the distorted mouth, covering it. "Nice going Joe." He grins. "Now you one of us, too." Joe does not yet understand. Now he feels a slip in the neck and the body swings like the clapper of a bell in his arms. Now he hears new footsteps behind him and a sudden skull-splitting screech. It is the scream of a woman. He thinks he recognizes it but it is too late, now it really is too late as the girl in his arms swings one last anguished time, as her knife slices at the dark with a flash and he sees a face reflected in the blade for an instant before it drops into the leaves. But he must know what he has seen. He has seen the face of a killer. It is the same face he has always seen.

The moonlight washes down on them all.

OF THE COLOR TURMERIC, CLIMBING ON FINGERTIPS

GERRY HUNTMAN

BALL'S PYRAMID WAS the ultimate climb for the three friends. It was a massive, ancient volcanic plug that projected over five hundred and fifty yards above sea level like a giant shark's fin cutting through the Pacific Ocean. It had been scaled only a handful of times, and always by the easiest routes. It took three years for Jason to get permission for them to even set foot on the declared nature reserve. His fiancée, Becky, and best friend, Dave, were as eager as Jason to climb the monolithic rock from the hardest, sheerest route. No "beta," as their craft described it—without the taint of any foreknowledge or advice.

The ocean wind swept across Jason, causing his hair to dance and his coat to flutter like a thousand butterfly wings. He was standing on a narrow ledge and had set several anchors in the rock to secure the group from being blown off the island. He glanced up the sheer face, rising four hundred and fifty yards, and then down the slightly off-vertical cliff one hundred yards to the sea. A large rubber dingy was moored to a rock outcrop, bobbing incessantly and maniacally in random directions, while much further out to sea was the *Osprey*, the charter boat from Lord Howe Island that brought the rock climbers to their Holy Grail. The boat would wait three days while they attempted the climb. The waves didn't cause too much trouble when they transferred from the twin-engine dingy through the pungent sea-spray to the slimy rocks at the base of the volcanic plug. The winds were too strong to attempt the summit this day, especially when they were climbing it the hard way.

With the noise of the sea and the frequent winds, there was little point in working with walkie-talkies. Jason was given a small flare gun to signal if the party was in trouble, and the captain of *The Osprey* had instructed the rock climbers to abandon their efforts and return to their dingy as quickly as possible if a similar flare emanated from the boat.

Jason noticed Dave, still scaling the easy lower cliff formation to join him at the narrow ledge, which was going to be their base camp. He was puffing, carrying most of the tent equipment, including porta-ledge devices enabling the three to sleep in their tents in safety. Jason laughed, as Dave—strong as an ox and nearly as large—always ended up with Sherpa duties. Dave wasn't overweight—far from it. The tall, ginger-cropped South Australian was stout and didn't have an ounce of fat on him. He would have made a great pro basketball player. They usually climbed together during the warmer months, and "fitness freak" Dave would supplement his winter training with some serious rowing on the River Torrens.

Becky was thirty yards behind Dave, taking it easy and enjoying the warm-up climb. She was very capable, probably the most technically skilled climber of the three, and fastidious with safety procedures. When climbing, she always had an intense, professional look about her, with her long dark hair tied back in a ponytail, popping from under her helmet, and brows creased in concentration above her expressive, brown eyes.

Dave finally pulled himself onto the ledge and carefully placed his large bundle on the widest possible location.

Jason swung his arm around, grasping Dave's hand with his own. "Thanks, mate. That was a big haul."

Dave wiped sweat from his forehead, despite the cooling winds. "Someone had to do it." He took a small swig of water from his Nalgene flask, and his countenance turned serious. "Mate. While Bec's still climbing—haven't had a single moment alone with you, 'specially with you two moving to Sydney—I wanted to tell you there's no hard feelings. I know I said it over the phone a few months back, but I want you to really, really *know how I feel*. When Bec broke up with me I was gutted, especially since—you know, my best friend and all."

Jason grasped Dave's shoulder with his right hand. "Hey, I didn't—"

"You don't need to say it. It took a while, but I realized that it wasn't meant to be." A small tear formed in one of his eyes, and a gust sent it streaking along his cheek bone into nothingness. "Jeez, I look at you two and all I can see is joy. Someone out there will do it for me, but Bec and I didn't have that chemistry."

They hugged, as they had always done since primary school when something important had been resolved or achieved.

"Whoa, am I meant to see this?" Becky asked over the whining wind.

"Just a tender moment," Jason said. "You can join us, if you want."

"Pass. Maybe we should get these portas set up. Haven't used one for years."

Dave moved toward his pack when out of a crevice a fat, black chitinous creature scuttled near his foot.

"Shit!" he yelped, and without thinking, crushed the

creature under his climbing boot. It was an insect, larger than a human hand, with six legs and a bulbous, pitch-black exoskeleton. Yellowy-gray liquid oozed from the mangled body, which even with the winds smelled acrid, like vomit.

"Christ!" Becky cried. "Do you know what you just did?"

"Ah. Not exactly."

"One of the reasons why this lump of vertical rock is a protected environment is because there might be twenty or so of these stick insects living here. And that's it. They used to crawl all over Lord Howe Island, but they were wiped out by rats introduced by a shipwreck. These are the most endangered insects in the world. You probably wiped out five percent of the existing population in the wild, dickhead!"

"Shit, I forgot. I just hate insects and spiders. What are we going to do?"

Jason crouched near the insect's corpse and squeamishly nudged it. "It's sure big. If a scientist or another climber finds the remains, they might ask questions. It was an accident, but I don't want trouble. I say hide it in the crevices—if we try to fling it out to sea, the wind might blow it back onto the rocks."

Dave was visibly relieved. "Thanks. It was an accident."

"Dumbass," Becky said, and slapped him playfully on the back. "But it was a mistake."

Jason used his boot to slide the creature into a small crack in the cliff wall. Some dirt and mold had accumulated in a small natural recess four feet above it. He scraped the material onto the ledge. Dave and Becky helped.

"What's this?" Jason asked, staring at his palms.

A layer of fine orange-yellow powder caked both his gloves. The others had the same, and they could see its source—a small area where the powder was thickly clinging to the wall of the recess.

Becky wiped her hands on her front shirt. "It looks almost like turmeric powder. You know, for curries."

"And as clingy," Jason replied. He sniffed it carefully.

"Almost smells like turmeric too." He kept rubbing his hands together, but little of the material was loosened from his Cordex gloves, nor the exposed areas of his lower arms. "I could be wrong, but I think it's a mold, or some kind of spore. Never seen anything like it."

Becky nodded. "Yeah, but that's weird. I read pretty much everything I could find about Ball's Pyramid, and I didn't get any reference to this. There's precious little that grows here, and these ugly buggers only survive because of a few solitary bushes near a tiny water source. I reckon this mold, or whatever it is, should have been in the literature."

"No one's climbed this rock at this time of year," Jason replied. "Maybe this stuff only comes out for a few days a year, set around some special time."

"Solstice," Dave stated, trying to wipe off the powder onto his trousers, and managing to get a smear on his face and onto his helmet. "I remember reading in the paper this morning that today is the Winter Solstice. Just saying."

"Could be," Becky said. She suddenly cried and jumped back, too close to the hundred yard precipice for comfort.

The insect, half covered in the material that was scraped from above, moved.

The three climbers stepped further away, unable to speak. Dave lightly whimpered, barely audible over the swirling winds.

The insect made a few loud scraping sounds, and walked off. Nearly walked. One leg was missing, several others were broken. Its body still had glistening flesh and yellow pus hanging out of its thorax. And yet it managed to crawl on its assembly of uneven legs. It grew in confidence and managed to actually scuttle along the ridge. Becky screamed and leapt over the creature as it waddled by.

"It was dead," Jason stated with urgency. "It was as dead as you can fuckin' get!"

The next day was perfect for climbing. The wind had died

down to almost a sigh and it was mild, a few degrees above the average for the year. The insect episode had been a topic of interest into the early night, but the climbers had chores to do and needed a good night's sleep for the day's long, tough climb. The collective view was that the insect was hardy and had successfully scampered elsewhere, ultimately to die. If there was time, they agreed to look for the body after their climb, to make sure it could not be found by anyone else.

They set off early in the morning with Jason at lead. It was, as expected, slow going as he took minimum risks and spent much of his time setting bolts and anchors for clipping in belay ropes. This was a high-grade climb, and it didn't take long for the three climbers to have their skills stretched to the limits and for the pleasure of the challenge to seep in.

At one of the belay points they took a break, hanging from their ropes, drawing in the view of the ocean, from nearly a thousand feet above sea level.

"Sublime," Dave said.

"Completely," Becky agreed.

"By the way, guys," Jason said, inspecting his hands and arms. "That turmeric stuff hasn't come off yet. It's gone through my gloves onto my hands, and it's also stained my lower arms."

"Tell me about it," Becky replied, with a tone of annoyance. "It went through my shirt and I've now got yellow boobs."

The two men exploded into laughter, and Becky couldn't help but join in.

"Got stuff on my hands and legs," Dave said. "I tried a bit of water to wash it off, and eventually it does clean up, but we can't waste our water."

They soon set off again, climbing the rock face of the island. At times they scaled small, protruding outcrops, but much of the climb was up sheer cliffs, dependent on fixing pitons, bolts, and other anchors into narrow cracks and gaps, none of which were ever climbed before.

Dave was in last position along the route, one he was happy to have. Jason knew his friend was a good, reliable climber, but he was the weakest with respect to technique.

"I thought The Totem Pole was a tough climb," Dave said, approaching the next belay point for clipping. He was referring to a nearly two hundred foot high rectangular rock in Tasmania that looked more like Cleopatra's Needle than a sea- and wind-eroded rock, and was considered one of the hardest graded climbs there was.

"Yeah," Jason shouted back. "It's like this face has five or six of them."

"More like—" Dave's feet slipped and there wasn't sufficient hold with his hands. He didn't cry out. He was experienced. Instead, he focused on bracing himself for the jarring of the fall when his rope extended to its length from the last belay point. As if the gods had frowned on the group, Dave's rope hooked over a small pimple of rock close to his descent path. When the climber reached the full length of his fall, stopping relatively gently due to the elastic nature of the rope, the portion that was hugging the rock formation pinged back to its straight position, catching Dave by surprise. Dave started twisting and swinging several yards to his right, failing to control himself as he was unable to catch hold of any part of the cliff.

"Rope!" cried Becky, which signified a problem with Dave's safety line.

He grabbed hold of a narrow crack in the cliff face with both hands, forming fists and jamming them in. He glanced up and saw that his belay rope had shredded when it ground over the rock it had hooked onto. He heard the rope snap as it was severed, and gritted his teeth when the full weight of his body concentrated on one of his fists. He separated his left hand from the gap, hoping to find some other purchase to grab onto, while his legs raced about, also seeking the sanctuary of a hold.

"Christ!" Dave breathed in and out quickly to build up his

oxygen levels for the struggle ahead. "Not sure if I can do this myself, guys! Would sure like some help!"

Becky was the logical rescuer. She was thirty yards diagonally above, while Jason was much higher.

Becky quickly readjusted her equipment, and carefully rappelled down until she got to the belay point where Dave fell prior to clipping. In seconds, she connected a figure-eight device and repelled from her new anchor point.

Dave started to lose it, screaming, "Shit! Shit! Shit! I can't get any holds! I can't keep this up for much longer!" His face had turned a bright red and Jason could see, despite the distance, a look of mortal terror in Dave's eyes.

"I'm coming!" Becky cried, stopping her descent several yards above Dave's altitude, but five yards to his left. She quickly scanned the vertical terrain and shook her head, having made the sober assessment. "I can't dyno across, Dave. The same kind of crazy rock that cut your rope will do the same with mine. I've got to set up a new anchor point."

"Quickly!" Dave grunted, hardly able to muster the strength to speak.

Becky expertly constructed an anchor by inserting a hex into a narrow space, attaching two cams. She completed the device with a sling and carabiner, and a spare, short belay rope. She unhooked herself from her original belay rope and grabbed hold of her new protection.

Inexplicably, the upper rock formation that held the hex disintegrated.

With the instinct of a seasoned climber, Becky grabbed for purchase with both her hands, but it wasn't good enough. There was a quick intake of breath as reality coldly encompassed her. She silently slipped down the sheer rock face.

"Becky!" Jason cried, stunned that another accident could have happened so suddenly, and then horrified when he saw that she had no protection.

Becky managed twice to slam her hands onto outcrops,

hoping against hope to stop her fall. Instead, it barely slowed her descent, and it caused her body to tumble.

With tears flowing down his cheeks, and despair screeching from his mouth, Jason saw his fiancée smash into a large outcrop one hundred and fifty yards below, followed by Dave falling, screaming, and trailing a useless umbilical cord.

Amazingly, she didn't bounce off the rock and career into the ocean. She was dead, unmistakably. The moment her head hit the rock, there was a six foot red wash glistening on the surface. Her body and limbs were misshapen, at odd angles, like a discarded marionette. Her helmet was nowhere to be seen.

Dave fell almost the entire distance to sea level, and with dignity totally ignored, shattered on the sea-washed rocks. The only saving grace was that it was too far to see the details. But it was hard for Jason to take his eyes away from Becky.

Jason hung there, not even remembering to secure himself, crying, swaying, and cursing God.

His eyes kept returning to Becky's body. He wasn't looking for something, nor hoping for the impossible. He just had to see her. It wouldn't be long before he would never see her again.

His gaze turned to the *Osprey*, wondering if they noticed the catastrophe, and saw no signs of activity. His eyes tracked back to the outcrop.

She wasn't there. Just a fan-shaped smear of drying blood and gore.

Where . . . ?

There was a shadowy movement slightly to the right of the outcrop.

He shifted his body and focused.

It was a climber. *Another climber*, his brain kept hammering at him. He swallowed and realized how dry his throat was. It was Becky. She had landed with her body in a sideways position, shattering her head. Her face—what was left of it—was distorted but unmistakably hers. A single eye stared upward as she climbed by grasping onto the smallest of ridges and gaps with her fingertips. Sometimes her boots would fail to find a ledge, but her fingertips—becoming ragged as she progressed—held her weight.

He was washed with a fleeting moment of insanity when he welcomed the idea of being with his Becky, but as she got closer he saw her state in more detail. The sheer horror of the thought of being close to such fresh ruin was overwhelming. He panicked. He unhooked his belay rope and climbed. For his sanity, for his life.

The adrenaline had worn off. His body was aching, bleeding, after several desperate lunges to get away from Becky. And yet she closed the gap, easily. She was very close now, only ten yards below him, and that single brown eye, which was fixed on her climbing, was now targeting him. She was dead, *she had to be dead*, but her eye was alive. As she knowingly gazed on him, a ragged, bloody smile formed on her tattered face.

"Jase, why are you leaving me?" Her voice was distorted, hollow like the grave.

He couldn't climb anymore. He was spent, and the universe collapsed around him, his sanity imploded into a singularity of hell. "Y—you're dead," he whimpered.

"No, you're wrong," said the fractured voice. She hadn't slowed her movement at all. In fact, she had picked up her pace.

"Y—your face, your body . . . broken."

"My heart beats, Jason. I want to hold you, to make the nightmare go away."

The thought of her being so close, to be inches away from her gaping skull and fragmented bones, caused him to almost faint with overwhelming horror. To kiss her lips, blue and cold . . .

Becky was only a few yards away, her blood-crusted, shattered smile inviting doom. "Embrace me. Stay with me forever."

Jason fumbled in his jacket pocket and pulled out the single shot plastic flare gun, something that had escaped his thoughts in his despair. He pointed it at the gap between Becky's chest and the cliff wall, firing at point blank range. He closed his eyes as the intense heat of the burning magnesium enveloped her breast, flinging her off the cliff.

To his dismay, while Becky fell, lighting up like a bonfire, her hands whipped out and finally, successfully grabbed hold of a protruding rock. The rest of her body slammed into the cliff, breaking more bones, and yet she held on. While grasping onto the cliff with one hand, she expertly fastened her body by rope to an anchor. She flapped incessantly at the fire encompassing her, trying to put it out, not once crying out in pain.

Jason thought she would come for him again, but she slowed down. The flapping became a few feeble swipes, and as the acrid smell of burnt flesh and hair rose up to him, she collapsed, hanging limply on her belay rope, still burning.

Jason set up a harness and sat in it, trying to recover. He ignored the smell of the smoldering corpse. It was now, it seemed, a real corpse.

Another movement came from below.

Oh no, sweet Jesus, no!

Dave's corpse was climbing the cliff face. He was some distance down, but he was a worse mess than Becky had been. His limbs and body were so broken he climbed in fits and starts, bones grinding against each other each time he moved. There was an odd whooshing sound that seemed to emanate from the body, and when it got closer it became apparent why—Dave's head had been completely shattered, and while remnants of both it and his helmet girdled his neck and shoulders, the sound was coming from his exposed windpipe.

Jason prepared himself for oblivion. He hadn't the strength left to climb, and he was certain his sanity was going to give way completely. Either way, or both, there was total darkness.

Dave moved—he had no eyes. He could not see. As the corpse was climbing higher, it also made wide horizontal detours, almost as if it needed to fully cover the area of the cliff face, to make sure it wouldn't miss anything. His ragged hands would reach out and feel for whatever it might find.

Me.

Jason was certain that this blind corpse would find him, and God knows what would happen next.

Dave reached the level of the cliff where the still-smoldering corpse of Becky hung. It moved first one direction, and then scampered like a crab toward her. His hand touched her blackened body. It moved quickly, urgently, over her torso, and found what remained of her face, which curiously was untouched by the flames. Gently, like a mother caressing a baby, the hand touched and followed the contours of Becky's face. The shoulders of the corpse slumped, and then a louder whooshing sound came from the gaping neck. It was almost emotional, a voiceless keen.

With supernatural strength, Dave's corpse pushed himself a dozen or more yards away from the cliff and fell, limply, into the sea far below.

You lied, my friend. You still loved her.

Jason climbed to the summit of Ball's Pyramid because it seemed the right thing to do. He wasn't in a fit mental state, but he risked it. Death didn't seem so poor a prospect as he once thought. The wind had picked up a little but he was able to sit at the top of the geologic wonder with some comfort, and observe his surroundings.

He saw another dingy being lowered from the charter boat into the sea. *They have binoculars. They know something is wrong.*

He looked to the northwest and saw Lord Howe Island, twelve miles distant. *People live there. And tourists visit regularly. Eight hundred at any one time.*

Jason knew that the turmeric-colored spores caused the re-animation of Becky and Dave. And the stick insect. How, he had no idea, but he guessed that Ball's Pyramid's isolated position, and the very narrow window in each year when the spores appeared on this most desolate of islands, had dramatically curbed its propagation. The three rock climbers were the first in thousands, if not millions, of years, to give it a chance to move on. He guessed that the reanimation of Becky stopped when the spores were all destroyed by the fire and heat.

He stared at his hands and arms, noting the yellow stains. He looked down at the distant corpse hanging from the cliff, where sea gulls were fighting over Becky's flesh. The crew of the charter boat would arrive soon, and regardless of how difficult it was, would do what they could to retrieve Becky's body. They might even be surprised by what they found floating in the ocean.

Jason checked his climbing gear and mentally charted a route back down that would make use of the anchor points already set in the cliff.

Jumping from the summit still seemed a sweet and strangely relieving idea, but the thought of reanimating chilled him like nothing on this earth.

He started the climb down, forgetting how exhausted he was.

He had a job to do.

KILL-BOX ROAD TRIP

PATTY TEMPLETON

JO AND FENN sat in a booth in the half-dark corner of Denny's. The lights flickered. There was a hole in the roof that looked like a heart. The linoleum floor was smeared with blood.

There were no bodies.

"Why do you have a black eye and rug-burn?" Fenn asked.

"He has worse," Jo said.

"Helluva way to get dumped." Fenn stirred her coffee with a straw.

Jo looked out the broken window, past the parking lot and the fizzling EAT HERE neon. "I didn't get dumped. We weren't dating. It was a two-night stand."

"Dude, what? Anything after one night is commitment. What the hell kinda name is Wilkes, anyway?"

"A good one. I kinda liked him. He had blue eyes."

"And offensively long eyelashes. How did you find that d-bag?"

The only other occupant of the diner was a worn-down waitress leaning on the charred counter. Her eyeglasses swung below her loose neck from a pearl chain.

"Bourbon Street Beer Garden. He had a skinny tie and his nose in a seminal study of philosophy."

"That was your first sign. Seminal, huh? You can't be dating sharp dressed men that jackoff in four AM dancehalls."

"Fenn? *Seminal.* Strongly influencing later developments."

"Did he have big later developments?"

"You're an idiot."

"Zing!"

"Shut up."

"Can I see his text again?"

Jo slid her phone across the table. Fenn caught it and read the text.

"I'm not all literary and shit, so excuse my analysis," Fenn started.

"Mmhmm." Jo kicked a slouchy boot at Fenn's messenger bag. It contained a *Penthouse Letters* and a copy of *Letters to E.T.*—both from 1987. Fenn liked to read by yearly themes.

"Did he mean you should be thankful he left before, and I quote El King Douche a la Texties, he sculpted you into a broken hag?"

"Mmhmm."

"What a dick, and why'd he send you breakup texts and then beat your ass?"

"He was trying to explain disappearing, but I caught him leaving. He thought I was still in the shower."

Fenn held up her empty coffee cup.

The waitress saw it and came over with the pot.

"'Kay. Two questions," Fenn said after the waitress left.

"Yeah?"

Fenn squinted an eye and leaned into the middle of the table, "One: why'd we haul-ass from Chicago to Colorado? I didn't ask on the ride because you had *Raw Power* on for sixteen hours. You ruined that album for me for at least a year."

"He took the box," Jo said. She poked at a thick cut on her palm.

"The black box?"

Jo nodded.

"What the ef, Jo? Not cool."

Jo stared at a crappy framed poster of James Dean and Marilyn eating at a diner.

The black box had been in the family since 1590.

"Nobody but our moms even know about it."

"That's what I thought," Jo said.

Pandora opened a box once. It contained a stream of toddler monkey piss compared to the contents of Jo's box. The evil of the world had to have a fat mama somewhere.

And she needed to be fed.

Daily.

Blood. Family blood.

"Why would he want it?" Fenn asked.

"Don't know."

"It doesn't do shit. Sometimes it makes that *Jurassic Park* raptor purr. I hate that." Fenn rolled her shoulders.

"What was your second question?" Jo asked.

"What'd you chop off of Monsieur Bagga-Dicks? You kept checking a light-up thing in your handbag. Your family's a two-trick pony: feeding and flesh tracking. Tell me we aren't in Colorado on a hunch, right? I got shit to do back in Chicago."

"Shit meaning Davey?" Jo asked. She threw a cold fry at Fenn, who caught it in her mouth.

"Hell and yes," Fenn said and swallowed the fry. "Davey is the shit I be doing. I'm like UH! Take it!" Fenn mounted a leg on the aluminum-edged table and shifted her hips back and forth.

The table rhythmically creaked.

Jo raised her fist and dropped an ear.

"Guh! Dude, I was makin' love right then, you can't be dropping ears all up on the table while I'm makin' babies with it." Fenn poked the ear with a fork. "Why an ear?"

"Last thing I grabbed before I passed out."

"You let that MF-er black you out?"

"Shut up."

"Pussy."

"Whatever. You weren't there."

"How was I supposed to know that Dude McPitchTent-and-Stroll was gonna steal your box?"

"Doesn't your family have some built-in danger warning? What good's an ancient family of deadly defenders without that?" Jo asked.

"Hell no. What? You think the world is magical? There's good, there's bad, and then there's a few tricks between. Shit, I just gotta keep my eyes open."

"Well, you didn't."

Fenn snorted.

"And I didn't," Jo continued, "and we're here now."

"What are we going to do about her?" Fenn sloshed her mug at the waitress.

"What about her?" Jo asked.

"Dude, she has one arm and half her neck-chest is hanging off. It almost got in my coffee. *Twice.*"

"She's still serving coffee, isn't she?"

"I guess," Fenn said, "but how? I restate: the world ain't magic and I don't believe in zombies."

"She's not a zombie."

"But why isn't she dead?"

"Maybe penicillin, maybe Jesus. Wilkes probably messed with the box. It doesn't like to be jiggled around."

"The box did this?"

"Why else would a Denny's be half destroyed, smelling like burnt hair?" Jo said impatiently.

"Will she die on her own?"

"How do I know? The box hasn't misbehaved in over four hundred years."

"Should we call your mom?"

"No. Definitely not," Jo said. "Even on chemo she could kick my ass."

"What about my mom?"

"No. She'd phone mine."

"Should we ask Flo, over there, if she wants to die?"

"If you want to kill her." Jo was not about to off a grandmotherly waitress with rhinestone, horn-rimmed glasses.

"Hey lady," Fenn shouted at the waitress.

The waitress let the glasses fall from her mouth and raised the coffee pot with her one arm.

"No. We're done. Lady, you wanna die?"

"They all died," the waitress said. She looked dazedly at the blood and absence of bodies.

"Yes," Fenn said, "but do you want to die?"

The waitress nodded.

Fenn pulled out her boot knife.

Actually, it was almost a machete.

The woman's eyes opened wide.

The coffee pot dropped from her hand.

The knife hit her throat.

The blood hit the grill backsplash.

Fenn's mom had taught her how to use a blade when she was eight. This was one of many reasons Fenn referred to her mom as *fucking awesome*.

"You done?" Jo called from the crane machine by the front door.

"Yep."

The crane made jangling noises and missed Jo's target.

"I wanted that orange bear."

Fenn smashed the glass with her elbow and fished out the bear.

"Thanks."

The two women walked out of the diner to their Olds 88.

The car started on the second try.

Wilkes's ear sat on the dash and glowed when they turned the correct direction.

~

"'Kay. Jo. Explain to me why we're standing in a dark, empty field?"

"It's not empty. Something has to be here."

"You're right," Fenn said.

"I am?"

"Yeah, past that ridge of trees lives a slasher family who will shove their junk into the sex-holes they've chewed into our bodies."

"You're pessimistic," Jo said, "and gross."

"You sure we're in the right spot? Can that thing lie?" Fenn glared at the ear.

"I don't think so."

"Don't think so?"

"Why would it?"

"You're the flesh tracker."

"Wilkes has to be here."

The two women looked around. Trees and dirt. Patches of grass. Stumps. Not even a string of barbed wire or a fencepost.

Jo's dress fluttered against her leggings.

Fenn scratched her ribs under her Rancid shirt.

The clearing was the size of a baseball field.

The highway had led to a gravel road. The gravel went to dirt. The dirt thinned to two faded ruts. Then the pines opened and they were in the clearing and the ear stopped glowing.

After thirty minutes of aimless walking, Fenn turned off the headlights and Jo heard her mutter about goddamn dying in the dark, but saving the effin' battery just in case.

Jo was pissed. Pissed at herself for not knowing what to do next. Pissed at Wilkes that even his stupid ear could screw her over. She turned in a circle with the ear in her upturned palm. Nothing.

"Hey!" Fenn said.

"Huh?"

"Know who might know what to do right now?"

"Huh?"

"*Your mom.* Let's call her."

"No."

"Not even to see why the ear won't work?"

"No."

"This blows."

"You're not helping."

"Yep. Hey, did you shoot Wilkes? You did, right?"

An owl screeched in the trees and Fenn's hand moved to the Smith and Wesson at the small of her back.

There was a crunching noise.

"I got him in the arm."

"There's something here."

Jo looked at Fenn, annoyed.

"Seriously, yo. I heard . . . crunching," Fenn said.

"Where?"

A Willow Man ran out of the woods.

"There."

Not a Willow Man.

Six willow men.

Red and repulsive, stretched and swollen. Soggy, wobble-shuffling, rotted bodies that looked like they'd mated with vines.

Fenn smiled.

Jo gagged.

The smell of bad eggs, dumpster grit and sulfur filled the air.

"Get to the car," Fenn hissed.

"But—"

The crunching. It was their muscles. Rubbing together. Tearing. A neck cracking, pepper-grinding noise.

Fenn rushed forward.

Jo ran back.

Fenn crossed the clearing and leg-swept the first Hieronymus Bosch beast, three feet taller than her. She knelt on its thin, clotted chest and chopped through all the cords that attached its head.

Jo didn't make it to the car.

The dirt shifted.

Skeletal appendages stretched out of the earth. Thousands of them. Fingers here. Hands there. Shins. Arms. Pieces. Remains. Shoving. Grabbing. Pushy little bastards.

The willow head rolled and hit a tree stump and the Giger-reject backhanded Fenn with one long, unjointed arm.

A bone-hand tried to pull Fenn's foot underground. Another went for her arm.

"What the hell?"

"Groundfolk," Jo shouted, then swatted a dead arm off her leg. A disembodied skull unburied itself and Jo kicked it across the clearing.

The five other grotesques gathered around Fenn.

There was a shotgun in the trunk. A baseball bat. A crowbar, too. And half a field of bones between Jo and the Oldsmobile.

A jilted Gunther von Hagens project grabbed Fenn and lifted her face to face.

Jo ran for the car.

Fenn planted her knife in the thing's forehead, then she twisted from its grip, slicing its body apart with her weight on the way down.

The halves, still connected at the top of the skull, slithered a V and attacked Fenn's feet.

Jo swerved around the pinchers. The goosers. The crowding Groundfolk.

Fenn wore bigass boots for a reason.

"*I.*" She stomped. "*Will.*" Stomp. "*Kill.*" Stomp. "*You.*"

Bones shattered. The beast howled.

Four standing, two down, none dead. The downed ones still twitched, looked like they might be able to knit themselves back together given enough time.

"Oh come on!" Fenn yelled as she chopped a foot off one and shot a globular eye out of another, only to have them both get up again. She backhanded a ground-arm hitting her ass with a jawbone.

Jo had the trunk open.

A bone-arm slammed it closed.

Others clawed the back of Jo's calves, shredding her leggings.

"Stupid pieces of crap." Jo grabbed a bone and swung it at the other Groundfolk. A ribcage split and skittered in two directions. Others slunk into the soil, only to reappear two feet farther.

Jo popped the trunk again and grabbed the shotgun.

Another skull tried to bite through her boot.

"*Yee* and *haw*!" Fenn yelped twenty yards away. She rode a tottering creature's shoulders. Fenn wrapped a razor-wire garrote around its neck.

Two others ripped her shirt and scraped her back trying to ply her off their friend. Their hands were slick as skinned ferrets. Sharp. Splat. Scratch.

The last Willow Man noticed Jo.

Fenn pulled the garrote tight. She jumped over its shoulder, planted her feet on its chest and leaned backwards.

The head came off and piked itself on a Groundfolk elbow. Fenn fell into the arms of one of the petulant puke-trees who'd ripped her shirt to tatters. She put her gun in its mouth, pulled the trigger and red meat exploded all over her face. The remaining Willow Man put her in a headlock. Fenn's back was to its gurgling chest.

Jo didn't like the Willow Man watching her.

"Shoot that shit," Fenn barked as she tried to get her elbow unstuck from her headlocker's ribs.

Jo let fly and the blast frayed the monster's thigh.

The willow thing stumbled. Spluttered. Screeched.

Fenn twisted to a panda-hug on the shithead's side and began to carve. She'd chop the MF-er in half.

The Groundfolk sucked themselves under the dirt. Every single one. Then they slammed themselves upward. The clearing exploded in earth-clods and gray bones.

Jo ducked the falling bones. Fenn got smacked on the neck with a femur. Then a pelvis.

That's when Jo saw the black, frothing hole near where a hip should've been on the Willow Man.

The Groundfolk poked. Nudged. Punched.

The Willow Man towered over Jo. Its half-torn thigh made it stand crooked.

Jo aimed for the hip hole and pulled the trigger.

He, it, exploded.

All over.

And didn't get back up.

"Sick." Jo pulled a tendon chunk out of her hair that knuckle-cracked and chuffed.

"Fuckin' how?" Fenn yelled.

"Black thing at its hip! Hit that!"

"Oh, I'll hit that."

Bone-arms clicked against each other. The Groundfolk snapped. Scraped. Worried one another's limbs. A wind knocked half of them over.

There were five shots.

Jo looked up and Fenn was covered in dirt, blood and meat clumps.

Fenn kicked the Groundfolk out of her way.

"Dude, I got to use my garrote! Then you lone driftered into town, and found the explode button, and we kicked ass!"

Jo held up her hand.

Fenn high-fived it.

Jo frowned at her stained dress. It'd been her favorite.

Fenn pogoed and clusters of chirping meat fell out of her hair. She picked a lump out of her bra.

The Groundfolk let the women have a small circle.

"Is this what happens when you don't feed the box on time?" Fenn asked.

"No. It's only midnight. We have till sunrise."

The Groundfolk clapped in mock-approval.

"My mom used to tell me stories to make sure I didn't screw with it. Snake floods, dour witches, Ebola, Groundfolk, mass poisonings, ant storms, hordes of ravens bashing themselves against people."

Fenn squatted by the meat mess in front of Jo. She nudged it with her pocket knife.

"Think we could make jerky outta them and infomercial it for megabucks to rich pricks interested in the occult? Be all, *Demon willow meat, bitches!*"

"Got to burn them," Jo said.

"Why?"

"Hunch."

"Like shooting at their hip things?"

"Yeah."

"'Kay, but you're buying me a new everything," Fenn said and shimmied her now-fringed shirt. Part of the drippings landed on Jo's shoes. "Guh. That hurt. How's my back?"

"Gross," Jo said after a look. "That crap .38 Special shoulder tattoo you got is totally scraped up. Nothing looks too deep."

"Freakin' hurts."

"Whiner."

"I repeat: this blows. Make that effin' ear work."

Before Jo pulled the ear from her pocket, the sky brightened a couple miles past the clearing's edge.

"We go that way," Jo said.

The Groundfolk were tired. They opened a path.

"Yes, ma'am," Fenn said and followed her friend into the woods.

"Am I seeing what I think I'm seeing?" Fenn asked.

The two women had followed the light through the pines, over a hill and come upon another, smaller clearing.

"If you're seeing the 1991 horse-diving drama, *Wild Hearts Can't be Broken*, playing at a homemade drive-in, then yes, you are seeing what I'm seeing, Fenn."

"Dude, how'd you know the year it came out?"

"Shut up."

"So, we going down there?"

"Yes."

"What if Wilkes has back-up?"

"You'll kill them, too."

"Sweet," Fenn said.

They walked into the drive-in.

"He's in there," Jo said with a nod to the concession shack.

"Whoever painted the hotdog and popcorn men sucked." Fenn pointed to the anthropomorphic food people adorning the shack's walls.

"If Wilkes is here, why isn't he killing us?" Jo asked.

"Guess he wasn't expecting two hot bitches covered in dead-man-willow-blood to walk outta the woods," Fenn said and took a step forward.

The concession shack swayed left. Creaked right.

Red light blared out of the cracks.

Brown liquid flushed out.

Someone in the shack gave a ragged, guttural yowl.

"After you," Jo said.

"Hmph." Fenn took another step.

The shack slammed forward. It moved about an inch.

The brown liquid continued to flood the field.

It was chunky. It quickly reached ankle high.

"Aww," Jo said, "These aren't watertight."

"Mine either." Fenn frowned down at her jump boots. Eight years old and full of holes.

Weevils and earwigs swam through the torrent. Skin molts and larvae clouded it. More than a few unidentifiable insects hopped the water top.

"What if that's not even Wilkes?" Fenn asked.

"It's him."

"It could be the redneck sex-hole family."

"Quit it."

"Now, can we call your mom?"

"No."

The shack stopped shaking.

The Dutch door half opened.

"Who's there?" said a tired voice.

"That's Wilkes," Jo said. She readjusted the shotgun on her shoulder and lightly swung the crowbar with her other hand.

Fenn drew her boot knife.

"Who's there?" Wilkes repeated.

"Screw you, jerk," Jo yelled.

A husky moan came from behind Wilkes and ended in a bronchial cough.

"Oh, it's you, Jo," Wilkes said. "Hold on."

He shut the Dutch door.

"The crawlies in the whatever-we're-standing-in are eating my boots. Might we move out of the gush?" Fenn asked.

"There is no out of the gush."

"Up there." Fenn pointed to the top of the shack with her knife.

The sound of splintering wood and saturated heaving came from inside, followed by a loud hiccup and a *thwack-wack-thud*.

"Bad idea," Jo said.

"Whatevs. Not getting eatin' by hell-bugs. Doin' it." Fenn ran through the brown tide.

Jo sprinted after. She threw the crowbar onto the shed roof.

Fenn cupped her hands, Jo stepped in and Fenn shoved upward. Jo scrambled onto the tin roof, hung her arms down and helped Fenn up.

"Good view of the movie, eh?" Fenn said.

Jo ignored the comment and scraped the pest-gush off her palms.

"Dude, I totally chopped off alotta heads tonight." Fenn smiled and pried a large hole in the tin roof.

"Yeah, your parole officer'd be real proud."

Red light spilled out of the hole.

The shack wavered.

The light faded to a dull yellow.

The smell of lavender-rubbed wounds and salt filled the air. And buzzing.

Fenn looked inside the roof hole.

A woman was duct-taped to a chair. Her stomach was cut open and the box was shoved inside.

The woman opened her mouth.

The buzzing grew louder.

"Ef," Fenn said and rolled away.

A stream of cockroaches barreled out until a cloud hung over the shack.

Wilkes yelped.

"Your ex has an old broad with the box shoved into her belly," Fenn said. She flicked a line of cockroaches off Jo's shoulder.

"Seriously?"

"Yep."

The cockroaches climbed on Jo's leg instead.

"Wilkes," Jo said, staring into the hole.

"What?" Wilkes sobbed.

There was a *Thwack. Wack. Umph.*

"What are you doing in there?"

"Don't want to—" *Whump.* "—talk about it," Wilkes said as he hit mysterious lumps in the brown water.

"Don't want to talk about it," a lilting voice mimicked.

Fenn looked in the hole.

The popcorn maker was still on. Puttering.

Grub worms leaked from the taped woman's unblinking left eye. Her hands began to bloat and twitch.

Wilkes swatted waves of grubs away from him.

"I need that box back," Jo said calmly.

"Can't give it to you," Wilkes said and sniffed. "It's stuck."

"In the woman?" Jo asked.

"In my mom."

"I'll put it in your mom," Fenn muttered.

"Shut up!" Wilkes screamed.

"Not helping," Jo hissed.

Fenn stood up and crunched cockroaches on the roof.

The cockroach cloud above Fenn disapproved and dive-bombed her.

"Shit, okay, Christ," Fenn said to the bugs. "Sorry."

She stopped stomping and the cockroaches stopped swarming.

"Wilkes, why is my box in your mom?"

"She was dead."

"Uh—"

"I made her better."

"There is no better from dead," Jo said.

"I know that now."

The roof shuttered. Fenn caught Jo before she rolled into the hole. Twelve cockroaches were smashed.

The cloud swarmed Fenn again.

"Fuck tonight, man," Fenn yelled. She stood still. Her back hurt like hell. Last thing she needed was goddamn cockroaches laying eggs in her scratches.

The cockroach cloud dissipated.

The roof creaked.

"Why is the box in your mom?" Jo tried again.

"I need her," Wilkes said and rubbed his forehead with his fists.

His mother's breasts swelled under her shirt.

Wilkes pointed his shovel at them.

Two mole rats burrowed out, bloody-toothed, and flopped into the brown gush.

Wilkes punched himself in the side of the head and sobbed again.

"It can't do that," Jo said.

"It did," Wilkes said. "She ate popcorn and said she missed me."

He looked at his mother. She blinked at him. A grub

worm fell. Wilkes looked at the roof. "She said her stomach hurt. I was getting her a drink of water and then shit flooded out of her mouth and her eyes went red so I duct taped her to the chair and freaked the fuck out. Okay?"

"How'd you know about the box, dickslag?" Fenn said.

"Dick what? What does that even mean? Fuck you."

Fenn thrust her boot knife into the hole. "See this? I'ma cut you with this."

"Oh yeah, girl? I'm real scared of a knife when my mom recently threw up two thousand pounds of insects."

He backed up against the wall as far from his mother as he could get.

"How did you know about the box?" Jo asked.

"My family used to be Keepers," Wilkes said.

Fenn looked in the cockroach hole.

"When?" Jo asked.

"You should know," Wilkes said. "Your family took the box from us."

"Your family caused the possessions?" Jo asked.

"What effin' possessions?" Fenn asked.

"1590, the men of Roanoke," Jo said.

"Their eyes turned white, their bodies went veiny and stuff kept trying to break free of their skin," Wilkes tiredly said.

"What le ef?" Fenn asked.

Jo took over. "They lost the use of their voices except for howls and grunts. They worshipped random trees. They attacked livestock, fisted holes into cows and ate them."

"Figures he'd come from cow-fisters," Fenn said.

"Shut up!" Wilkes punched the ceiling again. It sagged further.

There was a chirring. A groan. Then Wilkes's mother opened her mouth and said, "The women gathered the children. My boys found them. Everyone died. All of them eaten. My boys fit down their gullets what they could then threw what was left in the sea." Wilkes's mom sniffed a worm back into her nose and continued, "My boys burned themselves in boats so their bones wouldn't be found."

"Who was that?" Fenn said.

"My mom," Wilkes said.

"My mom," Wilkes's mother imitated. Then added, "I wanted *proper* blood."

Jo said, "A woman cut the palm of her baby and put it to the box instead of using her own hand. She had TB and didn't want to lose any more blood."

"Didn't like it," pouted Wilkes's mother. "Tasted like apples and fish."

"So you killed a freakin' colony over bad baby blood?" Fenn asked.

"Then I found one of Jo's great-great-whoevers in a fruit cellar, didn't I, my wittle, cutie-pootie-pie?" Her voice turned to a huffing rattle.

Jo nodded at Fenn.

Wilkes cowered further into the corner.

"Tasted like cherries and sunsets."

"How'd his family survive?" Fenn asked.

"Nobody's perfect," said Wilkes's mother.

"John White left Roanoke for supplies," said Jo. "He got back and everyone was gone. Wilkes, your last name is White, eh?"

"Yeah, Jo. It is."

"It is," parroted his mom.

Her chest-mole-holes leaked the brown that, formerly, belonged to her mouth.

"Jo," Wilkes said.

"What?"

"I might be sorry."

"Sorry, sorry," sung his mother.

"Screw sorry. Give Jo the box back," Fenn said.

Wilkes looked up. "I told you. It's stuck."

Jo and Fenn balanced on a roof that was now more not there than there.

"I tried."

"Not hard enough, jackass." Fenn dropped through the opening into the shack.

There were ticks in the water. The shack shuddered. The cockroach cloud plunged back inside Wilkes's mother. Her stomach ballooned outward and then flattened.

Fenn was knee-deep in revulsions. Two naked mole rats swam past her. They struggled. Their heads were heavy and kept dunking under.

"Fenn?" Jo said.

"I'm okay." Fenn spread open her fingers to crack them. She drew two knives from her thighs.

Fenn itched everywhere. Freakin' everywhere. She was gonna strip naked and rub against a goddamn tree when this was done.

"Get over here, asshole," Fenn said to Wilkes.

He climbed over his popcorn sack stack.

Fenn made a fist around one of her knife grips and punched Wilkes in the face.

He fell back with a splash.

"*Bitch!*" Wilkes held a hand to his split eyebrow. He shouldn't have. A tick climbed in the split.

Brown liquid poured out of Wilkes's mom.

"Fenn, there's no time," Jo said.

"That was for Jo's eye and my achin' back." Fenn added, "Jo, you watch his freakass ma."

Wilkes' mother sang, "*Watch me, watch, watch.*" Her hands fluttered. Jazz hands.

"Get up," Fenn told Wilkes.

"You going to hit me again?"

"On three, I'ma cut up your mom and you're gonna pull out that box and throw it to Jo."

Wilkes got up and stood in front of his mother.

Her body chittered and trembled.

The skin had grown tight and puckered around the box.

"At the end of 'go, go, GO,'" Fenn said.

"Fine," said Wilkes.

"Ready." Jo waited at the edge.

"Go . . . go . . . Go!"

Fenn pulled down her blades and cut each side around the box in less than three seconds.

Wounds can't babble, but these did.

Wilkes pulled the box free and threw it over his head.

"Got it!" Jo said.

It felt lighter than it was supposed to.

Wilkes's mom cheeped and quaked.

Then her swollen arm broke free from the tape.

And the other.

She stood.

"Go!" Wilkes said and shoved Fenn, hard.

He broke the lantern that hung by the door.

The brown gush caught fire.

Fenn fell through the Dutch door into the muck.

The naked mole rats followed after.

Wilkes's mother grabbed his one ear and rammed his face into the hole in her stomach.

A scream doesn't sound like a scream when it's buried in a body.

"Fenn," yelled Jo.

The chittering turned to glugging as Wilkes's mother filled his body with something. Something small. Something vibrating.

Wilkes thrashed.

Fenn stood up.

The concession shack burned.

Jo jumped off the roof.

Wilkes quit struggling. Things prickled in his mouth. In his stomach. He was weighted down. Things squirmed in his legs.

His mother smiled with her eyes closed, hands firmly holding his face to her guts.

Fenn shot Wilkes in the back of the head.

Jo watched as something crawled out of the hole.

Wilkes's mother grinned at Fenn and Jo.

"Can we go?" Fenn asked.

Jo shook the box. "I don't know. It's not heavy enough."

"I'll be home soon, moonpie," Wilkes's mom said to Jo.

The fire surged forward.

"Now. We go, now." Fenn dragged Jo through the bog water, over the hill, and into the woods.

The three miles felt like ten.

The Groundfolk left a clear path.

The earth sucked the bones up as Jo ran past.

The black box felt heavier as they entered the clearing.

Jo dropped it, walked two steps then fell over.

Fenn slumped against the car five feet away. She winced when her back touched the wheel well.

"We are not getting into the Oldsmobile like this," Fenn said.

"Got to."

"Gotta burn them first," Fenn shucked a thumb to the red Willow Men.

"Look," Jo said.

The forest was a fast-acting inferno. The fire was at the edge of the clearing.

"Get in." Fenn sighed.

Jo picked up the box. Barely. It was stupid heavy. She got in.

"You are on tick-duty." Fenn handed Jo her Swiss Army knife.

The engine turned over on the second try.

The car smelled like a rotting t-rex even with the windows rolled down.

"You got your box back," Fenn said as she pulled onto the two-rut road.

"I did."

"And we didn't die."

"We didn't."

"Is *it* in there now?"

"Yes."

"Is everything gonna be number-one-A-okay when you feed it?"

"Yes."

"How do you know?"

"Just do."

Fenn nodded.

Jo extricated a tick out of Fenn's cheek.

"Guh. Watch the money-maker, girl."

The black box gave a short purr.

Both women ignored it.

"I feel bad about the massive forest fire."

"Mmhmm," Jo said.

"'Kay. I'ma put it out there," Fenn said. "Why the ef would Wilkes think that he could bring his goddamn mom back from the dead?"

"No idea, but it kinda worked."

"You aren't okay, are you?" Fenn asked.

"No, I'm not.

"What now?"

Jo looked down at the box, then at Fenn.

"I'm going to call my mom."

FALCO WRECK

RAYMOND LITTLE

MANHATTAN—1983

JOSH WINCED WHEN he saw his old friend for the first time in two years. "What the fuck happened to you? You look like shit."

"Thanks," Sam said. "Nice to see you too, buddy."

"Hey, sorry, man. Come in." Josh led him through the apartment to the slick minimalist kitchen. "Coffee?"

Sam forced a smile that revealed a broken front tooth as he eased himself onto a stool. "You got anything stronger?"

"Sure." Josh ignored the urge to point out the fact it was ten in the morning as he grabbed a beer from the refrigerator and placed it on the counter before settling himself opposite his pal. "It's good to see you."

"Yeah?"

He watched Sam pull the ring with trembling fingers before tipping the can to his mouth. Of the old gang, Sam had always been the one to take everything to excess—alcohol, drugs, sex—but he'd had an air of invincibility about him, like a force field held together by his good looks and charisma. Josh could find no resemblance between that person and the shambling mess sat across from him now. His clothes were crumpled and stained, but worse than that was his face—aged, grey and gaunt. A thin, weeping scab ran from his left temple in a curve to his chin and his right eyelid was purple and swollen.

Sam lowered the beer for a moment and glanced around. "Nice place. Where's Penny?"

"At the hospital. She's on early shift."

"You married yourself a good one there. Heart of gold."

Josh leaned his elbows on the counter and lowered his voice. "Are you in some kind of trouble?"

"You could say that."

"Serious?"

Sam took another swig from the can, his gaze fixed on Josh. "I'm afraid I have some bad news, buddy. Real bad." The tremble in his hands worked its way into his voice. "It's Wes. He's dead."

Josh felt his stomach lurch as if he'd just dropped over the hump of the world's largest rollercoaster. "Shit. What happened?"

"The official word is that it was suicide."

"No." Josh thought of Wes, sweet natured, generous Wes. He'd last seen him six months or so before. Wes had called while on a business trip to the city, so the two of them had met up and hit the bars just like the old days. It was a good night, and he'd seemed happy. "I don't believe it."

"And you'd be right not to. Wes didn't kill himself."

"What are you saying?"

"I'm saying he was murdered. And I know who did it."

Josh studied his friend's battered features. When he spoke at last he realized that his voice had dropped to a gruff whisper. "Who killed him?"

"The same one who did this . . . " Sam touched the gash on his face. "And this . . . " he pointed to his blackened eye. "And this . . . " he undid his jacket and pulled his shirt up to reveal a mesh of crisscrossed lacerations cut deep into his torso. Blood oozed from an inverted circle where his left nipple should have been. "Our old friend Falco Wreck is back."

Josh felt his shoulders slump. He should have said it was impossible; Falco had been dead for twenty years. But he knew as well as Sam did that as far as Falco Wreck was concerned, nothing was inconceivable.

BOW CREEK, VERMONT—1962

"It's not just about the smoke," Sam said, his cigarette held loose between two fingers in a casual pose he took for sophistication. "It's about how you do it." He took a long drag, tipped his head back and blew a thin line of blue from his slightly pursed lips.

"Yeah, that's really cool." Josh nodded. "You look just like Betty Davis."

Wes spat a mouthful of Dr. Pepper onto the river bank to stop from choking. "Josh is right," he said when he'd stopped laughing. "You look like a dork."

"You two just wait and see." Sam smiled. "I'll be the one with my hands up Wendy May's sweater next term."

Josh exchanged a glance with Wes and raised his eyebrows. The two of them were in agreement on the dumb-assedness of smoking. If anyone was going to have any success with Wendy Big-Jugs though, Josh guessed it would be Sam. For a thirteen year old, Sam had an easiness in the company of girls beyond his years. To Josh, the opposite sex was still somewhat a mystery. He checked his watch. "Shit, I gotta go."

"Hey, come on." Sam flicked his butt into the river. "The fish are just starting to bite."

Josh pulled his line in and looked at the purple sky.

"What's the matter? Afraid of the dark?"

"Hey, leave him alone," Wes said. He looked at Josh. "You'd better get going."

"Yeah," Sam said. "And if you see that little freak, tell him to go fuck himself."

Josh forced a smile. "See you tomorrow." He rested his rod on his shoulder and set off at a pace, annoyed at Sam for being unfair, annoyed at himself for being such a pussy. It was okay for those two; they lived on Maple Drive on the western edge of town. They didn't have to go by the Wreck place.

He followed the curve of the river and glanced over his shoulder to check he was out of sight of his two friends before he started to jog. He could have cut through the woods and saved ten minutes, but there was no way he was setting foot in there alone. He skirted the edge of the trees until he'd circled them to the point where they met Pole Hill Road and stopped to catch his breath. At the top of the road—which was no more than an unmade dust track—sat a solitary white-painted building. The Wreck house. Josh scanned it, paying particular attention to the various angles of the rooftop where the little freak most often perched, but he was nowhere in sight.

The daylight faded a degree, and Josh noticed the low gray clouds rolling in from the west. He forced his legs to move and walked fast, aware of the noise of his own breathing and the soft tread of his sneakers on the dusty earth. He neared the Wreck place, staying close to the bushes that edged the road on its left to keep as much distance between himself and the house on his right. Deep shadows began to grow beneath the porch and the white-painted cladding turned violet in the encroaching twilight.

He was almost past the house, had almost let himself believe there would be no incident, when movement caught his eye. He shot a glance upwards and there, crouched like a cat on the front apex of the roof, was Falco Wreck. It was crazy to be frightened of a ten-year-old boy who had never done anything more than stare at him and whisper, but the kid gave him the creeps. It was too dark to see his features, but Josh knew he'd be grinning, his little teeth as white as his face, his shoulder length hair as black as coal. And there were the rumours. He looked away as the familiar whisper came to him on the breeze.

"*Look at me.*"

Josh concentrated on the track ahead.

"*Look what I can do.*"

That time, the whisper had been harsh, menacing, but worse than that, it hadn't come from the roof.

"*Look.*"

Josh turned and looked into the eyes of the boy standing six feet behind him.

"*Let me show you.*" Falco flicked his thick, pointed tongue in and out of his lips like a rattler tasting the air and grinned.

"No," Josh managed. He tried to turn away, but his body felt old and heavy as he looked into the child's eyes.

Falco came toward him, though he seemed to take no steps. "Look," he repeated. The black of his pupils grew until it engulfed his eyeballs, and Josh felt himself pulled to the edge of a cold dark void that made him gasp. "Just a taste, for now," the boy said, and the universe of black receded at his command until Josh was able to move at last. He stumbled backward, shamefully aware of the damp warmth spreading down the inside of his thigh, and whipped his fishing rod out in a wide arc.

Falco touched his fingertips to the cut on his cheek left by the rod's tip and smiled. "*One day, the penny will drop.*"

Josh turned and ran for home, the shallow, unreal laughter of Falco Wreck following him on the breeze.

BROOKLYN—1983

"Hey, here he is, Mr. No-Show."

Sam closed the front door and peered into the dim corridor. "Hello, Mrs. Martello."

"Hello nothing, you owe me a month's rent."

"Don't worry, I'm good for it." He passed the old lady by and climbed the creaking staircase. "I'll drop by the bank tomorrow."

"Tomorrow, tomorrow, always tomorrow."

Sam ignored her and felt for his key as he reached his first floor two-room.

"And by the way," he heard her call as he let himself in, "you look like shit!"

He flicked the light switch and kicked his way through empty cartons and beer cans to the bed, lifting a half-finished bottle of bourbon from the bureau as he passed. The room was a tip—worse even than its usual state—but tidying seemed to be a battle he could never win. He unscrewed the lid and caught sight of his reflection in the full-length mirror opposite as he sat on the bed. The old lady was right. His face was a mess but at least it drew the eye from his ill-fitting black suit and tie. He took a swig from the bottle and raised it to his reflection. "Here's to you, Wes. Sleep well, buddy."

"Here's to you, Wes. Sleep well buddy."

Sam shot a glance up at the far side of the room where the voice—a perfect mimic of his own—had come from. In the corner, hanging from a noose, swung the naked body of his recently buried pal. The bottle slipped from Sam's hand with a thud onto the rug as Wes, his face bloated and blue, turned one bulging eye to look at him. Sam clapped his palms over his eyes. "No! You're not real!"

"Look at me."

The voice had changed to the whisper of a small boy. Sam dropped his hands. Levitating in the corner, where the vision of Wes had been, was Falco Wreck, still ten years old, his black hair hanging over the sides of his pale face.

Sam had begun to sob. "Please, not again."

"Get the knife."

Sam opened the bedside cabinet drawer and pulled out the large carving knife, blood stained from its previous usage on his torso.

"Put your hand on the cabinet."

"Please, I'm begging you," Sam said as he followed the boy's orders.

Falco flashed his little white teeth in a grin. "Now, cut."

It took a while, but with a lot of sawing and hacking, Sam managed to remove his hand.

BOW CREEK, VERMONT—1962

The three boys clambered over the wall and dropped onto the long grass on a blazing August afternoon. Josh felt light in his head and grabbed onto the nearest gravestone to steady himself. A hand touched his shoulder.

"You okay?"

"Yeah, I'm fine." He forced a smile for Wes.

"We don't have to do this."

"Like fuck we don't," Sam said as he strode ahead. "Come on, I know exactly where it is."

Wes raised his eyebrows.

"I'm okay, really," Josh said, though he'd been far from all right since his encounter with the Wreck boy three weeks before. The five days immediately after the incident he'd suffered a fever that had kept him bedridden. He'd told nobody exactly what had happened with Falco, though his parents caught snatches from his sleep talking that they'd put down to illness-induced delirium. The slashes down his forearms that he'd kept concealed would have been harder to explain. "Come on."

The two of them followed Sam through the uncut grass between the weathered, lopsided gravestones of the old part of the cemetery.

"It's just bullshit, anyway," Wes said. "A stupid old story to scare the kids."

Sam glanced over his shoulder. "It ain't bullshit, and I'm gonna prove it."

They stepped through a gate into the well-tended new part of the burial ground, and Josh began to regret being there. Even if what Sam had told them was true, he wasn't sure he wanted it proved to him.

Sam stopped, counted the stones along the row they were

in and pointed. "Over there." He led them diagonally across the graves and knelt at a small moss covered slab. Josh and Wes dropped to their knees on either side of him.

"Wipe it off," Josh said. He watched Sam pull and scrape the moss away and felt sick at the simple lettering when it was at last revealed.

FALCO WRECK 1931-1941

"Shit," Sam whispered as if he'd surprised himself. "It *is* true."

"It don't mean anything," Wes said. "It's just a relative with the same name."

Sam shook his head. "It's him. My uncle Ted told me all about it. Falco died in his sleep, real sudden. Then, sometime after he was buried, people round town started seeing him around the Wreck place. You know Mrs. Wreck? She ain't his Mom. She's his little sister. But he ain't aged in the last twenty years."

"So what?" Wes asked. "You saying he's a ghost?"

"What else?"

Josh swallowed. "He ain't no ghost. I don't know what he is, but he's flesh and blood, just like us. I cut his cheekbone good when I whipped him with my rod."

"So who's to say ghosts can't bleed? Whatever that little freak is, we're gonna find out."

Josh felt goose-bumps break out on his arms. "How're we gonna do that?"

Sam stood and popped a cigarette between his lips. "We're going to ask him."

MANHATTAN—1983

"How's he doing?"

"Not good. He lost a lot of blood." Penny brushed back a stray lock from her husband's brow and kissed him on the cheek. "We're doing our best for him."

"I know." Josh hugged her. "Can I see him?"

"For a few minutes. He needs rest."

Josh pushed open the door and crept into the dimly lit hospital room. Sam was propped in the bed, oxygen mask on his face. Various drips surrounded him, pumping the necessary fluids into his veins, and a heart monitor beeped by his shoulder. The bandaged stump of his left arm protruded to one side, suspended in a harness.

Sam opened his eyes as Josh approached and pulled down the mask. "Hey," he croaked.

"Hey." Josh reached down and placed his palm on the back of Sam's right hand. A lump stuck in his throat at the sorry site of his old pal.

"Don't tell me . . . " Sam paused to run his tongue over his dry lips. "I look like shit."

"You've looked better."

"Thank Penny for me. She's the best." He closed his eyes for a few moments. "How did I end up here anyway?"

"I had you transferred. This is the best place in New York."

"And the most expensive. I'm broke, in case you didn't know."

"Don't worry. I've taken care of it." Josh felt Sam's hand turn and grip onto his fingers.

"You have to listen to me, Josh. He's going to come for you. He killed Wes, and he'll kill me when he's finished having his fun. Then he'll come for you."

Josh leaned close and lowered his voice. "Wes hung himself, Sam. And you—"

"I know. I cut my own hand off. But don't kid yourself. When he shows you the darkness, you got no choice."

Josh couldn't disagree. He remembered too well his encounter with Falco Wreck when he was a boy and how it had left him with a fever and the urge to scratch his arms with a piece of broken glass. And he'd been given only a glimpse.

"And the more he shows you," Sam continued, 'the more you want to harm yourself. The blackness gets inside you." He closed his eyes.

"Sam, what is the blackness? What can I do to stop him?"

"The blackness is him." Sam opened his eyes and coughed. "So dry . . . "

"Hang on." Josh wet his lips with a damp wad from the side table.

"It's so big, Josh, and so heavy, it's unbearable. And when it gets inside you . . . "

"It's okay, man." Josh held onto his friend's hand. "Sam, you've got to tell me. What can I do?"

Sam closed his eyes again and began to drift, taken by the morphine and codeine. "There's nothing you can do," he slurred. "You're fucked. We're all fucked."

BOW CREEK, VERMONT—1962

Josh glanced west at the disappearing sun and zipped up his jacket. The whole thing was a bad idea, but once Sam had made his mind up on something there was no talking him out of it.

"The lights are turning on," Wes whispered.

Across from the boys' hiding place in the bushes by the dirt road, a room that Josh guessed was the kitchen in the Wreck place shone yellow. The silhouette of a woman, her hair in a bun, crossed back and forth before disappearing from view. Further lights appeared in the rear downstairs rooms.

"What do we do?" Josh asked, trying to hide the tremble in his voice.

"We wait," Sam said.

They didn't have to wait for long. Within five minutes, as the evening sky turned a deep bruised purple, a small boy emerged from an attic window onto the roof and scampered on all fours to the front apex.

"Come on," Sam said, and the three of them stepped through the bush. A childish giggle floated down to them.

"He's seen us," Josh said.

"Good." Sam strode across the dust road onto the front lawn of the old white house. Josh and Wes exchanged a glance and followed. "Hey," Sam hissed.

Falco Wreck looked down at him and cocked his head to one side.

"Come down. We want to talk."

Josh looked at the kitchen window, afraid that Mrs. Wreck would hear them, but she was still in a back room. When he looked back at the roof Falco was standing straight up, his arms held out from his sides as if to keep his balance.

"Come down," Sam repeated. "We want to ask you something."

Falco looked down at Sam, smiled, and began to tilt forward.

"What's he doing?" Wes whispered.

Josh took a step back. "I don't know."

Falco continued to tilt, his whole body straight, until he was hanging from the roof at an impossible forty-five degree angle. All three boys began to back away.

"Not fucking possible," Sam muttered.

"Come on," Josh tugged at his friends' sleeves. "We need to get out of here."

"What are you?" Sam asked.

"Why don't I just show you?"

Josh squeezed his eyes shut. "Don't look at him!" The silence he received in reply from his buddies told him all he needed to know; Falco's eyes would be black and Sam and Wes would be paralyzed on the edge of the dark abyss. He turned away, opened his eyes, scanned the lawn, and saw what he wanted. He took three strides, scooped the baseball sized stone in his hand, swiveled and pitched it upward with all his strength. The rock bounced of Falco's temple with a dull thud. The spell on Sam and Wes was broken immediately and they regained their senses in time to hear the sickening snap of the strange boy's neck as he hit the lawn head first.

"Black . . . " Wes uttered as he dropped to his knees, a drool of saliva hanging from the corner of his mouth.

"It's okay, it's okay," Sam said, to no one in particular.

Josh approached the bent body on the lawn. Falco's head was twisted further than was natural so that he was looking over his own shoulder, his dead eyes wide as if surprised at his own fate.

"I killed him," Josh whispered.

"Come on." Josh felt his elbow pulled. "We gotta get out of here."

"I killed him."

"Shut the fuck up!" Sam hissed. He yanked Wes to his feet. "You didn't kill him, Josh. He's been dead for fucking years."

Josh felt himself pushed and jostled until he found himself running alongside Sam and Wes. When they stopped at last at the back of old Bill Tyson's farm he dropped to his knees and threw up. He heard the sound of Wes sobbing nearby.

"Listen to me, both of you," Sam said. "We were fishing by the river, all evening. We were nowhere near the Wreck place. Everybody knows he's always fucking around on that roof. It'll just look like he fell and broke his neck."

"But I—"

"No buts," Sam said. "Whatever he was, he was fucking evil. He got what he deserved."

MANHATTAN—1983

The moment the phone rang in his apartment, Josh had a bad feeling.

"Josh?"

He felt his pace quicken at the tone of his wife's voice. It was flat, devoid of her usual bounce. "Penny, what's wrong?"

She began to sob.

"Penny, what's happened?"

"The boy came to see us. He's such a small boy."

"Are you still at the hospital?" Josh fought to stifle the panic in his voice. "Are you with Sam?" Penny was silent. In the background, Josh thought he heard a whispered voice. "Penny, who's there with you?"

"I'm in Sam's room. He's dead. I'm sorry, Josh."

"Penny, listen to me. You've got to get out of there. Go to the nurses' station, the reception, anywhere where there are other people."

"I killed him. The boy showed us the darkness. Oh, Josh, it was so heavy and so cold, and Sam begged me to do it. It was the only way."

"No, no, no." Josh ran a wrist across his damp cheeks, aware of the hopelessness growing in his gut. "Don't listen to the boy. Don't even look at him."

"There's so much blood. I cut him, and cut him. Poor Sam."

"Get out of there, Penny!"

"It's too late. The boy wants me to give you a message. He says to remember what he told you in Bow Creek." Her grief overcame her then, and she struggled to speak her last words. "Goodbye, Josh. I love you."

"No, Penny, wait!"

The line went dead, and Josh ran from the apartment, the words of Falco Wreck from all those years ago resounding in his mind:

One day, the penny will drop.

WHITSTABLE, ENGLAND—2013

The sea was calm, a red hue reflected over its surface from the fiery September evening sky. Josh took a long sip of his beer and looked down on the last of the beach-walkers from his seat on the wooden veranda of the Neptune Inn. The pub had begun to fill with diners and drinkers both inside and out—the blazing heat of the afternoon had turned into a humid evening with just a hint of breeze and the locals had descended onto the sprawling beachfront restaurant and bar to enjoy it. He glanced at his watch. The man hadn't made an appearance yet.

Josh pulled a pair of spectacles from the breast pocket of his jacket, slipped them on and opened the leather file on the table before him. He flicked through the reports, correspondences and photos, and retrieved a hand written note. It was dated from thirty years before, and though he'd read it so many times he could recite it word for word, he studied it once more. It was a short note, given to him several weeks after the funerals of Sam and Penny, released subsequent to the inquest into the death of Wesley Barnes. He held it under the glow from the little table lamp.

Dear Josh,

He is back, and he has shown me it all. I'm sure you and Sam are next. I know what he is. Falco Wreck is not a boy. He is the void that surrounds existence, the sheer nothingness, and it is so heavy and vast and cold. You will never understand until you have seen it, and once you have, life is unbearable. The layer between existence and the black void is paper thin. Life is so small a spark of light, and the dark, cold nothingness is so big. You can't beat it, buddy.

So long,

Wes—April 3rd 1983

Josh returned the sheet of paper to the folder. It was

more than a suicide note—it was a heads up from his old pal, despite the hopelessness he must have felt when he'd written it. It told Josh what he was up against and had served him well since that worst of nights in New York when Penny had thrown herself from the seventh floor window of Sam's hospital room after slashing him to death. The fact that the body of an unidentified young boy was found gripped in her embrace on the blood spattered sidewalk gave the newspapers added headline fodder for weeks.

It seemed that Penny had saved his life, or at least bought him some time. Falco Wreck had returned from death twice before that Josh knew of, and he was sure he'd be back again one day to finish what he'd started. He'd been gone for thirty years, though, and Josh hadn't wasted a moment. He drained his beer glass and nodded at the man who had sat opposite without a word. The man was young, and solemn, with an expression of hopelessness that Josh recognized. As the man opened his unseasonably heavy coat to retrieve an envelope, Josh saw the bloody cuts protruding over the white collar on the man's neck. His body would be covered in them.

"Her details," the man said. "And a photo."

Josh gripped the edge of the offered envelope, but the man held it tight. "You're doing the right thing," Josh assured him.

The man let it slip from his fingers and wiped a tear from his cheek. "God have mercy on us both." He rose from his seat and stalked away.

Josh opened the envelope. The photograph revealed a young woman, her hair a shock of red curls, her eyes dark and sultry. He turned it over and read her name on the back—Emily Keane—and her address. In smaller writing in the bottom right hand corner, the simple inscription, *Born 06/08/1970, Died 03/01/1995*, was set in brackets. He slipped it inside his leather folder.

Emily Keane. Dead since 1995 and yet still walking around this quaint little English seaside town. Josh added her name to the others he'd encountered. Jake Smith. William Hathaway. Mary Leone. Falco Wreck. He would kill her, just as he had the others. It wouldn't be permanent—they always came back—but it would give her victims a little more time.

The force that drove the darkness embodied in Falco Wreck and his kind was jealousy of life, of that Josh was sure. And Wes had been right; existence was such a tiny spark of light that could never win. But Josh would hold the dark tide back wherever he could, for he knew that every second gained for every soul on this side of the thin veil was another moment in paradise.

DREAMS IN A PINK LIGHT DISTRICT

KYLE S. JOHNSON

I WAS THERE again, a child window shopping, just looking, thanks. Trick-or-treating with a realistic mask, drawing stares. The women, bored and smoking, perking up as I passed, moving to me too late, going back to their waiting. My eyes were up this time, all whiskey confidence. Why was I there again? Curiosity for a dead cat, a lee from the wind, just because, because. As if thrown there by fate: a face, eyes on me, not judging, but expecting. Already on her feet, pressed against the glass, bathing in the harsh pink glow, the next in a long line of mistakes. She leaned out through the doorway, her voice a whisper, a shared secret: *hi*. She led me in and I didn't think twice. Guided me to a chair, so I sat. The parlor was small and sparsely decorated. A fan to take the edge off of the night's repulsive heat, some shelves with toiletries, a water cooler, pictures of dogs, cats, and Jesus tacked to the walls, and yeah. I asked her for her name, my Korean flimsy, shaky. Her confidence was a razor, *I speak English*, leaving it there. I asked her once more in my native tongue, no less flimsy, and she said I could call her Pick-Mi because I had. It was good enough. Somewhere nearby, the subway cars squealed and rumbled out of the station, packed with people going places that weren't small, quiet, pink-lit, or dangerous.

NIGHT TERRORS III

Pick-Mi was all legs in red thigh-high boots that climbed up under a skirt that did little to conceal, barely a lampshade. She jostled her pack, fished out a cigarette, offered me one. I shook my head, ever the choirboy. She sat close, those endless legs crossed and comfortable as she blew smoke rings into the pink light. Where to begin? Taking it slow, she rattled off her pitch, a bored, rote grimoire of *yes* and *no* and *do* and *don't*. A drunk staggered by outside, business suit and tennis shoes and bad hair, stopping and slouching and staring into our little cerise aquarium. He cupped his hands to the glass, peered in, scowled. Neither one of us were moved, all too accustomed to our fishbowls and our gawkers. Surly and mean, the *ajumma* bounded out of the darkness and shouted him into retreat with her fast talk. No fight left in him—it was Friday after all—and he was on to the next fish tank and the next bored display piece, look but don't touch. She repeated herself: *What do you want, military boy?*

She took my money up front and stuffed it into the front cover of a book whose Korean title I couldn't translate. Like a dime store horse rumbling to life, her face broke into a thin smile, a bit of put-on pleasure, all part of the package. So small a change, so vital to her configuration, and it was then that the voice in my head spoke in that whisper, the only voice I had left that didn't shout or bark. There's a sucker born every moment, love is Vaudeville, love is carny-rigged, but the lights had made it so easy to find, so cool inside. The birth of the next mistake, she took me by the hand and led me back, and it was over before I was aware of the night's hot drone. She had already won.

Behind the door: a red room, bed big enough for two, mostly empty wardrobe. Hearts on the wallpaper, my coat on the hangar. Twenty minutes, maybe more, since the last hot belt of Jameson, my confidence wearing off as she undressed casually, a wholly sexless act, while ridiculous questions and observations poured out of me. She laughed at it all, dismissively, until something I said stopped her cold. Sitting on the edge of the bed, her long red boot half slid off, her face upturned, scowl etched on: *Nobody forces me to do anything. Ever.* I apologized, but she wasn't ready to accept it yet. *You know, you're not the first to think he has to save me. I know you. You are not unique. A typical missionary. Rescue me from my primitive culture, make me an honest woman, take me to civilization, clean apartment and church on Sundays, the babies.* She'd practiced this, taught herself the words, still not perfect, but close. *Were you forced here, military boy? Did you have a choice? I want to be here. I chose this. I don't answer to a CO or the MP. I don't have curfew. I am freer than you could ever hope to be.* Feeling hot then, muscles twitchy and tingling, a hint of sweat creeping in cold, my quiet companion inside and whispering oh yes, she's the one indeed, she's always been. She, boot removed, new cigarette, blowing her smoke at me, checking her phone: *Look. You have twenty-seven minutes. Do you want to talk or do you want to do this?* I took the obvious choice. A steady fool, but nevertheless practical. Action did the talking for a while. Breathlessness. Weightlessness. Delirious movement, punctuated by a cold shame that I did my best to ignore. From within came the other voice, belonging to me but not my own, the one that didn't whisper, chiding me along.

Finished, laying there beside each other in red and sweat, my head swimming, still drunk, quite drunk, but what else was new. Checked my phone—23:58. It hadn't taken long at all. Time enough left. Quiet for a while, and she offered me a smoke again. I declined, and it was pushing play on a VCR, her argument resuming, *mise en scéne*, right at the good part. *Would you be here if you really had a choice?* I came here on my own, didn't I, and I picked you, Pick-Mi. *You know what I mean.* There are always circumstances, it's not like I was drafted into this. *And neither was I.* I wasn't insinuating—*I know perfectly well what you were trying to say, I'm not stupid, you know.* Yeah, I figured that much. *So you chose this country? Chose Korea?* No, but I chose the walk. Chose the street. Chose this box, this room, you. *Yes, you did. But so did I.* Maybe we aren't too different after all. Maybe I'd surprise you. *I doubt it._*

I tried to change tack then and there, seeing the pattern emerge, so I asked her where she learned her English. She took a moment, smoking, thinking, and with a little look of satisfaction: *The traffickers who took me from my parents and my God-fearing home and put me to work servicing bored, boneless men like yourself. They made me learn English so I would make them more money, of course.* It hurt a little more than it probably had any right to, but there's whiskey for you. Staring off into nothing and losing myself in the red lights, not sure that I wanted to be there any longer, knowing I needed to be. *University. I'm studying to be a doctor.*

Ah, well then. *What, you don't want to know my university?* Would you want to hear about where I went to school? *So he does learn. Maybe you can surprise after all.* Old dogs and new tricks.

She laughed, the first and only genuine thing she'd allowed me to that point, and the phone had my attention again as the numbers slid imperceptibly into a row of zeroes. A fresh start, clean slate, born anew. Noticing this, like adhering to a cue: *Yes, you have enough time. But if I may, can I suggest my special service?* Not giving me time to answer, not needing a confirmation, already knowing, she stood, and in the red light of the room, naked and dappled in shared sweat, everything was different again.

She lifted her hair and let it fall over her chest, baring her shoulders to me, revealing the chaotic jumble of scarification canvassing her back. A jagged, raised-relief constellation map, every mark and line intended and necessary. At its center, her white hot burning sun, an ivory ring dangling between her shoulder blades. Moving backward toward the bed, she sat on its edge and looked at me over her shoulder.

Go on, pull it. You'll see. Time a factor, always, the ever-moving pool, I ignored hesitation, ignored the urge to question, just went with it, riding neural impulse, I took it in my fingers. Pulled it gently, drawing out the string, long and taut, her muscles twitching and bristling and tightening slightly. *Let go.* So I did.

The string contracted back into her. A slow, headache crawl. She was saying something as it recoiled, but her voice was miles away, using her native tongue, that language I couldn't wrap my head around. Before the ring reclaimed its place at the center of her universe, as the numbers on the phone clicked again into double-zero-colon-zero-one, I could feel myself following that voice over the air, through nothing-everywhere space, could feel myself falling back onto the soft, warm sheets. The red room bled into black, my eyes closing, no longer in my control. I remained there in the dark for a moment as the dream took me, letting it take hold, until her voice climbed up from the abyss, closer, finding my ear: *Open your eyes and see your surprise.*

Awareness, wave after wave, a barrage. Like being born. I was standing, clothed in my fatigues, and alone. These sensations were immediate, but not the most jarring. The secondary impulses hit harder: the chill of autumn, the haze of morning drumming haplessly against thick, glum fog. Open air, free to roam, lapping against the gray and pushing it along. Then the noise came: people passing, heel-to-toe clicking, muttered conversations, laughter from somewhere distant. The low purr of engines, and then the next tier of awareness, the yellow knife of headlights cutting through the curtain. Dark gray splotch-people, moving like watercolor spreading across an easel, going places in the hidden, living city beyond the fog.

The building loomed there, Mustang red and chrome, too familiar and too obvious to be anything but. Without seeing, only knowing, I climbed the steps and pulled the handle. The telltale jangle of bells hanging above the frame, the creak of the door against the jamb. Pages from a dog-eared book, lines from a remembered song. I stepped inside to find the interior only slightly less fog-hazy, but I knew where I was going, didn't I? I found the stool at the counter and sat. A face pushed out from the gray miasma, familiar, cheerful and heavily made-up, *Oh, my. It's been a while, kiddo. What was it then? Coffee, black? Eggs over easy, wheat toast, hash brown with peppers?* You've got it, and I folded my hands over the laminated menu, sticky with syrup.

I accepted the logic of these dreams, decided to claim what I could for myself, they were at least partially mine after all. The coffee came quickly, piping hot, but thin and weak. No control over that. Clattering and sizzling sounds from the kitchen, and I drained the mug quickly. My tongue screamed, died. The woman came, I'd forgotten her name if I'd known it at all, and she let out an impressed little sound as she filled me up.

From what I could see, the place seemed cleaner, newer, like I imagined it would have been in its heyday. There were people in the booths and down the counter, hidden but given away by coughing, sneezing, the low drone of hushed conversation, the uneven tempo of silverware clinking against plates.

A quick chime from the little bell above the door. I didn't have to lift my head to look. I already knew who it was. Heavy boots found the stool next to mine, pulling close to the counter, the woman's voice warm with familiarity, his gruff and quiet. He led, to the point, *grits, two biscuits, gravy, two fried eggs, bacon, coffee*, and she snorted, *oh, you big spender*. I didn't want to look. Didn't need to, either. So I didn't. I could see him anyway, that shiny crown cresting against thinning waves of sandy hair. I could see myself seeing myself reflected in the mirrored aviators that only came off for special occasions. The rough hands, scaly, almost reptilian. Still there. A mug against the counter.

Sipping noises. Grunted approval. Throat being cleared. Then a silence, ticking by like accumulating interest on a silent debt, past due. Where are you, Pick-Mi? I think I'll have that cigarette now.

You're looking well.

Thanks.

Things are going all right?

Yeah. It's not too bad.

Of course it isn't. That's the point.

How's Mom?

I haven't seen her today.

How was she yesterday?

She slept through most of it. Sleeps most days. Nights, too. Today, she'll be at the parade, I'm sure. You'll find her there.

Parade?

Yep. We're celebrating. She'll be there.

Okay.

Have they made a man of you yet?

I don't know.

Want my opinion?

Not really, if that's okay.

You're not.

He sipped his coffee and, a nervous tic, I followed suit. The woman brought me the plate, still smiling, not attuned to the tension or ignoring it, and I started knifing at the eggs, letting the yolk bleed out and run into the edge of the toast.

Those clothes? They don't make you a man. You need to do better. Need to do more.

So what would I need to do?

And you'd start listening to me now?

Try me.

He was chewing loudly, struggling with the food, breathing hard through his nose in quick, satisfied gusts. I was grinding coffee between my teeth.

You want to know the secret? How I came home a man?

-263-

I'll tell you, but you're not going to get it out there babysitting . . .

Babysitting. I'd heard it plenty before I shipped out. Code: not good enough. Not valid. Just babysitting.

. . . a line in the sand that they're tough enough to draw but too chicken-shit to cross.

The sounds of celebration roiling together from the street outside pressed against the glass, wanting in, rising to a fever pitch. Children squealing, men and women selling things, buying things, look at this, look at that. I sipped the coffee dry and steadied myself on the stool.

There's a darkness, boy. Maybe we're born with it, I don't know, but we all have it. But it's not just that. We share it with someone. That's your other. We don't know who, and we don't know where they are in the world. But they're out there, and they've got the other half of it. I found that other half on the Red River basin. He was a boy, maybe seventeen, I don't know. Not much younger than I was, really. We were all young, even the old ones. He had a gun, I had a gun, and I did what I needed to do first. I saw it in his eyes, saw it pouring out of that big hole I put in his chest. All the rest of that darkness. Poof. Gone. That's how you do it. You need to find that shadow and take it back. Then, well, do with it what you wish.

I'd lost my appetite, so I pushed the plate away. He kept talking, the words making less sense, sounding less and less like that voice that I knew, more and more like another I heard calling out from another place, sweet and practiced and pleased.

I had little else to say to him. As far as I knew, the well had run dry when we shook hands at the terminal two years prior and the only thing I could muster, still so regrettable because it had sounded half sincere: thanks, Dad.

There's another way, you know.

I stuffed my mouth full of Tabasco-slopped egg, the sticky yellow running down my chin. I left it there, defiant.

You could kill me.

I said something garbled, not really words, but I determined that it was a sufficient reaction. I heard him lift the steak knife from the counter, could hear it split the air as he waved it about his face.

I'm not saying it would be easy. But wouldn't that make you a man? Isn't it necessary? Kill your father, and what choice do you have? Boys kill their fathers every day, and so they must take their place. It's always a slow death. Bed-pissers. Liars. Freeloaders. A thousand little cuts. I'm already bleeding. You've already made me so weak, my boy. So just finish it already. Take the goddamn reigns, own up to it. Kill me once and for all. Put me down deep. Finish it. Be a man. Don't you want to make the old man proud? Isn't it what you've always wanted?

I followed my own rules of decorum, of logic, took control of the dream, slapped some money on the counter and, without looking, not once, I left the diner with my dream-father shouting after me, challenging me to kill him.

Outside, the fog had thinned enough that I had a better look at the town I once called home, once loved, had to escape. Much of the street was like I remembered it. The concrete divider separating people going this way or that, stretching like an artery down the junkie arm of the town. The shops, squat and simple, where I spent too many afternoons skipping lectures and spending money, not caring.

The revelers scrambled on the sidewalks, wearing their masks, brandishing noisemakers and trinkets. A man with the head of an oryx brushed past me, paused in recognition, and chose to continue on without a word. Across the road there was a row of vendor booths, proprietors spilling out of the rickety wooden boxes, hoisting their wares above the curious buyers, selling themselves. I moved closer, stood among the rabble with my arms crossed. Each held Styrofoam trays wrapped in plastic that held sliding, wet hunks of viscera, colorful and glistening. A woman was bellowing out, her head a television screen on a snow station, her voice was white noise. *Our brave searchers found one of the great labor-gods sleeping in the wood, tired from cleaning up messes! They bound her in her rest with the strongest of ropes, and they've taken great pains in retrieving these morsels for you! Even now, they are out there digging into her flesh, beneath the bone! These are the cheapest god-bits you are going to find, and how fresh! How delicate they are!*

Her competitor, a glowing, twinkling nebula upon his shoulders, ripped open one of his packages and dangled the meat, curiously blue, in front of him. In his fingers, it bobbed, expanded, contracted, alive and struggling to flee. *No, no! Buy here, my friends! The true color of the work-god is blue! My men are not cowards, no, they felled one of the giants in the mountains with great stone. We have no need for rope, for submission! The prize is in the battle, my friends! My god-meat is tough, muscles strengthened by action! My competitor wants to sell you soft, stringy meat! Sleeping meat? Where is the charm? Where is all of that glorious effort?*

Through and around the crowd, children bounced and sang and chased each other while wearing the tired rubber faces of old men and women. They each held knives above their heads, stabbing downward at the air, running after one another in a Mobius strip, never catching their neighbor, never running out of air to breathe. Their high voices, shrill and joyless, buzzed in unison behind unmoving mouths. Their song told of their intent: they sought to kill that which made men weak, which prevented them from ascending, that ancient black thing, to take the flesh of intermediary gods as souvenirs. My hands itched for something, so I stuffed them into my pockets.

A bell pealed from somewhere distant, and the fog rolled in to swallow it all up. The footsteps, sales pitches, songs of deadly children, muffled screams from the diner, all evaporated into the mist. There was silence for a long time, and all I could do was fall into the nickelodeon in my mind, see all the ways I could spill the blood of my father, all the pictures we would paint together with his red.

There came a rumbling, something heavy from down the road, creaking and groaning. Because it only seemed logical, I took shelter behind a lamppost and tried to wish myself as thin as possible. It emerged like a war elephant lumbering through a bog, its erect trunk pointing, leading. The old Sherman was a museum relic, dinosaur bones on puppet strings, dancing. Hungry from its slumber, it chewed the asphalt of the street and expelled the waste in thick plumes of black smoke that mingled with the gray of the fog, darkening everything. Rust red armor, porous and chitinous, breathing, alive. Dangling from the skirt and draped over the hull were bodies of Korean soldier-boys, ones like me, sleeping in their vomit, their faces corroding in the puddles, their smooth hands gripping their empty green bottles of *soju*.

Men in suits dragged behind it, connected by leather straps, bound at their wrists. The faces were different, but only slightly, each smiling beneath perfectly coifed hair. Their pockets bulged with promissory notes, small bones, shiny candy wrappers. One of them stepped in a puddle of what had once been a soldier-boy's face and, though he tried to hide it, his face soured into a vicious glare. The others affected similar faces, a domino effect of contempt for everything and everyone that wasn't there. I wanted to cough, but I held it in, and the tank rolled on, the men glowering behind it, no longer in the mood for theatrics.

The man in the garish lime tuxedo emerged from behind the procession on the opposite sidewalk, arms down, hands folded over his waist. In that moment, I sensed that he had always been there, always observing. He was looking in my direction, and I could see that his eyes were little more than thin cracks in the shell of an egg. The crack that served as his mouth widened, threatening to shatter him. He lifted an arm and gestured behind him, guiding me toward a towering, sloping citadel of obsidian that had taken the place of the dollar store where the day manager used to sell pot out of the stock room, maybe still did in some other plane of existence. My hiding spot useless, the delirious parade having passed, I followed his suggestion, and the air burned hot as magma as I passed him.

I stepped into a velvet antechamber. The walls were littered with scrolls, every page with cryptic sigils and lewd figures drawn in the margins. The woman at the desk, plain and plump and unaffected, smiled wide and asked me if I'd like a room. I told her that I suspected I had an appointment, because I did. She thumbed at her Rolodex and confirmed what I already knew. She would be waiting for me in the room at the top of the stairs, just through the double doors. I nodded my thanks, walked through, stepped inside.

Everything was deep in red and painfully clear. The wallpaper hung down in long, dry strips like fish scales, hearts and all. The floor was a pliable mesh of crisscrossing steel, the cold breath of the earth rising to claim the room from below. A grand staircase of polished oak climbed up into a dark vanishing point. It had no banister, but pikes on either side of each step, topped with the cleanly severed heads of men, dead eyed and rictus grinning. I knew them to be her past clientele, unified in our dirty secret, only for us to share. I climbed the stairs, the red washed away by the black, and though I couldn't see their heads, I could feel them watching without knowing, could feel their smiles conspiring. The door was easy and weightless, and I stepped inside.

I wasn't surprised to find myself in the very bedroom of my childhood. Posters on the wall that only my closest friends knew about, my secret admiration of things that would have put me lower on the food chain. Stacks of comic books I never had the chance to read, movies I never got around to watching. The window was thrown open and the curtain wafted with a dusty breeze that smelled like the sea. There was the bed. With it, the smell of dried urine that never seemed to go away. The smell that followed me, haunting, chasing, for so many of those years, across oceans. And there, upon the bed, she sat, her back to me, scars healed. She was playing with the sheets, twisting the fabric in her hands.

Was it as good for you as it was for me? Are we done here? *Is that how you say it? Was it as good for—*Are we done here? *Yes. Yes, I'm sorry, but we don't have any more time left to explore. It's very late and you have to be on your way.* What is this? *Whatever it has to be. Whatever you make it. I helped, of course, but I wouldn't take any credit. This is you. It is what you need it to be. So. Should I make you an appointment for next weekend? Sooner? There is so much left for us to see.* What makes you think I'll be back? *Because you will. You have more to find. So many places to go. It wouldn't be the first time.* Okay, well, I think I'd like to go. *Sure. You want to go. I know. You know where the door is.*

The drawstring, the one that had been on her back, was wrapped in my fists, the line drawn taut in between. I sighed. She didn't budge.

Why does it always have to come down to this? *And why shouldn't it?*

I didn't have an answer. I went to her. My palms brushed against her collarbones and the soft, cold flesh drawn tight across. She was steel, no warmth. She didn't fight, because she'd done it before. I didn't resist, because I thought maybe I had done this, too. Nothing substantial, only the third act. Then: wakefulness.

I gathered my jeans, hurrying, knowing that the last train would be at the station in eight minutes. Pick-Mi was in the wardrobe, throwing on a silk robe. She would have to change again, climb back into those tall red boots, slip through the hoop of the skirt, sink into the chair in her little foyer, smoke her cigarettes, and wait at the window for maybe somebody, maybe nobody. Her night would not be over until the hot sun burned Seoul's drunks down to ash, turning them into pumpkins, into management, movers-and-shakers, toy soldiers. The sun always came, promised like that next mistake, and I wanted to think that was when she was free to craft the escape she needed but never claimed to want.

She followed me to the door and didn't say a word. I returned the favor. I knew where to find her when I needed the gift of sleep, the architecture of our dreams. When the time would come, she would have a different name, always did, always with a new personality affected, but the coordinates never lied. The train would get me back to the garrison with time to spare, but I was never really there when it carried me away. I was still somewhere else, beneath the hot mantle of a pink-lit earth, being watched from a high tower as I ascended the stilled chest of a murdered janitor god whose work was never done and would never be finished.

FED

JESSICA LILIEN

"**SHE'S NOT EATING.**"

"She's gaining weight."

"*How?*"

The doctor laughed and put his hand on her arm. He was not her regular doctor. Her regular doctor was a smarmy asshole who had chuckled and told her to "do me just one favor—*Don't. Google. Anything.*" He had then sat back in his chair, very pleased with himself, and laughed, and when she hadn't laughed with him, he explained to her, very seriously, that "Many women often . . . " and she stopped listening. This was soon after the baby had started moving inside her, struggling, and it was horrible, it was foreign and terrible, it wanted out of her as much as she wanted it out.

"This is normal," the new doctor told her. "Everything is normal at this stage!" He threw his hands up in the air and laughed and Beth didn't look down at the table, the little metal table like in a veterinarian's clinic. Neither of them were touching it; it might as well have not even been in the same room.

It was ugly when it was first born. Actively, offensively ugly. Beth wasn't sure how many people knew that: how ugly babies are at first. Even after the snot and gore and shit was wiped off of them—and that *did* have to be done—even after *that*, their skin was blotchy and flaky, covered in something waxy that you wouldn't want to get under your fingernails. It stuck in their hair. Their eyes were insectile and evaded contact; they were ashamed of themselves and angry. Their hands and mouths were alien and needy and everyone was smiling at you, proud of themselves for removing it successfully and presenting it to you, waiting for a reaction. Beth knew how she was supposed to react. But she didn't want its mouth anywhere near her. She feigned great pain, and they took it away from her, and someone else fed it at least.

The books told her that the baby would wake her up every two hours, so when she woke up on her own, late on the first morning it was home, she thought it was dead. But it wasn't dead. It was asleep, and then it woke up, and its face was wet and slick with what looked like sexual lubricant, not saliva. She wanted someone else to clean it off. Eventually it started to cry and she changed its diaper.

Mark was doing this thing—had been doing it while she was pregnant, too—where he would touch her and smile *gently* at her. She didn't know when he'd started to do that thing, at which trimester or which inch of her stomach she gave up to him. He hadn't ever done that before, smiled like that. She didn't think he meant it (whatever it meant). She thought he probably *thought* he should do it. But he wasn't saying so, if so, and he just kept doing it, and she didn't know how to tell him to stop. He was gone when she woke up that first day. He wasn't at work, she knew, but he was gone somewhere, and he had left the two of them alone, even though, as far as he knew, it was dead. He didn't know. He was a feminist, he said. He had taken four weeks' leave (though he wouldn't, in the end, actually use it all; he would go back early). She had taken four months. She worked for a very progressive firm.

Her body felt loose and heavy, as though she was wearing

a pelt, another body on top of her body. She imagined that she could feel her cunt hanging, swaying, like a man's genitals. She cupped her hand between her legs. It was fine, it felt fine. She hadn't torn; it had been an easy birth. No drugs—no time for them, it all happened too fast—but she hadn't needed them; it had been easy. It had been expelled out of her like vomit: one quick wrenching moment of nausea, eyes closed, clenching, her body doing something she didn't tell it to do, something hard, and then it was gone from her. She'd felt not empty but violated, full of rubber gloves and blood.

Eventually she wrapped it up and took it out of the nursery and into the kitchen and made herself coffee, and Mark came home; he'd bought them fresh whole wheat bagels and lox and fat-free whipped cream cheese. This was what their mornings were like for a lot of mornings in a row, or some version of it: sometimes he made scrambled eggs instead; sometimes she put her fingers inside of herself to check and see if there was anything there. Foreign objects. Small lost bits of unsharp metal or mold or dead fruit flies.

After breakfast, they would spread one of the soft, expensive new playmats on the floor and the three of them would lay there. Mark would talk to it, and she was expected to talk to it, offer it objects, try to get it to hold things or look at things, just look at something. She wore her old college volleyball shorts, a T-shirt, no bra. Her tits were strange, heavy things, someone else's tits, not hers. Firmer and higher and prettier than hers, but there was something wrong with them, and they stained her shirt wet and they hurt. She worried that there were things living in them, one big round wet alien in each one, turning and turning and growing and leaking. Everything was wet and dirt and hairs stuck to everything. She didn't know where all the hairs came from; she didn't think they were hers.

She pricked herself with needles to make her nipples bleed and she called it mastitis; she wasn't sure if she was using the word correctly but she'd read it in a book and Mark looked concerned and didn't make her feed it. They had formula, bought before it was born, and they used that and fed it with bottles. Sometimes it ate, at first; often it was disinterested, and formula pooled in its mouth and rolled down its cheeks and chin and grew crusty behind its ears. It smelled like basements and yeast infections.

She wanted to turn on the TV when they were on the playmat on the floor. She didn't know what was an appropriate length of time to stay there. She would close one eye, sometimes, the eye away from Mark, and angle her head up and play a game like she was a TV camera so she wouldn't see it, but Mark wouldn't realize what she was doing. He would think she was looking at it, too. She wondered if he was thinking, too, that he could have performed these duties—talking to it, offering it objects—just as well with the TV on, with a book in one hand. It wasn't something they were both required for, which required the full attention of two adults with advanced degrees. She practiced angling her head and thought about it, about how much longer she should stay there.

Its fingernails were repulsive: sharp and white and very clean on small moving wrinkled fingers. She was expected to trim them.

Their nights were undisturbed. Mark never mentioned it; she didn't know if he knew that wasn't how it was supposed to be. Maybe he thought they were very lucky and didn't want to jinx it, or maybe he didn't know. The baby never cried. The baby never asked to be fed at night. Her breasts throbbed as though filled with rotten teeth, and for the first few nights they leaked and stained not only the sheets but the mattress underneath; she was embarrassed. After a few nights they stopped leaking. They still hurt, they were still heavy; she imagined the milk hardening and crystallizing inside of her, turning to cement, locking the aliens in place like bugs in

Lucite, dinosaur bones in stone. If you cut one of them off of her, you'd get a clean cross-section of it, curled up as though asleep. She imagined holding it in her hand: the round unyielding ball of the front of her breast, the nipple soft in her palm, a rough hard bloodless stump protruding from her body still, a tree stump, an amputated forearm.

She brought it in to work eventually; that's what women did. Her secretary made noises over it. Her secretary was too young. She watched them both, silently.

"She's not eating," she said.

Someone else's secretary looked up, concerned. Beth knew that her skin had gone bad, her hair was not right, but she thought it would be okay, it was only to be expected.

"It's normal," the other person's secretary said. Beth thought that woman had children, too. Everyone did, though. It was a thing women did. "Look at those cheeks! Look how healthy she is! Everything is normal at this stage!"

The baby's cheeks were unnaturally soft where they were not chapped from being always wet.

Beth had not gotten used to the baby's name, did not think of it by name. (She thought of it as a loaf of sourdough bread, rising uncovered on the counter. It smelled of sex and bacteria and was soft and sticky in a way that caused tiny black specks of dirt to become embedded in it, and it was her job to keep it clean or people would disapprove of her.) When other people called it by name, it took her a moment to remember what they were talking about. When other people asked her for its name, she tried to pretend she hadn't heard them.

People asked often. It was gaining weight at an alarming rate and the people at the park took notice, cooed and fawned over its wrists, its calves, the soles of its feet. Its wet vaginal mouth in its face, pushed together into a sucking-thing truly obscene by the fat balls of its cheeks.

"Who is feeding you?" she asked it.

The woman kneeling beside the stroller glanced up at her, startled, then smiled, nervous, complimented her, and left.

Beth had meant to join a . . . a group? Of some kind? A mothers' group? A playgroup? Le Leche League? She didn't know which one was the one people were supposed to join, but after a while it didn't seem to matter anymore. She went to the park, but she had to consciously work to go at different times of the day, on different days of the week, to different parks sometimes, to avoid the groups of women who would get to know her. She didn't know why she did this. She had forgotten what she did when she went to work. What takes up a person's time? All she could think of was "email," but that couldn't be right, could it? Could you just read and write emails all day long? What was it that she used to do? It was very important, she remembered.

The baby was quiet at the park, it lay on its back in the stroller and stared, shocked, at a fall of colored balls and rings hanging above its head. She had stopped carrying bottles with her when she took it out. It didn't eat. It hadn't eaten anything in weeks.

What came out of her breasts was not milk, at first. It looked like paint. Later it was thinner and looked like something from a sick person. It tended toward blue, which they told her was normal, and if you left it in the refrigerator it separated into cream and the part that was not cream became even bluer than before, and Mark would try to make jokes about it. They said, too, that sometimes there was blood in the milk, a burst capillary, a cracked nipple (a person's nipple can crack, she marveled, *like ceramic*) and this, they told her, was fine for the baby. If it bothered her, she could leave it to separate in the refrigerator—the blood would sink—and she could pour the less-bloody milk off the top. But a little blood would not hurt the baby, they told her. Blood sinks in milk, she learned. Cream rises and blood sinks. That the human body could create food within itself disgusted her. She hated the idea of anything consuming something like that.

"Have you fed her already?" Mark asked.

"No. Have you?"

"No," he said.

Had he started to notice? What would he think of her? Still, the baby grew fatter. She wasn't a bad person if the baby kept growing fatter. Its eyes grew clearer, more defined; they seemed to be able to focus on things. Beth looked away.

Mark noticed first when it started to grow teeth.

"Isn't this early?"

"Everything is normal at this stage," she told him.

Later, she put her finger in the baby's mouth, and it bit her, hard. Did it think this was her breast? Beth smiled at it. She had tricked it, and she was pleased with herself; she felt mean and good. The baby goggled, it did not seem to notice or mind, and the pleasure wore off. Beth removed her finger. The baby's arms flailed, its head popped to one side and then the other. It seemed unable to control its own movements, but it seemed very strong. Its belly was round and soft. She put a hand on it, carefully, and she felt something inside of it move. Just its heartbeat, she told herself, flinching her hand away. She changed its diaper. It was shitting lustily, growing daily, happy, learning how to smile. Someone was feeding it.

There is a thing that grows in you, that someone else puts inside of you. It hurts you, makes you sick, literally feeds off of your body. Somehow another living thing has gotten inside of you. Even after they remove it, they just give it back to you, and you are expected to take care of it, to take very careful care of it and keep it from getting too warm or too cold, to make sure it stays clean, not to drop it or throw it. It might have killed you; people die from them, still, all the time.

Three different people had given her, as a gift, a very

expensive plastic toy giraffe from Sweden, or Denmark, maybe—somewhere cold and liberal—which smiled with its tongue out as though it suffered a disease. She gave one of them to the baby and it chewed divots into its neck, legs, backside. An ear came loose and she watched to see if the baby would choke on it, but it didn't. She didn't think this was supposed to happen; she thought that maybe this was not normal. Her mother-in-law had given her a solid silver engraved teething ring from Tiffany, but she assumed this sort of thing was decorative only, not for actual use. It was engraved with the date the baby was born, but no name. It was still inside its blue box, in the baby's top dresser drawer. Beth wanted to give the baby the Tiffany teething ring, shove a slab of cold silver into its mouth and see what happened, see if the baby could chew divots into that, too. She worried, though, that it might actually do that. The baby sometimes reached its hands toward her, as though to grasp her body. Sometimes the baby waved the giraffe at her, perhaps offering it to her or showing her what it had done. Sometimes she heard noises at night that were not the baby.

"Milkteeth" was a word she thought of one day, looking at them. She couldn't remember what the word meant. Were they just baby teeth? Or were they something more specific? Beth's mother had saved all of Beth's teeth as they fell out of her head as a child, Beth's and her sisters' also. Beth's mother still had three small white cardboard boxes sitting on top of her vanity table, each one containing a collection of teeth, each box for one sister. They were unlabeled, but Beth's mother knew which box contained the teeth of which sister. Some of the teeth were not completely clean. Beth had heard, somewhere, that if a tooth was knocked out, and you had to take it to the dentist to have it replaced, you should keep it in a glass of milk. Beth's brow knotted. That didn't sound right. That couldn't be sanitary. Maybe that was an old wives' tale. Beth used the tip of her finger to move the baby's lips back, to examine the teeth. They were small, but they seemed very solid, very strong. They were not overly sharp-looking, certainly not pointed. One of the giraffe's feet had come off, chewed loose at the bent knee. Beth had given the baby a second giraffe and thrown the first one away, taken it immediately out to the big green trash can behind the house, afraid that if she left it in the kitchen garbage can, Mark would see it and think that it wasn't normal. The baby was looking at her, had figured out how to focus on her eyes. Beth removed her finger from the baby's mouth and used the hem of her shirt to rub it clean, rubbed slowly until the skin around her nail felt sore, and still the baby watched her.

Breast milk goes bad. Blue breast milk is fine, and bloody breast milk will not hurt the baby, but if you leave breast milk in the refrigerator and no one eats it, it spoils and turns to chunks and it stinks. Beth threw the breast milk away, poured it down the sink, and made herself smell it as a punishment. The baby was behind her, on the kitchen floor, in a car seat, strapped down, pounding its second giraffe— headless—rhythmically against one leg of the kitchen table.

She realized at some point that the correct question was not "Who is feeding you?" but "What are you eating?" and she did not ask that question out loud. Someone might hear a question like that.

She realized at some point that eventually she would have to return to work, which meant a nanny or a daycare, which meant that someone would notice. Someone would have to notice that the baby did not eat.

She realized at some point that it was happening at night. That the baby had tricked her, had let her sleep through the night in order to keep her from seeing it happen. If she just stayed awake, all night, she would find out who was feeding it.

The baby had stopped making noise behind her. Was it dead? She did not turn around for a long time. Eventually Mark came home and she pretended she was normal.

ABOUT THE AUTHORS

Kevin David Anderson's stories have appeared *in Dark Animus, Dark Wisdom, Darkness Rising, Dark Moon Digest*, and many other publications with the word "dark" in the title—which is kind of misleading because he's a happy, lighthearted person who lives with his family in Southern California. Anderson's novel *Night of the Living Trekkies*, from Quirk Books, earned positive reviews in the *Los Angeles Times*, the *Washington Post, Fangoria*, and received a starred review in *Publishers Weekly*. He's latest book, *Blood, Gridlock, & PEZ: Podcasted tales of Horror*, is his first short story collection filled with tales that originally appeared in audio form on podcasts like *The Drabblecast* and *Pseudopod*. Anderson is an Active member of the HWA, with a BA in Mass Communication, and fifteen years of award-winning marketing experience. Check his web site and blog for news of his upcoming novel, *Night of the ZomBEEs*, a zombie novel with BUZZ—www.KevinDavidAnderson.com

Richard Farren Barber was born in Nottingham in July 1970. After studying in London he returned to the East Midlands. He lives with his wife and son and works as an Operations Manager for a local university.

He has written over 200 short stories and has had short stories published in *Alt-Dead, Alt-Zombie, Blood Oranges, Derby Scribes Anthology, Derby Telegraph, ePocalypse— Tales from the End, Horror D'Oeuvres, Murky Depths, *Midnight Echo, Midnight Street, Morpheus Tales, MT Biopunk Special, MT Urban Horror Special, Night Terrors II, Siblings, The House of Horror, Trembles, When Red Snow Melts*, and broadcast on *BBC Radio Derby, The Wicked Library* and *Pseudopod*.

Richard's first novella, *The Power of Nothing* was published by Damnation Books in September 2013 and his second, *The Sleeping Dead* was published in August 2014 by

DarkFuse. His website can be found here
www.richardfarrenbarber.co.uk

Jennifer Brozek is an award-winning editor, game designer, and author. Winner of the Australian Shadows Award for best edited publication, Jennifer has edited fifteen anthologies with more on the way. Author of *In a Gilded Light*, *The Lady of Seeking in the City of Waiting*, *Industry Talk*, and the *Karen Wilson Chronicles*, she has more than sixty published short stories, and is the Creative Director of Apocalypse Ink Productions.

A freelance author for numerous RPG companies, Jennifer is the winner of both the Origins and the ENnie awards. She is also the author of the YA Battletech novel, *The Nellus Academy Incident*.

When she is not writing her heart out, she is gallivanting around the Pacific Northwest in its wonderfully mercurial weather. Jennifer is an active member of SFWA, HWA, and IAMTW. Read more about her at www.jenniferbrozek.com or follow her on Twitter at @JenniferBrozek.

Jay Caselberg is an Australian author based in Europe. His work has appeared in multiple venues and languages worldwide. His most recent novel, *Empties,* a novel of brutal psychological horror is due out soon. More can be found at http://www.jaycaselberg.com.

Peter Charron lives in Western New York with his wife, sons and Maine Coon cats. Although a pharmacist and operations expert by trade, he much prefers writing fiction. He is interested in the anomalous and enjoys digging through the long forgotten boxes in the attics of Anthropology, History, Mythology and Technology. Peter's short fiction has appeared in several print publications, e-zines, and anthologies. He is currently preparing a novel for publication.

Dennis Etchison is a three-time winner of both the British Fantasy and World Fantasy Awards. Many of his short stories may be found in the collections *The Dark Country, Red Dreams, The Blood Kiss, The Death Artist, Talking in the*

Dark, Fine Cuts, and *Got To Kill Them All & Other Stories,* several of which are now available as ebooks from Crossroad Press. He is also the author of the novels *Darkside, Shadowman, California Gothic, Double Edge, The Fog, Halloween II, Halloween III,* and *Videodrome,* and editor of the anthologies *Cutting Edge, Masters of Darkness I-III, MetaHorror, The Museum of Horrors,* and (with Ramsey Campbell and Jack Dann) *Gathering the Bones.* He has written extensively for film, television and radio, including scripts for John Carpenter, Dario Argento, *The Twilight Zone Radio Dramas,* Fangoria Magazine's *Dread Time Stories* and Christopher Lee's *Mystery Theater.* He served as President of the Horror Writers Association (HWA) from 1992 to 1994. His latest books are *It Only Comes Out At Night,* a career retrospective edited by S.T. Joshi (Centipede Press), *A Little Black Book of Horror Stories* (Borderlands Press), and *A Long Time Till Morning,* an anthology of dreamed stories co-edited with Peter Atkins.

Taylor Grant has been a professional storyteller in one form or another for most of his adult life. His work has been seen on network television, the big screen, the stage, the web, newspapers, comic books, national magazines, anthologies, and heard on the radio.

Co-Founder of publishing company Evil Jester Comics, Taylor is also the co-author of *Evil Jester Presents,* the critically acclaimed, bestselling comic book. His dark fiction has been published in two Bram Stoker Award-nominated anthologies: *Horror Library Vol. 5* and *Horror For Good,* as well as *Cemetery Dance Magazine. Fear the Reaper, Of Devils and Deviants, Blood Type, Nightscapes Vol. 1, Box of Delights, Tales from the Lake Vol. 1,* and *A Feast of Frights from the Horror Zine.*

Eric J. Guignard writes dark and speculative fiction from the outskirts of Los Angeles. His stories and articles may be found in the disreputable publications reserved for back alley bazaars. As an editor, Eric's produced the anthologies, *Dark Tales of Lost Civilizations* and *After Death . . . ,* the latter of which won the 2013 Bram Stoker Award®. Read his novella, *Baggage of Eternal Night* (a finalist for the 2014

International Thriller Writers Award), and watch for many more forthcoming books, including *Chestnut 'Bo* (TBP 2016). Visit Eric at: www.ericjguignard.com, his blog: ericjguignard.blogspot.com, or Twitter: @ericjguignard.

Gerry Huntman is a writer based in Melbourne, Australia, living with his wife and young daughter. He writes in all genres of speculative fiction, although most tend toward dark. His latest short fiction sales include *Lovecraft eZine, Aurealis Magazine, World of Horror* anthology, and *Best of Penny Dread Tales* anthology. He is publishing a young teen fantasy novel, *Guardlian of the Sky Realms*, late in 2014.

Kyle S. Johnson lives in Cincinnati, Ohio, in a house on a street. Usually, there are cars parked along the street. People walk their dogs on the sidewalks when the weather is nice. There are fewer people walking dogs when the weather isn't so nice, but it doesn't seem to affect the number of cars very much.

Jack Ketchum is the pseudonym for a former actor, singer, teacher, literary agent, lumber salesman, and soda jerk—a former flower child and baby boomer who figures that in 1956 Elvis, dinosaurs and horror probably saved his life. His first novel, *Off Season*, prompted the Village Voice to publicly scold its publisher in print for publishing violent pornography. He personally disagrees but is perfectly happy to let you decide for yourself. His short story "The Box" won a 1994 Bram Stoker Award from the HWA, his story "Gone" won again in 2000—and in 2003 he won Stokers for both best collection for *Peaceable Kingdom* and best long fiction for *Closing Time*. He has written over twenty novels and novellas, the latest of which are *The Woman* and *I'm Not Sam*, both written with director Lucky McKee. Five of his books have been filmed to date—*The Girl Next Door, The Lost, Red, Offspring* and *The Woman*, the last of which won him and McKee the Best Screenplay Award at the prestigious Sitges Film Festival in Spain. His stories are collected in *The Exit At Toledo Blade Boulevard, Broken on the Wheel of Sex, Sleep Disorder* (with Edward Lee), *Peaceable Kingdom* and *Closing Time and Other Stories*. His novella *The Crossings* was cited by Stephen King in his speech at the 2003 National Book Awards. In 2011 he was elected Grand Master by the World Horror Convention.

Jessica Lilien has work published or forthcoming in *Lumina Journal*, *Clackamas Literary Review*, *Columbia: A Journal of Literature and Art Online*, *Morpheus Tales*, *Madcap Review*, and *Trivia: Voices of Feminism*. Her short story "After Saco River" was one of the winners of the LUMINA XII 2013 Fiction Contest, judged by George Saunders. He called it "very strange." She lives in Brooklyn.

Raymond Little has been published in anthologies in both Europe and the USA. "Falco Wreck" is his second outing with Blood Bound Books, and he is currently working on his novel *Phantasmagoria*. Ray lives in the south of England with his wife Julie, whose encouragement allows his mind to cast its net into the darkest pools. Sometimes, he catches monsters.

A lifelong reader, fan, and collector of horror and science fiction, **Simon McCaffery**'s stories have appeared in magazines including *Black Static*, *Lightspeed*, *Space and Time*, *Tomorrow SF*, *Wily Writers*, and *Alfred Hitchcock Mystery Magazine*. Anthology appearances include *Book of the Dead 2: Still Dead*, *Other Worlds Than These*, *Mondo Zombie*, *Rocket Science*, *100 Wicked Little Witch Stories*, *Appalachian Undead* and *PSYCHOS: Serial Killers, Depraved Madmen, and the Criminally Insane*. He lives in Tulsa, Oklahoma.

John McNee is the author of numerous strange and disturbing horror stories, published in various anthologies, including *Blood Rites, Tales from the Bell Club, Ruthless, D.O.A.* and *D.O.A II*. He is also the creator of Grudgehaven and author of *Grudge Punk*, a collection of stories detailing the lives and deaths of its gruesome inhabitants. He lives in the west of Scotland—where he is employed as a magazine writer—and can be sought out on Goodreads and Twitter.

Matt Moore believes horror fiction should both thrill and make you think. His short fiction, poetry and columns have appeared in print, electronic, and audio markets including *On Spec, AE: The Canadian Science Fiction Review, Jamais Vu, Leading Edge, Cast Macabre, Blood Rites,* and the *Tesseracts* anthologies. He's a three-time Aurora Award nominee, frequent panelist and presenter, Communications Director for ChiZine Publications and Chair of the Ottawa Chiaroscuro Reading Series. His short story collection *Touch the Sky, Embrace the Dark* was released in 2013. Find more at mattmoorewrites.com.

Rachel Nussbaum is a young writer and artist living on the Big Island of Hawaii. She's had artwork and writing published and featured locally, but this is the first time one of her short stories has been included in an anthology. Currently, Rachel is attending University, studying English, art, and animation. One day she hopes to write and illustrate her own novels and comic books.

Aric Sundquist is a graduate of Northern Michigan University and holds an MA in Creative Writing. His stories have appeared in various publications, including *The Best of Dark Moon Digest, Evil Jester Digest Vol. 1,* and Blood Bound Books: *Blood Rites.* Currently he lives in Marquette, Michigan. Visit him at: http://aricsundquist.weebly.com/.

Steve Rasnic Tem's latest novel *Blood Kin* (Solaris, March 2014), alternating between the 1930s and the present day, is a Southern Gothic/ Horror blend of snake handling, ghosts, granny women, kudzu, and Melungeons. In 2015 PS Publishing will bring out his novella *In the Lovecraft Museum.* Also forthcoming is a giant 225K retrospective horror collection from Centipede: *Out of the Dark: A Storybook of Horrors.*

Patty Templeton is roughly 25 apples tall and 11,000 cups of coffee into her life. She wears red sequins and stomping boots while writing, then hits up back-alley dance bars and honky tonks. Her stories are full of ghosts, freaks, fools, underdogs, blue collar heroes, and never giving up, even when life is giving you shit. She won the first-ever Naked Girls Reading Literary Honors Award and has been a runner-up for the Mary Wollstonecraft Shelley Award. Her debut novel, *There Is No Lovely End*, was published this year.

Paul Tremblay is the author of five novels including *The Little Sleep, Floating Boy and the Girl Who Couldn't Fly* (with Stephen Graham Jones), and *A Head Full of Ghosts*. He is also the author of the short story collection *In the Mean Time* and co-edited (with John Langan) the anthology *Creatures: Thirty Years of Monsters*. His short fiction and essays have appeared in the *Los Angeles Times* and in numerous "Year's Best" anthologies. He lives outside of Boston, Massachusetts, with his family and without a uvula. www.paultremblay.net

A Wisconsin native, **Dean H. Wild** lives in the town of Brownsville located in the east central part of the state with his wife Julie and their cat, Siegfried (Ziggy). His work has appeared in the HWA anthology *Bell, Book & Beyond*, as well as *Vivisections, Extremes 5, Fantasy and Horror from the Ends of the Earth* and *Nine: A Journal of Imaginative Fiction* among others. He also occupies the Assistant Editor seat for *The Horror Zine*. When not writing, editing or proofreading for one project or another, he is busy working on a novel. It is with great pride he takes his place among the family of Blood Bound Books authors.

Made in the USA
Charleston, SC
20 April 2015